Future King

A Novel

Larry Pontius

This book is entirely a work of fiction based upon a legend that has long been a matter of public conjecture. The author intends no harm of any kind to anyone living or dead.

Cover artwork by Jordan Hess.

For Harriet,
the most beautiful woman
in my world

"I will tell you something else, King, which may be a surprise for you. It will not happen for hundreds of years, but both of us are to come back. Do you know what is going to be written on your tombstone? *Hic jacet Arthurus Rex quandam Rexque futurus.* Do you remember your Latin? It means, the once and future king."

— Merlyn

From the T.H. White novel
The Once and Future King

1

At precisely 6:12 p.m., an alarm shrilled through the corridors of Jodrell Bank Observatory near Manchester, England. Deputy Director Margaret Kinsey cursed under her breath and scooted her chair back from a spilled cup of hot tea.

"Near Earth Object?" she said to herself. "Is that possible?"

She shook her head and cursed again. It had to be another muck-up by the controller, but she didn't need the scrutiny an alarm on her watch was certain to bring. She did what she could to save the work on her desk from the tannin flood, quickly brushed off her gray wool slacks, and hurried for the control room.

Dr. Hiram Feinberg was coming out of the door as she got there. A heavy set, graying and bearded sixty-two year-old, Feinberg was the oldest and most experienced of the astronomers at Jodrell Bank. Margaret Kinsey was glad he happened to be there tonight, but right now he was in the way. Beyond him she could see the chair at the array control computer. It was empty.

"Where's the duty controller?" she shouted over the alarm.

Feinberg frowned over the half glasses sitting on the end of his decidedly Jewish nose. Pointing over his shoulder into the control room, he yelled, "In there! The Lovell is on remote!"

Damn! He was right, of course. They were on automatic pilot. The Deputy Director had known that before she started running up the corridor, but didn't want to accept it.

The IBM mainframe was controlling the enormous seventy-six meter Lovell radio telescope, and it was the computer that had tripped the alarm. There wasn't any controller foul-up, no simple human error she could sweep under a bureaucratic rug. Something was out there, something large enough to present a threat, and it was on a collision course.

"I'll get the alarm," Feinberg shouted, "and meet you in the Observing Room." He moved off down the corridor in a burly shuffle.

By the time Margaret Kinsey reached the O.R., the high-pitched wailing had stopped. Moments later, Feinberg joined her to help. The imaging equipment gave them a picture in a little over three minutes; a telltale smear of light pointing a long, bony finger toward earth. But what was it, and on a trajectory to where? Dr. Feinberg was more comfortable with the Observing Room computer. Deputy Director Kinsey decided he should ask the questions.

The computer complied with a rushing stream of information. The contact was an asteroid. The raw numbers for the dimensions and weight were too abstract. They needed a visual idea of the size. The Deputy Director suggested two pianos. They settled on something about the size of a Hummer, traveling at 24.867 km per second, approximately 89,521 km per hour.

"My God," said Margaret Kinsey. "I tell my students all of the Near Earth Objects have been mapped. Where did this come from?"

"Perhaps it was just created," Feinberg suggested. "Or the orbit is so long we haven't encountered it in hundreds of years, before anyone was recording events."

He was still typing the rather complicated instructions that would provide the distance of the object when the alarm tripped again and they both flinched.

Margaret Kinsey couldn't resist a glance upwards which she knew was useless. "Hurry, doctor," she urged. "We need time to do anything constructive."

Finishing the instructions, Feinberg smacked the enter key. "There. Now let me see if I can shut down that noise again."

"Turn it off completely," the Deputy Director said.

He nodded, went out into the corridor, and turned off the entire alarm system. By the time he returned, an estimated distance had appeared on the screen: 44,761 kilometers. Below it blinked another set of numbers. The estimated time of impact: thirty-one minutes, forty-four seconds. The seconds were counting down with each blink.

"Two for one," Feinberg said ruefully.

"How could it sneak up on us like this?" Kinsey asked, an angry edge in her voice.

Feinberg glanced at her. She was an attractive woman, but the clenched jaw didn't serve her well. "It's just a rock and some gases, doctor," he said. "They don't sneak anywhere." He thought for a moment. "It might have been hidden by the moon. Or it might be a Lovell program anomaly."

She didn't respond.

He reached his hands out over the keyboard again, then hesitated. "What do we do when we have the coordinates? Ring the local authorities and tell them a Hummer is falling on them out of the sky?"

Margaret Kinsey was silent.

"You know the destructive force we're talking about," Feinberg reminded her. "This thing will create a crater half a kilometer wide, fifteen or twenty meters deep. Everything in that area will be vaporized." He glanced at the computer screen. "In thirty-one minutes and eight . . . seven seconds. If it's here in Great Britain, do you want to count on the Home Office to warn them?"

"Perhaps it will shatter when it strikes the atmosphere and the pieces burn up," the Deputy Director offered.

Feinberg looked at her, his weary umber eyes peering over his half glasses. "God help us if it doesn't." He took a breath and began to type.

The computer answered in longitude and latitude: fifty degrees forty-five minutes north, four degrees thirty-nine minutes west. They lost precious time finding a map with Dr. Feinberg musing that it wasn't surprising; their primary interest at Jodrell was in the opposite direction. However, he was out of quips when they located the impact point the computer had projected. It was a little more than 340 kilometers away; a rock outcropping on the southwestern coast of Cornwall named Pencannow Point.

"Bugger all," the Deputy Director said.

Feinberg raised an eyebrow at the mild profanity, but was silent.

"I think that's one of the places that cult of nits waiting to be saved by aliens has staked out," she said.

Feinberg shook his head. "I don't follow it much. What with the unemployment and the shortages and all, I guess people just need something to hold on to." After a moment, he added, "Looks like they may become casualties of more than The Troubles."

Margaret Kinsey stared at him a long moment. There wasn't time for the Home Office and their public relations division. The world would have to find out afterwards. She picked up the phone.

2

"UFO twits coming in the windows," Constable Nyles Langston said in disgust as he hung up.

The Duty Sergeant, John Willis, didn't look up from the copy of the *Globe* he was reading at the other desk in the small office of the police station in Crackington Haven.

"It's bad enough we've got them crawling all over the rocks up at Pencannow Point," Langston said. "Now they're ringing the station, from Manchester, mind you. And not just some ordinary nutter. This one's an official at some bloody bank. *Deputy Director*, mind you."

Sergeant Willis continued to read.

"Says there's a bloody asteroid coming; going to hit right up there on the point."

Willis looked up from his reading. "Asteroid? I thought it was aliens who were coming."

"Just as crackers, if you ask me," Langston groused.

The sergeant laid down his paper. "You said a bank?" he asked with a curious frown. "What exactly did he say?"

Constable Langston waved the question away with a derisive flick of his hand. "Not worth writing down. It was a woman. She says we're going to be *vaporized!*" He opened his eyes wide, blew out with a whooshing noise, then laughed.

"What bank?" Willis asked.

Langston sighed. "Jordon or something like that."

"Jodrell?"

"Yeah, that could be it."

The sergeant rolled his eyes. "You bloody lummox," he said.

"They're coming!" someone yelled.

An arm stabbed the sky, pointing to the west above the dregs of orange on the horizon. "Up there!"

A child giggled with excitement.

"I see it!" another voice shouted.

And a second arm shot up from the crowd of twenty or thirty people huddled in the cold wind whipping over the rock point that rose 131 meters above the sea.

"It's a ship! A saucer!"

Stillness settled over the group. Women squeezed their husband's hands. Fathers hoisted youngsters on their shoulders for a better view. The point of light grew brighter. Larger. Closer.

Stalking ahead of Sergeant Willis, his billy swinging in a clenched fist, Constable Nyles Langston reached the crowd first. "Get your bloody arses off this point now, you layabouts!" he ordered, and everything seemed to happen at once.

Suddenly it was daylight. Gasps arose from the crowd. Children screamed as people scattered, and someone hollered, "Look! They're sending out smaller ones from the mother ship."

"Off this bloody point, I tell you!" Langston yelled over the commotion. Then the sky blew up.

❖ ❖ ❖

As Dr. Margaret Kinsey hoped, the asteroid had broken up when it hit the atmosphere, turning into what was largely a spectacular and harmless light show. However, one tumbling chunk of black quartz weighing nearly a kilogram failed to burn up with the rest of the pieces and stayed unerringly on the course it had been on for over fifteen hundred years. This last remnant came screaming to earth and crashed into the rock cliffs of Pencannow Point with the explosive power of a dozen sticks of dynamite.

Ironically, Constable Nyles Langston was the hero of what soon would be called the Pencannow Point Incident. He managed to flush the crowd of alien gazers away in time to avoid serious injury to anyone but himself. He also kept his head when the emergency crew arrived.

"Bloody lucky you knew how to tie this tourniquet on your thigh," said one of the paramedics as they carried him to the ambulance. "You would have bled to death for sure."

Langston nodded with a sick smile. "Training," he managed, but when he asked himself how the tourniquet got there, he wasn't sure. Did someone or something come out of the crater after the blast? He wasn't sure.

3

Marjorie Langston was exhausted. She had worried through three hours at the hospital before the doctor came to assure her Nyles would be all right.

"You should be proud, Mrs. Langston," the doctor told her when he finally joined her in the waiting room looking weary and drawn himself. "Your husband is a hero for saving those people."

She smiled. "That's my Nyles."

"He's asleep," the doctor said. "There's nothing you can do here now. I suggest you go home, get some rest. We'll call you when he wakes. You can see him then."

When Marjorie got home, she tried to eat something, but her stomach was in knots. There wasn't much in the fridge at any rate, and none of it was appealing. She knew she couldn't sleep; not without taking her mind off Pencannow Point. Certainly, the telly would be no help in that regard. All it broadcast into Britain's homes these days was more worry. Tonight it would be how an asteroid had nearly killed them all, and about the constable who was in hospital with grave injuries. She slumped tiredly into her chair in the living room and retreated to her one haven. Reaching a paperback romance from the nearby bookcase, she began to read.

❀ ❀ ❀

The evening had grown cold. Marjorie Langston was now huddled in her chair, the book open in her lap where her hands had drooped when she finally dozed off. As she slept, something slowly tugged her back to consciousness, a warmth that soothed the tension from her chilled arms.

She turned once in the chair, resettled herself, and smiled in her sleep. A moment later, she first blinked, then opened her eyes.

A man was there, in the shadows beyond the chair lamp. It seemed like Nyles, but how could it be?

"I need your help, love," he said.

The voice had the timber and rough edge of her husband's; enough that she didn't realize it wasn't his. It belonged to the one who had tied the tourniquet and saved Nyles Langston when the asteroid struck, the one that the fiery celestial body had finally released from his long imprisonment, as he had foreseen it would. The figure in the shadows was the prophet, the advisor and wizard to a High King of Britain fifteen centuries ago. This was Emrys Myrddin, the enchanter who came to be known as Merlyn.

As he watched Marjorie Langston struggle to understand, he thought of the enchantment of another woman long ago in the service of another Pendragon. This night's slight of mind would also bear fruit, but not a child. Tonight it was the King's magician who was in need, and he wasn't seeking her bed, only her assistance.

"Nyles?" she said hesitantly. "Is that you?"

"I must go to London," Merlyn whispered.

A quizzical look came over her face. "London?"

"The King needs my help."

"The King?" She frowned. "But Nyles— "

"I need you to drive me to the rail station," he interrupted, stepping out of the shadows. "But I must change first."

He was draped in what seemed to be a long, slightly tattered, hospital gown. His straggly hair and beard appeared to her as the unkempt locks and stubble of her husband. She glanced where the bloody bandage had been wrapped around his leg when she first saw him in the hospital. It was gone.

"But the doctors told me it would be days before you were walking," Marjorie said.

"They were wrong," said Merlyn. He smiled warmly at her. "You know your brute of a husband."

That was her Nyles. She couldn't stifle a smile of her own. Then suddenly she was in tears. "I was so worried about you, Nyles," she said, sobbing as she moved from the chair and embraced him.

"Everything will be all right now," he said.

She held to him for a moment, then pushed away with an impish grin. "You could use a shower," she said.

After fifteen hundred years in a cave, I shouldn't be surprised, Merlyn mused to himself, but only nodded. "It will have to be quick."

Marjorie suddenly put a hand to her mouth. "Oh no," she said. "The car keys. When Sergeant Willis told me you'd been hurt, I searched everywhere, but I couldn't find mine. He had to bring me along to the hospital, and I took a cab home tonight." With tears welling in her eyes she went on. "They gave me what was left of your clothes, Nyles, but they said there were no keys or wallet." She sobbed again. "I'm sorry."

"Don't worry, love." He took her in his arms and kissed her. From somewhere he produced a wallet and set of car keys and winked. "You warm the car while I bathe and change. Then we must hurry."

4

The drive from Crackington Haven to the rail station at Bodmin Parkway took nearly an hour. For the first few miles Marjorie Langston pecked at Merlyn with questions about why he had to go to London and what it had to do with the King. He fended them all off with the same impenetrable answer: it was police business and he couldn't tell anyone, not even his life's love. Between the questions he surreptitiously marveled at their vehicle, an old Volkswagen Golf, and the British road system. He had hundreds of questions of his own, but they would have to wait for another time. He couldn't risk revealing his lack of common knowledge in this future and perhaps disturb the enchantment.

However, as they approached Camelford he sensed a feeling he hadn't had in more than a thousand years, a dark foreboding that beclouded his mind momentarily and led him to speak of a past only he knew. "It's over there," he said softly, pointing out into the countryside on the passenger side of the Volkswagen.

Glancing once, but keeping her eyes on the road, Marjorie Langston said, "What's over there?"

"Slaughter Bridge," Merlyn murmured. "Not far from Camlann."

She turned and looked at him now. His face was pallid, his eyes glassy. She reached over and touched his arm. "Nyles? Are you all right?"

The touch of her hand woke him from the reverie. He shook his head slightly and smiled as warmly as he could manage. "Yes, love. I was . . . I was just thinking about King Arthur. They say that's where his last battle took place."

She turned back to the road. "Since when do you know about that kind of stuff?"

"I must have read it. In one of your books," he tried and got away with it.

"Oh, you!" she said, rolling her eyes. "My books are a better comfort than that telly you sit in front of every night."

He huffed appropriately and asked what had been on tonight about the asteroid. When she told him she hadn't watched the telly, Merlyn took the lead, conjuring a story of whole cloth about how he had chased the people off the point and the ride to the hospital, deepening the enchantment. After a while he grew quiet and yawned. "I'm tired," he said. "Do you mind if I get some sleep on the way?" It was a good way to steer clear of any more mishaps, verbal or otherwise.

"Of course not," she agreed. "I'll wake you when we get to the station."

Merlyn turned his face to the window and tried to get comfortable. His yawn hadn't been entirely an act. He *was* tired and he knew there were others sleepless this night, playing out the dark drama he had foreseen. He must be rested if he was to change the last scene, and it would take much more than the enchantment of this young woman.

5

King Charles pushed the heavy damson-colored draperies aside and leaned close to the glass, looking keenly into the darkness below.

"Did you hear that?" he asked.

Prime Minister Alistair Saxon cocked his head. "I beg your pardon, Your Majesty?" He pointed to his ear with a deprecating smile. Then he rose from the chair Charles insisted he use rather than standing during these long private meetings and moved to the window. "What did you say?"

"I thought I heard something," said the King. "Damned inconvenience, this electrical trouble. Black as ink out there." He let the drapery fall and turned to the Prime Minister. "It sounded like a shot, gunfire."

Saxon knitted his unruly eyebrows. "I should think not, Your Majesty. More likely a backfire from a cab or lorry."

Charles gave him a skeptical glance. "They're still out there, aren't they? Even in this rain."

"The rain has stopped."

The King was silent, waiting.

"A few," the Prime Minister admitted after a moment. "Farmers pro-testing the freeze on milk prices. I'm sure they mean you no personal harm, but I wouldn't trust the fates so completely."

With no hesitation, he stepped across the bounds of royal etiquette and took the King's arm, guiding him away from the window. Charles frowned, but allowed Saxon to move him toward his desk, which was uncharacteristically awash in papers.

"I appreciate the thought," the King murmured. It was as close to an expression of warmth as he could manage. Always stiff and distant in his personal relationships, Charles had become painfully so since his ascension to the throne.

Saxon acknowledged the comment with a nod and a muted smile. "There is good news to report, regarding that incident at Pencannow Point," he said. "Only a fragment of the asteroid made it to earth, and there was only one casualty: a constable who is expected to recover fully."

"I'm relieved at that news, Prime Minister, but changing the subject is not an answer to my concerns."

Saxon released the King's arm and moved back a step. "As you know, Your Majesty, *my* overriding concern is for Great Britain who requires her sovereign." After a breath, he added, "And order."

Charles eased himself tiredly into the dark Moroccan leather chair at the desk. They had come full circle, back to the subject they'd been arguing for nearly half an hour. He shook his head and sighed. "That won't do, Alistair, won't do at all. Order is not what this Emergency Powers Act is about." He shook his head again. "No, it's about power, the concentration of power. To put it bluntly, too much concentration. Too much control in the hands of one human being."

The Prime Minster took a calming breath and tried once more. "The Americans and some few others may have finally found their way out of this world-wide financial disaster. Even that is being questioned in some corners," he said. "However, this country is still faced with grave problems, Your Majesty."

"And cannot afford another," Charles retorted. "Particularly one that, in the long course, could produce a final malaise."

"With all due respect, Your Majesty, if someone is not given the power to end the fuel shortage and several of our other problems almost immediately, what happens in the long course will be academic. Great Britain will be no more."

Saxon had returned to his chair in front of the King's desk and now leaned forward and placed a bound report on the polished oak. "According to this study from the Home Minister, our petrol supply will be depleted in less than three months. And that is if we continue the strict rationing we now have on private vehicles."

Charles ignored the report and shuffled through the papers on his desk, picking up, then discarding documents, talking as he searched. "I did not wait through more than fifty years to assume this responsibility only to shirk it at the first sign of trouble."

"But, Your Majesty, these matters—resolving strikes, managing resources—are not the proper concerns of a monarch."

"No, no," the King muttered, an edge in his voice now. "I'm talking about *this*." He grabbed several bound pages and thrust them at the Prime Minister. "Have you actually read the proposed draft of this legislation?"

Saxon didn't move to take the document. It was a long moment before he said, "It is not a draft, Your Majesty. That is the Act as both houses of Parliament have approved it."

Charles drew the offered pages back and looked off toward the window where he had parted the draperies, where he thought he'd heard gunfire. The air was thick with silence. Finally, the King broke it. "I see," he said flatly.

Turning back, he took his time looking for the passage in the Act he wanted and found it. "Then you expect me to give my assent to language such as this?" He adjusted his glasses and read. "'Promulgations deemed necessary by the Emergency Commission shall not be in any way delayed nor modified by proceedings in British Court of Law, nor by unapproved public acts of protest of any kind.'"

"By the legal maneuverings of special interests," Saxon explained. "Or damaging strikes."

The King looked at him over his glasses. "That's one interpretation."

"The only one which shall be made, I assure you, Your Majesty."

"And that is because Sir Alistair Saxon, Prime Minister of Great Britain, is to be Chairman of the Emergency Commission? What if this excellent chap should fall ill? Or, heaven forbid, die?"

Saxon moved to speak, but the King put him off with a gesture. "What if he was to snap, to simply . . . go off his trolley?"

The Prime Minister gave a harsh, barking laugh. It wasn't attractive.

"I'm afraid I don't see the humor, Alistair," Charles said grimly. He tossed the document into the litter on his desk. "Frankly, in my opinion, this is an open invitation to a dictator."

The word hung in the air, spoken and gone, but still absorbing the faint hum of the heating system, the distant hoot of traffic.

Finally Saxon said, "Surely, sir, you do not believe I would do anything to bring harm to Great Britain or her people?"

Charles stared into the Prime Minister's slightly florid face. In the two years since he'd asked Alistair Saxon to form a government with his New Liberal Party, he had never been able to gauge what lay behind those hooded, agate eyes. He knew the theory on short men and their compensations, their egos. Did it apply here? Most likely, but wasn't that quite possibly what the country needed; a Churchillian bulldog, as the tabloids always portrayed this squat, fleshy, stubborn little man? What would he do if given complete leeway? What could he do?

At length, the King smiled, although without warmth. "No, Prime Minister," he told him. "I do not question your motives."

"Thank you, Your Majesty," Saxon replied, a layer of tension melting away.

"However, there is a larger issue here that I must question," Charles said, giving a slight shake of his head. "I'm sorry, Alistair. I've decided to speak against the Emergency Powers Act."

Saxon gazed at the gaunt, aging face for a few seconds, then took a deep breath and exhaled deliberately. The discussion was over, he knew. There would be no easy solution. "As I am sure Your Majesty is aware, it has been more than three hundred years since a sitting British monarch refused assent to an Act of Parliament."

"Queen Anne in 1707; The Scots Militia Act," Charles said.

"You understand what I must do, Your Majesty?"

"Fully, Prime Minister. Your responsibility is to follow the wishes of your party."

With a curt nod, Saxon added, "And, in this case, the majority of the Members of Parliament. But I want you to know that it does not diminish my loyalty to you, Your Majesty."

"Accepted," the King said, nodding. He looked for and found a leather-bound calendar in the pile on the left side of his desk. "You will arrange for my presentation to Parliament?"

"Of course, Your Majesty. When would be appropriate?"

Charles referred to the calendar. "I would prefer to make it as soon as possible. Let us say, Monday next. That will give me tomorrow and the weekend to prepare."

"Very well, Your Majesty."

The King closed the calendar and the subject. "Can I offer you something to brace against the chill; a brandy? I saw snow flurries this afternoon." He rose from his chair and buttoned his tailored herringbone suit.

Saxon was up quickly from his chair. "Thank you, Your Majesty, but I must away." He glanced at his watch. "In fact, I'm late for dinner now, with old classmates from Oxford. A seasonal tradition we never miss. If you'll pardon me?"

"Good night, then," Charles said. He turned and walked toward a door at the rear of the room, an exit to a small study with his personal library, fully stocked liquor cabinet, and private telephone, all of which he was retreating to more and more as he struggled with public and private problems.

As the Prime Minister entered the outer office of the King's chambers, his aide, Richard Thorn, looked up. Saxon shook his head. He had also made his decision. "Arrange a meeting, at the usual place," he said.

Thorn glanced at his watch.

"Tonight!" commanded the Prime Minister.

6

The meeting place had been chosen months before by Alistair Saxon, borrowing the worn security axiom, *hide in plain sight.* It was a conference room on the top floor of a five story red brick structure on Milbank Street, less than a kilometer south of the Houses of Parliament. The building was privately owned, but had been leased by one department of government or another for more than forty years, the last six by the Home Office. The comings and goings of the influential was normal here and the government employees paid little attention.

A cold drizzle had started falling while Richard Thorn made his phone calls. The rain added to the ease with which the meeting participants slipped through a side entrance and made their way unnoticed to the fifth floor.

The last to arrive was General Sir Ian Baker-Smythe, Chief of the General Staff and Supreme Commander of the British Armed Forces. The General was fifty-eight years old, of average height, and holding his own in a battle with nature to retain the hard body he'd carved as a young drill instructor thirty years ago. His salt and pepper hair was cropped short with no sideburns. Under his damp raincoat, which he hung up at the door, he was dressed in street clothes, a soft, gray cashmere jacket with charcoal slacks and turtleneck sweater. The casual attire created the opposite effect, emphasizing his ramrod military bearing.

"I trust this is important," the General said to Richard Thorn, while the aide tended a hastily assembled bar just inside the conference room. "I have a dinner engagement with Admiral Reardon."

Thorn handed the General his usual gin and bitters. "Charles intends to speak against," he said quietly.

The General's smile, which had been perfunctory in the first place, evaporated. He handed back the drink. "Call my wife; tell her to make my apologies to the admiral."

"Very well, sir," replied Thorne.

"We're waiting, Ian," Alistair Saxon called in agitation from a high-backed chair at the head of a polished oak conference table.

Baker-Smythe strode across the room and sat down, taking his place at the right hand of the Prime Minister, the seat of power. He nodded to the others at the table. They included another member of the military and three of the most powerful civilians in Great Britain.

To the General's right was Major General Jock Cabot, Commandant of the Royal Marines. Cabot was in his late forties, a muscular six-footer with a shock of dark hair and a strong, weathered face. He'd been perhaps best described several years ago by a *London Times* reporter who wrote, "Close your eyes and think of the kind of man you want protecting Britain. That's Cabot." The Major General reported directly to General Baker-Smythe and was in command of one of the finest fighting forces in the world.

Whether by accident or mutual avoidance, the military men were alone on their side of the table with two empty chairs. At the opposite end of the table from Saxon was the oldest man in attendance, Sir Geoffrey Kitterage. A rail of bones covered by taut, chalk white skin and a sagging suit he could swim in, Kitterage was what was left of the legendary Chairman of United Kingdom Communications, PLC. At seventy-two, despite his crumbling appearance and health, he was still very much in control of the sprawling media conglomerate he built, which included TV3, the second British commercial television network, and *The Word*, Britain's most popular tabloid newspaper.

Around the table on Kitterage's right sat a small, compact man, a chain smoker in a wrinkled, ash-dusty blue suit. This was Nigel Gibbon, Director General of MI-5, the vaunted UK security service. Although as head of British Intelligence he was appointed by the Home Secretary with the approval of the Prime Minister, Gibbon reported to no one, on everyone.

Finally, another empty chair over, sitting at the left of the Prime Minister, was the Rt. Hon. Michael Lyme, MP, arguably the key member of Saxon's cabinet. As Home Secretary, Lyme was responsible for the internal affairs of England and Wales, which included just about everything: the police service and criminal justice system, immigration, counter terrorism, and the civil emergency services. A gangly thin man with a pale in-door complexion, the Secretary appeared to wear a permanent frown.

Bearing down on the frown now, Lyme snapped across the table at the late arriving Baker-Smythe. "Some of us have plans for this evening, General. If this is the timely fashion in which you run our armed forces . . ." Pausing in mid-rant, Lyme took a breath, glanced at the Prime Minister, then backtracked. "I'm sorry, Ian, but I'm in the middle of a dozen issues."

"And about to become entangled in another, I would guess," said Nigel Gibbon. He gave a small, knowing nicotine smile and offered Lyme a nearly empty and crumpled packet of Players. "Smoke?"

The Prime Minister interrupted whatever eruption might have ensued. "I am not interested in discussing the decision that I have made today," he announced without preamble. "This meeting is to inform you of it and to coordinate the actions which now must be taken." He paused only briefly, then went ahead. "As of two hours ago, I am irrevocably committed to Thunderbolt."

More than one chair creaked, but no one spoke.

"We can wait no longer," Saxon continued, drumming the urgency into the table with a stiffened forefinger. "If we are to save Great Britain, we must act now. In the next three days."

His words hung in a thick silence, but only for a breath. "I believe your decision is hastily taken and ill advised," Sir Geoffrey Kitterage said flatly.

Saxon knew the billionaire was accustomed to speaking his mind and being listened to. It was one of the initial reasons he wanted him in this group; that and his grip on what the average Briton saw on the telly or read in the daily rags. Now, based on the man's constant interference and foot-dragging, he considered him a serious mistake.

"As usual, our communications expert has turned off his hearing aid," the Prime Minister said derisively, eliciting a cough from someone. He then turned to General Baker-Smythe, purposefully showing his back to Kitterage. "Ian, I'm expecting you to take the lead on this and . . ."

"I would appreciate the opinions of the other members of this group," the old man asserted, unabashedly cutting off the Prime Minister. "What do you think, Michael?"

Before Michael Lyme could open his mouth, Saxon whirled on Kitterage. "You are out of order, sir!"

Kitterage rose defiantly in his chair. "Out of order? Has it now become out of order to seek a reasonable, civilized solution to a problem? Have we come that far down this dark tunnel?"

"I tried to reason with Charles," declared Saxon. "It's too late for reason."

"You don't know that," Kitterage shot back.

The Prime Minister glared at the old man. For a moment it seemed as though he would reach the length of the table and strike him. Then the rage was gone. He settled back in his chair. "Nigel, if you will?" he said simply.

The Director General of MI-5 leaned over and lifted a slim digital voice recorder from the briefcase next to his feet. While the others watched, he placed it on the table and pushed the play button. The voices were unmistakable.

"I did not wait through more than fifty years to assume this responsibility only to shirk it at the first sign of trouble."

"Charles," Kitterage whispered.

"Quiet," shushed Michael Lyme.

"As I am sure Your Majesty is aware, it has been more than three hundred years since a sitting British monarch refused assent to an Act of Parliament."

"I'm sorry, Alistair. I've decided to speak against the Emergency Powers Act. You will arrange for my presentation to Parliament?"

"Of course, Your Majesty. When would be appropriate?"

"Let us say, Monday next. That will give me tomorrow and the week-end to prepare."

That was it. Nigel Gibbon pressed the stop button.

"My God," murmured the Home Secretary, staring at the recorder. "Right in his chambers."

Saxon ignored the comment. "I think His Majesty made it clear enough. He intends to stand in the way of the Emergency Powers Act and every plan we've made. Crushed under the heel of a man so weak he nearly wasn't crowned King because he couldn't control a young wife. That's irony for you."

He looked directly down the table at Kitterage. "And if Charles has his way, how then will you swallow your competitors, sir? How, without your precious concept of government supported mergers, which is waiting for the Chairman of the Emergency Powers Commission to implement?"

"I don't give a *damn* what Charles intends," said Kitterage. He was angry, red faced. "Men can be made to change their minds; even kings."

"In three days?"

"In three seconds, with the right incentive."

General Baker-Smythe moved in his chair. "Not this stiff-necked bastard!" he declared. The animal hostility in the statement shocked the room into silence. In the hush, the General took the second step. "Someone should break it for him."

"But this is monstrous!" sputtered Kitterage. "We are talking about the King of England."

"England has outgrown the Royals!" Baker-Smythe threw back at him. "Surely, her problems have."

The Prime Minister suddenly slammed the flat of his hand on the table. "Gentlemen, I will have order here!" he demanded. He waited a moment, then sat forward in his chair, still focused on Kitterage. "And just how would *you* suggest we get Charles to relent from this stupidity? From dragging us all, the whole of Great Britain, down with him?"

Kitterage didn't hesitate. "By getting his attention."

Saxon sighed and slumped back. "Make sense, sir. Or leave us."

Now it was Kitterage who bent down to a briefcase next to his feet. He fumbled in it for a moment, then brought out a manila folder and placed it on the table. "The prospect of millions of people seeing these with their morning tea will give him pause, I believe. And reason to reconsider."

He gathered himself for the effort and slid the folder down the table toward the Prime Minister. It stopped in front of Nigel Gibbon.

"Thank you, Nigel," Saxon said, holding out his hand.

Gibbon picked up the folder. After a moment of obvious inner struggle, he pushed it along to Saxon.

The intelligence man needn't have concerned himself about getting a look at what was inside the folder. The Prime Minister opened it and spilled the contents out onto the table for everyone's perusal. There were thirteen photographs in all. They had a number of different backgrounds, but the subject in each was the same: Camilla Parker-Bowles. Most of the shots were unflattering. In all of them she was naked.

For the first time during the meeting, Major General Jock Cabot spoke. "How did you get these?"

The question released Kitterage's first smile. "MI-5 isn't the only organization in Great Britain with spies," he said. "They were taken with high-powered lens or by hidden cameras. At Highgrove in Cotswold, Clarence House in London, and other locations."

"Are you suggesting you would publish these?" asked the Prime Minister.

"Not if he values his corporation," Michael Lyme said. He shook his head. "Our obscenity laws prohibit it. Especially with the Royals involved. The courts would fine UKC out of business."

Kitterage smiled again. "I would threaten. And also explain what would happen if the photos *accidentally* found their way to the Internet."

Major General Cabot looked pointedly at Baker-Smythe, but the General simply laid down the photo he'd been examining.

After a moment the Prime Minster said, "And you would personally help His Majesty to understand the ramifications?"

"Tomorrow," answered Kitterage. "Leaving two full days if they are needed. I'm sure I can arrange an audience through my own contacts, having nothing to do with anyone here tonight."

Saxon glanced around the table from one face to another. They were non-committal except for General Baker-Smythe, who had made his inclinations obvious to everyone.

"I'm not against it," the Prime Minister said finally. He stood and passed the photo he was holding to Michael Lyme. "Thank you, gentlemen. Richard will phone you when and if you are required." Then he smiled broadly. "And please don't try to pinch any of the photographs for your personal collections."

They all dutifully chuckled at the Prime Minister's attempt at locker-room humor, which served at least to relieve some of the tension in the room. Then they passed their photos to Kitterage and collected their belongings.

Major General Cabot and Nigel Gibbon, neither in any apparent hurry, drifted to the makeshift bar and Richard Thorn's attentions. After a short private conversation with the Prime Minister, Michael Lyme joined them, insisting he could only stay for one drink.

Both Sir Geoffrey Kitterage and General Baker-Smythe excused themselves and walked out into the hallway. They were waiting silently for the lift when Alistair Saxon stuck his head out the door.

"Ian, I'd like you to stay a moment," he said.

The General glanced impatiently at his watch. "I'm trying to reschedule a dinner engagement."

"It's not a request."

"I see," Baker-Smythe said tightly. "Yes, of course." He moved stiffly back inside.

The Prime Minister suddenly seemed to notice Kitterage standing at the lift. "Oh, I'm sorry, Sir Geoffrey. Didn't Richard tell you? The lift has apparently gone out again. You'll have to use the stairs." He pointed down the hall. "Sorry," he said with a shrug. Then he turned and went inside.

Kitterage smiled mildly to himself, unperturbed by the Prime Minister's rudeness, gratified that the General was most surely about to receive a richly deserved reprimand. Too bad he couldn't stay to eavesdrop, he thought, never imagining how wrong he was. The old man headed for the stairs. He had an appointment to schedule.

7

Marjorie Langston gently shook Merlyn's shoulder. "Nyles, we're here," she whispered.

"Uh?" he murmured.

"Bodmin Parkway; we're here."

He looked out the window at what he assumed was the rail station. "When does the next train leave?"

"I let you sleep while I checked. The next one to Paddington station is in fifteen minutes. It's the last London bound train tonight."

He sat up. "Then we have to get a ticket."

She let a smile spread across her face as she held up his wallet. "And you need money for that," Marjorie said. She waggled the wallet.

Merlyn stared at her for a moment, then sighed and slumped slightly in his seat.

She waggled the wallet again. "The truth, Nyles."

The truth, Merlyn thought. Yes, perhaps it was time for the truth. It had always been one of the best tricks in his hat. He looked off a moment, then turned back to her. "You have to promise not to tell anyone."

"I promise," she said with a smile.

He took a deep breath, and with a grimly serious look, began. "All right, the truth. I'm not really your husband. I'm the ancient Wizard, Merlyn. I'm here to bring Arthur Pendragon back from Avalon to save England in this time of great need."

As he rightly guessed she might, Marjorie began to softly giggle, and as the giggle grew into laughter she threw the wallet at him. "Nyles Langston, you're hopeless!"

"Hopelessly in love," he added as he scooped up the wallet. "Now let's get me a ticket and get you on your way back home so you can get some sleep."

Inside the station, without Marjorie noticing, Merlyn encouraged her to take the lead in the purchase of the ticket and finding the right place to wait for the train. When it arrived, they kissed again and he promised to be in touch in the morning. He boarded the train, found a seat, and waved at her through the window. She waved back as the train began to move. Then she turned and headed through the station to the parking lot.

Merlyn watched her go, knowing that she would sleep well and, when she awoke, there would be a call from the hospital, from her husband Nyles. It would all have been a dream. The Wizard smiled warmly. He liked Marjorie Langston.

As the train gained speed and moved through the night toward England's destiny, Merlyn settled back in his seat and calmed himself. There were two more things he must attend to before this day began in earnest.

8

It was hours past the time the old man normally retired. However, Sir Geoffrey Kitterage still sat at the enormous mahogany desk that dominated the room he called Communications Central. It occupied most of the ground floor of the town home in the exclusive Mayfair section of Westminster, not far from Buckingham Palace. He'd lived here for the past twenty years, since his first success with the launch of his daily newspaper.

An eclectic mix of past and future, the room was furnished with fine art and antiques, equipped with a bank of oversized plasma television screens where he kept tabs on his TV3 Network and its competitors.

The rain had stopped again, he noticed as he stared out the window into the night. Perhaps it was a harbinger of a better day tomorrow. He turned back to the desk. The envelope he had taken to the meeting with the Prime Minister was there. He lifted it. A lightweight for such heavy dealings, he thought. Did he have the right? Was it right?

The mahogany long case clock standing in the corner of the room struck the half hour, its muted chime seeming loud in the silence.

Kitterage glanced at the George III antique, circa 1785. It was one of his favorite pieces. He let his gaze shift to the platinum atomic clock perched on the corner of his desk with its automatically correcting digital display of times across the meridians.

"Perhaps it is time for change," he said to the empty room.

He put the envelope with its volatile contents into his briefcase. As he closed it, there was a soft knock on the door.

"It's Holcombe, sir," said a voice from the other side.

Clarence Holcombe was his personal aide and a confidant of twenty years. "Come in, Clarence. I've been waiting for you." As the aide entered, Kitterage motioned him to a chair and asked, "What word have we, Clarence? Have you managed it?"

Holcombe nodded with a contained smile. "Yes, sir," he said. "As we hoped, I was able to reach Henry Duckworth, His Majesty's appointments secretary, at his rooms in the Palace."

Kitterage give an agreeable snort. "That phone book of yours is worth your weight in gold and I shall see that you get it."

The aide gave him another slim smile. "Then, sir, I shall forego my diet beginning now."

Kitterage leaned forward to the man. "So, tell me what you've arranged. Are we on for tomorrow?"

"The King has cancelled nearly all of his scheduled appointments. Duckworth wasn't forthcoming as to why, but I assured him it was imperative, of importance to the nation's security, and he agreed to add you to the short list His Majesty approved. The appointment is set for eight-thirty tomorrow morning. However, Duckworth warned that he may have to wedge you in and suggested you be available from eight onwards."

Now Sir Geoffrey Kitterage smiled broadly at his old friend across his desk. "Have a trifle with Devonshire cream, my good fellow. Have two."

He sat back in his chair, almost exuberant, feeling the old, familiar sensation of adrenalin coursing though his body. It had been a long time since he faced a truly good fight. "What's that song from those American chaps, Clarence? You know the Camelot fellows, Lerner and his friend." And then it came to him and he smiled again. "I wonder what the King is doing tonight?"

❖ ❖ ❖

The only light came from the fireplace, a flicker of embers. The inch of cognac left in the bottle of Louis XIII de Remy Martin, still warm from an hour of sitting on the brick hearth, wavered between amber and bronze. The Italian Murano crystal snifters were both empty now.

Queen Consort Camilla sat up on the soft wool of the muted gray afghan spread on the hearth, drawing her bathrobe closed against a chill that had invaded the room. Charles rolled up on an elbow, his naked back to her, and stared into the leftovers of the fire.

"I can't possibly leave until it's settled," he said.

She sighed. "I'm not asking you to. But the whole family doesn't have to be punished. We asked the boys to take time off from their lives, but they haven't been able to enjoy a day of the holiday we promised ourselves. Nor have I, for that matter. Why shouldn't we go ahead? You can join us later."

"We've been over this. It will be an historical moment, every detail recorded, examined. It would be unseemly if the family appeared to treat it as unimportant, blithely flying off to Jamaica on the eve of the confrontation."

She pulled her robe closer to her body. "Really, Charles," she said. "You are being a bit puffed up over this, even for you."

"Damn it, Milla!" he said. "I've asked you not to speak to me in that tone. I forbid it!"

"As husband . . .or King?"

He sat up abruptly, fishing in the dim light for his clothes. "The subject is closed," he said flatly as he found his trousers and struggled into them. "I have work to do." Taking the bottle of Remy Martin and a snifter with him, he moved to the desk. "I would appreciate it if you returned to your bedroom."

Camilla silently rose and padded in bare feet to the door of the private study. "I won't be bullied, Charles," she said as she let herself out.

❖ ❖ ❖

Not far from Westminster or the Palace, in the private study of General Sir Ian Baker-Smythe, another discussion had gone long into the precipice night, edging toward the abyss. Ironically enough, it had also been laced with snifters of Remy Martin. The sole guest of the General was Jock Cabot, Commandant of the Royal Marines. Cabot now set his warmed snifter down and turned a page in the document before him, studying it again.

"We've been over it three times, Jock. Do you have a problem with the order?" Baker-Smythe asked.

Cabot looked up. He shook his head. "It's completely clear, sir. I've already personally picked the leader of the Special Ops team–Major Rhys Mallory from Commando Forty in Somerset. They are on their way to London as we speak. And all the ancillary requirements are in process."

"I didn't ask you that. I asked if you had a problem with it."

"I'm a marine, sir. I don't have problems with my orders."

The General gave a grunt of a laugh. "You're also Jock Cabot." He picked up the Remy Martin bottle, poured a quarter inch more into both of their nearly empty snifters, and had a drink from his. "If your people perform as ordered, there will be only minimum *collateral damage* as the Americans say. And we will have the advantage required for a successful campaign."

A dim flare in Cabot's eyes only slightly betrayed his feelings. "Have no doubt, sir," he assured the General. "They *will* perform."

"And you?" Baker-Smythe asked.

"Don't insult me, General. It's too late at night." He downed his cognac. "Now, if you'll excuse me, sir, I have things to attend to."

The General stared at him a moment, then smiled and nodded. "Goodnight, Commandant," he said. "And good luck."

9

The taxi driver at Paddington Station was a bantam of a man in his mid-fifties with thinning hair and bad teeth. He hadn't moved from his nest behind the steering wheel nor invited Merlyn to get into the cab. He checked his watch, then eyed the Wizard suspiciously through the open passenger window.

"You want a lift to Hyde Park at two o'clock in the morning?" the driver said. "It wouldn't be to rob me of my night's takings and my life, I suppose, now would it?"

Merlyn raised an ironic eyebrow. "An old man like me?"

The driver gave him another once over. "Then, what is it?"

"To keep a promise made long ago," the Wizard said, his voice sounding old now, seeming to come from the past. "To say something to a Major General."

"In the bloody middle of the night?"

Merlyn looked off into the darkness, then back at the driver through the window. "At the War Memorial at Hyde Corner," he said. "This was as soon as I could get here."

The driver's frown softened slightly. "They took their time building it, sixty bloody years." After another moment he said, "My father was in it. The war against the Nazis, I mean." He paused again. "Well, near as. He had a trawler and helped float some of the boys back from Dunkirk in 1940."

"Men fight in their own ways," said Merlyn.

The taxi driver stared at him a moment longer, then put the pistol he'd been holding under his coat in the glove box and started the car. "Get in, then," he said with a shrug. "Hardly worth the fare, but an old man shouldn't be walking alone this time of night. Not with trash about that would slit a throat for a quid."

"Do you all carry weapons?" Merlyn said once he'd climbed in and they were under way.

The taxi driver gave a caustic laugh. "Only those of us who want to live through the night."

"Somebody should do something about The Troubles," said Merlyn, probing for the depth of the disaffection. He gave it a breath, then added, "Whatever it takes."

"He'd be a hero, that somebody," the driver said. "A bloody hero."

And a man to bring an end to England thought Merlyn. The Wizard closed his eyes and concentrated. The one he would speak to was already there. He could feel it. There was no time to lose.

The solitary figure stood about midway along the curved face of the War Memorial, where the word Gallipoli had been carved into green granite from Western Australia. Merlyn recognized the stiff military bearing, the lank, masculine form he'd seen in his mind's eye. He moved silently through the darkness toward the island of light where Major General Jock Cabot stood with his back to him.

As the Wizard drew near, Cabot sensed something; the shadow of Merlyn's hand on his shoulder, an unheard whisper in his ear. With a small shiver he turned and stared into the night. There was nothing there. But when he turned back to the memorial an old man was before him, a bearded apparition.

"Why are you here, son?" Merlyn whispered.

Cabot jerked back instinctively and glanced around to see if anyone else was near, but there was only the enveloping night. He turned back to the shade before him. "Who are you?" he said.

"Whoever you want me to be," whispered Merlyn. "Your grandfather who died at Gallipoli with eight thousand of his countrymen?"

"How do you know that?"

"Your father told me."

"He's long dead."

The Wizard nodded. "Yes, in the first wave at Sword Beach on D-Day. Good men both of them. Doing what they believed they must."

Cabot knew this confrontation was in his own mind, but he didn't like it. "What do you want?" he asked with a slight edge in his tone.

"What do you?" whispered the Wizard.

The Major General stared at him for a long moment before answering. "To do my duty," he said finally.

Merlyn spread his arms wide, as if taking in the whole of the curved granite surface behind him and the hundreds of battle names carved there. "So did they all, and even more," he said. "To do what they knew was right, no matter the cost."

"The times have changed," Cabot said, his anger now clearly showing. "England must change."

"And what is right? What they gave their full measure for? Must that also change?"

"I don't care who you are," said Cabot, "I don't have to listen to this." He wheeled and started walking away into the night. After a few paces, he swung back to say something else and caught his breath. The old man was gone.

"Bloody hell!" the Major General breathed. He shook his head, then turned again and disappeared into the darkness surrounding the memorial.

As he moved away, Merlyn heard him curse, "Damn you, spirit!"

Merlyn held his hands in the cold, crystalline water that poured over the carved granite squares of the War Memorial and wondered if the human heart was ever so pure. He wondered if he had lost Cabot to the mirage of power, to false loyalty and pride. He would know soon enough, but now there was another detail he must see to; the old soldier. The Wizard wet his face with the water from the memorial, took a deep breath, and once again closed his eyes.

10

Seventy-four year-old Sergeant Major Trevor Warwick was up early, as usual. He'd fixed his tea and toast and carried it to the Recreation Lounge. He wasn't waiting for some decrepit know-it-all to wander in and take over the telly. He had seniority. He'd been at the Camelford Veterans Home longer than any of those worn-down skeletons; at least longer than anyone still ambulatory. He had rights. He had . . .

"Trevor Warwick, what are you doing up already?" Harriet Claiborne said from the door. "You know the Lounge isn't open until 8:00." She looked at her watch. "It's only 7:50."

"I'm guarding my news on TV3," he said, compensating in volume for the hearing aids he needed, but regularly refused to wear. "If I don't, that moron Kay will try to turn it over to that damned talk show."

"Quiet," she said, glancing toward the door to the hallway. "You'll have everyone poking their noses in here, including the nurse supervisor."

He had a sip of his tea and set it on the table next to the chair he'd commandeered in front of the television set. "You know, nurse Harriet, you have the most beautiful eyes I've ever seen; dark as your raven hair," he said. Patting the arm of the chair, he smiled. "Wouldn't you like to join me?"

Harriet knew seducing the young nurses at the Camelford Veterans Home was a constant, harmless theme with the Sergeant Major, but she still always flushed. Since she blossomed at thirteen she'd been embarrassed by looks from men. This morning she also couldn't help smiling. Trevor Warwick and his feisty brawl with old age was one of the reasons she loved her work.

She gave him a mild disapproving look. "How would you like your vitamin B-12 shot, Sergeant Major?"

He grimaced. "That's mean. How old are you?"

"*Young* enough to be your granddaughter."

He huffed something under his breath and leaned out to turn on the telly. "Not as old as I look, young woman. Not as old as I . . ."

The opening of the door interrupted Warwick as Commander Clive Kay entered the lounge carrying his tea and two pieces of smoked kipper balanced on a napkin.

"Damn," the Sergeant Major cursed under his breath.

Clive Kay was nearly six feet five and rake thin with long limbs. His last name and elegant look had provided him with a lifetime of mean, effeminate taunts and a combative attitude he still harbored in his seventies.

"What are you doing in here?" Kay demanded of Trevor Warwick. He looked at Harriet. "This is frightfully unfair. It isn't 8:00 yet."

"I guess he caught us, my dear," said Warwick. "We'll have to admit the affair."

"Sergeant Major!" the nurse chided.

"I won't have this!" Kay declared and moved toward the television set. "If you think you can control . . ."

"I was here first!" Trevor Warwick snapped as he struggled out of his chair and stepped in front of the advancing Kay. Then suddenly the Sergeant Major frowned and reached for his left temple. He sucked in a breath in pain.

"What is it?" Harriet Claiborne asked. She started to move toward him.

Staggering toward the nurse, he mumbled, "The King . . ." and collapsed.

Harriet was down with him immediately. His skin was already growing clammy. His breathing was shallow. Taking his wrist she felt for a pulse. It was there, but fluttering. "Trevor, can you hear me?" she said. "Hold on Trevor, I'll get help."

"My God, what is it?" Kay asked.

The nurse gave him a heated glance and shook her head. "Just stay with him," she told the Commander.

As Harriet started to get up, Trevor Warwick's arm jerked in a reflex action and struck her hand. She turned to him and his eyes opened. "Ring Tom," he said, slurring the words. "He's needed by the King."

11

The call to the SoHo flat in London came just as Tom Warwick stepped into the shower. Something made him turn off the water, wrap himself in a towel, and answer it. He had to sit down afterwards. It was Camelford; the call he knew would come someday, but he still wasn't ready for it. There wasn't any question about what to do. His father needed him and he would go to him. However, he was frustrated by the waffled diagnosis the doctor gave, and the other problem the man seemed to be implying.

While he showered and got dressed, he put a plan together. There wasn't much to it. He'd simply have to miss some of his classes at the University. Most of the professors were fairly liberal about attendance. He was sure his wife, Vivian, could manage on her own for a few days. They would just have to decide whether he should take a train or the Mini.

The ten-minute walk from the second story flat on Beak Street to the McDonald's on Oxford where Vivian worked took Tom Warwick halfway across SoHo. It was ten minutes of worrying, imagining the worse like the hypochondriac he knew he was. When he finally pushed through the doors into the restaurant, he was relieved to see Vivian out front, backing up the crew serving the early breakfast crowd. At least he wouldn't have to scare some poor kid half to death by asking for the manager.

His wife smiled when she saw Tom. As he reached the counter, she moved in to take his order. "Hey!" she said. "You're up early. Coffee, a sausage biscuit, and hot cakes?"

"Just coffee, thanks," he said. "Can we talk?" He pointed through the preparation area to the back where the cubbyhole that passed as the manager's office was situated.

Vivian Warwick frowned. Where was the famous bottomless pit of the starving history student she'd been supporting for the past year? She nodded and motioned him around. Then she leaned over the warming area and shouted for the assistant manager.

As soon as they were in the small office in the back, Tom told his wife about the call from Camelford.

She grimaced. "What did the doctor say? Was it a stroke?"

Tom tipped up his paper cup and had a slurp of the steaming coffee. "You know how they are; never straightforward. He called it a neurological event."

The look on his face told her he was holding something back. She knew to wait. You couldn't push Tom on some things: masculine, self-worth issues.

After a moment he said, "I think there could be something else besides whatever happened this morning."

"Like what?"

He looked at her, then glanced away. "Alzheimer's, at least the first signs."

"Is that what the doctor said?"

He shrugged. "No. But he made a point of telling me my father appears *confused*. He told me not to worry about it. Twice."

Vivian smiled. "Well, then, don't worry. It must not be anything serious."

Tom turned and, for the first time, met her eyes. "He thinks he had a meeting with King Charles."

"Your father?" she said, her eyebrows arched in surprise.

"He keeps talking about the King needing help." Tom had another swallow of coffee. "*My* help."

Vivian couldn't stop a giggle from popping out. She immediately sucked in a breath and apologized. "I'm sorry, that just came from nowhere."

Tom shook his head with a bitter smile of his own. "It gets worse. He apparently thinks the King is in Camelford. Says I have to come and help him–*the King*. To do what, I have no idea. According to the doctor he never gets that far."

"You're going, aren't you?"

Tom nodded. "I was going to ask if you needed the Mini, but on the walk over here I was thinking I don't know how long I'll have to stay. Can you call and check the train schedules?"

Five minutes later she had a train number and departure time for the trip from Paddington Station. "It's three hours and forty minutes to Bodmin Parkway, through Bristol and Plymouth," Vivian said. "You'll have to take a taxi from Bodmin to Camelford. That's another half hour or so." She looked at her watch. "But you don't have a lot of time. The train leaves at 9:15."

"We can't afford it, you know?" said Tom.

"We'll just put it on the credit card. You can get some cash on it, too."

After a moment of staring off, he straightened his shoulders. "All right."

She opened the top drawer of her desk and fished the credit card out of her purse. "Use as much as you need," she said as she passed it across the desk to him. "Now, it's already after 8:00 and I've got work to do. Eat or go," she said, pointing to the front of the restaurant. "And never darken these golden arches again."

It was just upbeat enough. Tom smiled and relaxed for the first time since the phone rang this morning. "Maybe just an Egg McMuffin for the road. I've got to get back to the flat and pack something." He stood and started down the narrow corridor toward the serving area.

"And a small juice," she said. "You haven't been getting your vitamins."

"I'll ring you tonight. Tell you what *the King* has to say," Tom called back, trying to put a light touch on what had been a dark day so far.

They both laughed, but neither would have if they had known what they were being drawn into.

12

Sir Geoffrey Kitterage had been waiting nearly an hour. He wasn't good at it. People waited for him, not the other way around and there was also the matter of his buttocks. They ached. At seventy, he thought, no man's boney ass was made for sitting and shouldn't be subjected to it, for Country *or* King. After changing positions for what seemed the twentieth time, he stood and wandered the waiting area outside Henry Duckworth's office.

"Waiting for an *appointments secretary*," he muttered to himself. He picked up a magazine from a table, riffled through it, and tossed it back down. As he was about to sit down again, the door to Duckworth's office opened and the appointments secretary stepped out.

"Deeply sorry about this wait, Sir Geoffrey," Henry Duckworth said, deferentially. Then he smiled. "However, I've just now had a phone message from His Royal Highness. He wonders if you would mind joining him downstairs in the dining room. He would like to stretch his legs, and he hasn't been able to have breakfast yet."

The invitation drew a restrained smile and a nod. "Tell him I would be delighted," said Kitterage.

"Very good, sir. If you'll wait just a tick longer, I'll inform him."

Duckworth disappeared back into his office and the old man walked over and picked up his briefcase. In a few seconds the secretary returned. "Please follow me," he said to Kitterage and started off down the hallway. "His Majesty will use his private lift and meet us there."

At that moment, standing at a stainless steel table in the kitchen that served the dining room, the youngest son of the King, Prince Harry, said, "Father will be furious."

"About you being out all night again?" asked the Queen Consort, Camilla.

Harry gave a low chortle. "I don't think so. The teenager you're thinking about is now a lieutenant in the Blues and Royals. You know what I'm talking about; it's this plan of yours to run off on holiday without him."

"Drink your orange juice," ordered Camilla. She put a half-eaten piece of dry toast on a plate at the table. "It won't hurt him. A little blood flowing through those veins might even help." She picked up the toast again and took a bite. "Bring out his human side," she said, talking through the toast.

Harry rolled his eyes. "Camilla, you are a trial."

"I am the woman who is taking you to the airport in a shiny red Jaguar convertible. William will be sorry he chose to stay behind and go hunting with your uncle, when he learns of it." She put the toast down again and took his arm. "Now, let's be off before someone notices a car has been pilfered from the Royal garage."

"We'll never get away with it," said Harry.

"This from a young snipe who got away with dancing in a Nazi uniform?" Camilla retorted. "A soldier who was secretly deployed as a Forward Air Controller in Afghanistan without his father's approval?" She huffed a chuckle, then went on. "We'll not only get away, but to Heathrow and thence to Kingston via Air Jamaica. An old friend, Jonathan Vick, works at their office in Chelsea. I rang him up at his home last night. He's been kind enough to arrange our passage. Under assumed names, of course."

"But how?" Harry said.

She chuckled again. "In the red convertible."

"You can't just drive to Heathrow," Harry said incredulously.

"Who's to stop me?"

"But–you're the Queen Consort of Great Britain."

"Precisely," said Camilla. She smiled, absolutely glowing with the intrigue. "Now, pick up those bags if you please and follow me. Our chariot awaits at the staff entrance in the south wing."

Harry gulped the last of his juice, stuffed a strip of bacon in his mouth, and obediently lifted the two suitcases. They were across the kitchen at a door leading outside to a small garden when the sounds of angry voices stopped them.

Camilla raised a finger to her lips and returned across the room. She eased the door to the dining room open and suddenly caught her breath. It was Charles. He was livid, arguing with someone out of her line of sight.

"Just what the hell do you think you are doing?" the King demanded. "This is ridiculous! Completely unacceptable."

Camilla pushed the door open enough to see the other man. He was dressed in khaki fatigues, pants tucked into his black boots, a black beret slanted on his head. She recognized the Special Forces uniform from reviews she'd made at military bases. Two men dressed the same were standing behind him. All three carried automatic weapons with bulbous black attachments on the barrels.

She thought the soldier in front was going to speak, but instead he did the unbelievable. He shot Steven Sunderkind, one of Charles' personal bodyguards from Scotland Yard. The gun made only a low coughing noise, but the security man was sent flying backwards and crashed into the wall behind him. He slid to the carpet, leaving a smear of red on the white wall. The ghastly act seemed to be a signal, a release to the other two soldiers. Both opened fire.

One killed Sunderkind's partner, who had jammed his hand inside his jacket, but never got it withdrawn. The other shot Henry Duckworth, who was standing next to Charles, then turned and brought down an older man who had yelled an obscenity and was hobbling toward the door to the hallway. The bullets stuck him between the shoulders, toppling him forward on his face.

Through it all Camilla had a sense of Charles, a peripheral vision. He'd flinched, but stood tall, stiffly facing the killers. Now the Special Forces man who fired first and started the massacre spoke to him in a stage voice, as if he was playing to an audience.

"It's safe now, Your Majesty. We've gotten them all. The assassins are dead."

Charles actually took a step toward him. "This is outrageous!" he declared. "There were no assassins. You fools have killed my appointments secretary and two agents from Scotland Yard." He pointed at the body of the man who had tried to run. "And that man over there is Sir Geoffrey Kitterage, one of our most respected businessmen."

Charles looked around at the carnage and shook his head. "Absolutely unbelievable." Turning back to the Special Forces man, he demanded, "Where is your superior? By God, I will not stand for this!"

"I'm afraid you will, Your Royal Highness. And a bit more," the Special Forces man said. He motioned the King menacingly toward the door to the hall with his weapon. "I'll have to ask you to move to a more secure location now, sir. For your own safety. We've chosen a room at the rear of the Palace overlooking the gardens . . . and the heliport." Turning to the other two men in khaki he said, "All right, round them up. The Queen Consort and William, Catherine, and Harry should be in their quarters upstairs. Prince Andrew and his brood are visiting. And don't forget Fergie is here to see their daughters. They'll all be in the south wing."

"Sir!" one of the soldiers said, and both moved silently toward the door.

"And be quick about it," the lead man called. "I want the whole family there when the choppers land." He glanced at his watch. "In sixteen minutes."

Camilla held her breath while she softly closed the door. She was shaking, sick to her stomach with fear. Every instinct told her to gather Harry and run, but she knew she couldn't. There wasn't a hope that she'd make it, not physically. She would only slow him; slicing into whatever slim chance he had of escaping. And where could the Queen Consort hide? No, this time Charles would be right. Her place was with him. He would need her.

To her relief, Harry was still standing by the exit, tense, but apparently unaware of what had happened in the dining room. As she hurried toward him, she dug into her purse. She must have some money somewhere.

"What is it, Camilla?" Harry asked. His eyes were bright, full of the scheme they were launching. "I couldn't hear from over here. Was that father? Has he found out? What was that popping? It sounded like a silenced weapon."

She took him by the shoulders, squeezing, her nails digging in. There wasn't time to explain. This had to be on faith, on what he'd been taught.

"Listen to me, Harry. This is serious, no play-acting. There are soldiers in the palace. They've killed some people. They've got your father and they're after William and you. You've got to run, get away."

"What?" Harry said, frowning.

"Now!"

"But Camilla..."

"Damn you, Henry Charles Albert David!" she whispered harshly. "I'm not Camilla. I'm the Queen Consort, and you are an heir to the British throne. Perhaps the only one now. England must have her Kings. Run!"

The frightened look on her face, the quaver in her voice, snapped him out of his stupor. It was the black tale he and William had been told and retold. The Roman Emperors, the French Kings, the Russian Czar; only it wasn't a story. He dropped the bags and hesitantly turned to the door.

"No, wait!" Camilla blurted. "Take your bag, and . . . here." She pressed several folded bills and some coins into his hand, ten pounds, six pence. It was all she could find. "Don't try to reach anyone we know. Anyone, you understand? They'll be listening, watching."

He picked up his bag and stared at her silently; conflicted, the taste of fear in his mouth. Then he stepped outside and was gone.

The Queen Consort didn't watch him move away, but turned back into the kitchen immediately. She put on fresh lipstick, straightened her hair and dress, then picked up a piece of bacon and walked calmly into the dining room.

13

According to his nametag, he was Major R. Mallory. He was efficient and emotionless. That was all they knew about the leader of the commando unit that had taken them captive. Now, crowded together near the Palace heliport with the rotor blades of a huge Sea King MK4 helicopter battering the air, they discovered his coolness couldn't be taken for granted.

The team of four men he'd sent to search once more for Prince Harry had returned shaking their heads. Major Mallory approached Camilla, a grim expression on his deeply tanned face. "You lied to me, madam. That was a mistake," he shouted over the noise. Then he slapped her.

It was a glancing blow, designed so, but with enough shock and sting to bring tears to her eyes. Camilla grimaced, but didn't bring her hand to her cheek or cry out in pain.

However, the Duchess of York, standing near the Queen Consort, was never one to fight instinct. "Animal!" she shrieked in fiery defiance and swung at the Commando leader with a wide roundhouse.

He dodged it easily, then turned to check on the men. Only one had lost control–Prince William. Two soldiers had roughly put down his lunge toward the leader with the butts of their automatic weapons. The Prince was left with a taste of his own blood as a caution against further aggressive moves and a young wife with tears welling in her eyes.

Mallory turned back to Camilla. "It's hopeless, you know," he yelled. "He can't hide with that face. We'll find him. You haven't accomplished anything except to put Prince Harry in danger." Now he spoke to a man wearing a headset, a radio strapped to his back. "Get Command! Tell them we're minus one, the spare. We're departing for D One."

The radioman acknowledged with a quick nod and started talking into the microphone curved in front of his face.

A few moments later, in a bomb-hardened underground site near Luton, fifty kilometers northwest of Buckingham Palace, General Ian Baker-Smythe leaned over a map table and drew a circle with a yellow marker.

"If he is on his own, we'll find him somewhere here, in the center of the city. On foot." He shook his head in a derogatory statement. "They never teach the Royals anything of practical value. He knows how to chase a skirt, look down on commoners, and dress up like a Nazi. But he won't have any idea how to rent a car, take a bus, anything like that."

"What if he's not?" said Nigel Gibbon. "On his own, that is." He stubbed out a Player's in the overflowing ashtray in front of him.

The General gave him a distasteful glance. "The rest of the family is airborne, on their way to D One. The staff has all been accounted for. There's no one else. He's alone."

"I understand a vehicle from the Royal garage was found parked near an exit to the perimeter fence. Fully fueled, with the keys in the ignition."

Baker-Smythe shook his head in irritation. "That has already been explained to my satisfaction. A bag of the Queen Consort's clothes, including bathing attire and sundresses, was also found. It's obvious we caught Camilla in another of her snits, planning to slip the royal noose, incognito. To the south of France with some lothario is my guess."

"Or somewhere else with Harry," Gibbon said. He raised an eyebrow in query.

"Either way, it's immaterial. She didn't make it. And the Prince has been left to his own devices."

The MI-5 Director lit another Player's. "Officially the boy is not out there. Finding him is not an assignment for the bobby on the corner. Absolute trust is required, only those who can be relied on to remain silent. That kind of manpower is limited."

"Save your excuses for the Prime Minister and pray you don't need them," the General said angrily, fanning away smoke. "How many men will you have, and when?"

Gibbon paused, feigning the calculations he'd readied hours before to cover this and several other possible eventualities. "With the Yard and my own resources . . . twenty, possibly thirty. The first units will be on the streets within half an hour. For your information, at least six will be females." He smiled, exposing dark nicotine stains. "Young and pretty."

Baker-Smythe didn't give him the satisfaction of a comment on the women. "I'll be available via mobile phone until I reach London," he said. "After that, you can reach me at Ten Downing Street, the private number. We're meeting with the Home Secretary." He got up to leave.

"You will, of course, want us to see that no harm comes to him," said the Director of MI-5.

The General kept walking, his back to Nigel Gibbon. "I will, of course, want you to find the young bastard . . . and keep him from destroying England."

14

Harry had started to run as the Queen Consort commanded, but stopped even before he was beyond the shadow of the palace. "What the bloody hell are you doing?" he whispered to himself. It wasn't youthful rebellion; it was common sense, his training kicking in. Camilla was right; he had to get away. But he couldn't make it alone. He'd need help.

He fished his mobile phone out of his pocket, thought for a second, then pushed one of the speed dials. On the third ring a sleepy male answered.

"Lo?"

"Michael, it's me," said Harry.

Dead silence. Then Michael Christian, a close friend from school days, sputtered, "Hey! I thought you were off on holiday. Where are you?"

Harry ignored the question. "Have you heard anything? On the telly or the radio?"

"What do you mean?"

"About me . . . or my father?"

"Is something wrong?"

It was taking too long. Harry jumped ahead. "Look, Michael, I need your help. Can you meet me?"

Harry heard the flap of bedclothes being thrown off. A wide-awake Michael said, "You got it. When and where?"

"Now," Harry answered, and a place suddenly popped into his head. "At The Stag."

It took a moment to sink in. "You mean that bar on Bressenden Place? Close by Victoria Station?"

"That's the one."

"It's too early, man. No one will be there. They won't even be open yet."

Nodding, Harry said, "I know."

"But, Harry, The Stag is a *gay* bar. We don't go there."

Harry repeated himself, this time with a slight smile. "I know."

"Bloody bonkers," Michael said under his breath. Harry could almost hear him shaking his head.

"And, Michael, bring a hat."

Twenty minutes later an old, maroon Honda pulled into the car park across from the bunker-like pub hidden down a back street near Victoria Station. A few seconds later Michael emerged, crossed the street, and joined Harry in the short, darken tunnel at the entrance to The Stag.

His *hide where they don't expect you* strategy and the completely uneventful walk over from the Palace had given Harry enough confidence to joke. He glanced at his watch. "You took your time. What'd you do, have breakfast first?"

"I had to find a hat," Michael quipped back. He smiled and pulled a black, wool ski cap out of his pocket and handed it to his friend. Then he turned serious. "So, what's this about?"

"I'm . . . not sure," said Harry. He took a breath and then stepped into it. "I think my father has been abducted. Maybe Camilla and William too."

"Holy Mother of God," Michael muttered.

That was as far as they got. Over Michael's shoulder Harry saw a black Land Rover SUV pull to the curb in front of a no parking sign across from The Stag. The driver and passenger were out of the vehicle immediately, heading toward them. They were both dressed in black raincoats.

Instinctively, Harry jerked his mobile phone from his pocket and looked at it. "Shit!" he spit out and threw it into the street. As he started to run, he sensed Michael moving in the opposite direction, toward the men in the raincoats.

"No, Michael!" Harry yelled, but it was too late. He didn't see the collision; only heard the muted grunts of a struggle, then the cough of what he assumed was a silenced weapon. On the one glance he took over his shoulder, all three men were on the ground. Harry thought of turning back. He had to help Michael. Then one of the raincoats started to get up and he knew he couldn't. He had to survive–for England.

It was only seconds until Harry turned the corner onto Buckingham Palace Road. Despite the still early hour, traffic in the road was heavy and the walkway was thick with people. He slowed to a fast walk, constantly checking over his shoulder. When a passing older couple looked at him strangely, he remembered the ski cap and pulled it on, down over his ears. At the first chance, he crossed the road, putting the traffic between him and whoever was behind him.

He kept expecting someone to point and start shouting, soldiers to jump out of some doorway and chase him. But no one paid him any attention. The streets were a blur of tourists with their cameras and maps, the homeless holding out their cups, and mostly just a crowd; business people carrying briefcases, shoppers loaded with packages, mothers dragging children somewhere they didn't want to go.

It was nearly five minutes before he saw the man in the black raincoat. He was on the other side of the street, looking across, and keeping pace. Harry began to walk faster. The raincoat was caught in a crowd. He tried to keep up, but there were too many people. He bumped into a woman with an armful of packages and she stumbled and fell. The man hesitated, started to help her up, and Harry bolted.

The man in the black raincoat shoved the fallen woman back down and came after Harry. In a few steps he broke out of the crowd into the open where he could stretch his legs. Harry glanced over his shoulder. It looked like the man was gaining. Suddenly the man changed directions. He started across the street, on an angle to intercept Harry.

Harry tried to move faster, his legs driving, arms swinging wildly. He crashed into a man, sending a briefcase flying. Someone grabbed at his sleeve to stop him, but he jerked away and stumbled on, dodging people coming toward him. Harry took another frantic look over his shoulder. The man in the raincoat was nearly across the street. As he closed the last few feet he began to smile.

Then suddenly there was a squeal of brakes, and the man's eyes widened in surprise. He yelled something, but it was drowned out by a sickening thud as the taxi hit him, cart- wheeling his body into the air. He came down head first on the back of his neck and lay there motionless.

As the crowd began to form, Harry saw a mobile phone or radio on the ground next to the man. Had he used it? Harry searched for a face, someone looking his way. There was no one. The scene in the street had everyone's attention. He backed away slowly.

Harry walked off the pain in his side, still constantly checking behind for the black raincoat or anything like it. To make sure, he took the next three cross streets, going right then left, then back to the right, stopping to look each time he changed direction. Finally, he relaxed enough to shake off some of the fear. Maybe the man hadn't used the radio, he thought. Maybe they'd lost him. Even if they had, it was clear that he had to get off the streets and find a place where he could get warm and think; somewhere he could figure out what to do. Maybe at the next intersection, he thought.

Running had turned the thin windbreaker that was supposed to ward off the chill of the Jamaican night into a damp freezer. Harry turned up the collar and pulled the ski cap down until it was sitting on his eyebrows and over his ears and started moving. Near the next corner, with his head down, shoulders hunched up, he didn't see the young woman or realize she'd stepped deliberately into his path.

She gasped softly as they banged into one another. Harry managed to keep them both on their feet, but his bag went sailing. It popped open when it hit, spilling clothes and toiletries onto the walkway.

"Sorry," he sputtered.

"No, no. It's my fault. I wasn't watching where I was going," the woman said. She crossed to his bag, bent over, and started picking up his clothes. "Let me help."

Harry's eyes widened at the view her short skirt provided. He gulped and scrambled to help her. Once he was down by her, she turned and smiled at him. She reached over and ran her hand down the arm of his windbreaker. "Are you cold, love?" she said. "I've got a place close by where it's warm."

She smiled again. This close, Harry could smell her perfume. It was strong. Her make-up was overdone. Suddenly he realized who, or what, she was. He felt himself blushing. "No thanks," he said.

She frowned. "Are you gay?"

Harry just looked at her. He could feel the blood rushing to his face.

"No, I don't think so," she said. She hooked a finger in her top and pulled it enough to expose part of a breast. "You got any money, love?"

He hesitated, but only a second. "Not for you."

The girl's voice suddenly went cockney. "That's my bleedin' day, ain't it?" She stood, tossing a handful of clothes into the air. Then she stalked off, complaining as she went. "First, it's a Kraut tourist with nothing but Deutschmarks and now I'm spending time with a bloody jerk what wants something for nothing."

"Hey!" Harry yelled after her, trying to sound angry.

What he felt was stupid and humiliated, and not just by the hooker. The light had changed and people were walking past, gawking at him. He pulled the ski cap down again and struggled to get everything stuffed back into his bag. The clasp was broken. He had to take a shirt out to tie around the bag to hold it shut. Finally, with the bag clutched under his arm, he was ready to move on.

Across the intersection, on the opposite corner, he saw a park. Somehow it looked familiar. When the light changed again Harry crossed the street and found a bench. He was tired and cold, and now that he thought about it, hungry. How long had it been since Camilla insisted he drink that glass of orange juice, since he ate that piece of bacon? He wondered where she was now. Where was he?

And then suddenly he knew. This was Bedford Square. He'd been here long ago, with his mother and William. On a cold day just like this. The three of them had spent forever wandering around an old building full of Egyptian mummies and old statues. He remembered it was warm inside, with rooms where almost no one came, where he could rest and think about what to do. Harry turned on the bench. He could see the building. He picked up his bag, glanced around to make sure he wasn't being followed, then walked across the park and into the British Museum.

15

Only the barest of accounts had been given out. No names, no number of dead. Nothing about the attackers. Nothing about King Charles or anyone in the Royal family, except that they were alive and well. The media had hammered all day long on the few details they'd been given until, like words repeated incessantly, they hardly made sense. It gave the speechwriters time to craft the proper explanation, patriotic, believable; something short and simple that the people would accept without too much questioning.

Now, at 7:00 in the evening, teatime for most English families, when the television audience peaked, it was ready. The production assistant squatting in front of the TV3 camera which was feeding the other British networks from the second floor office at Ten Downing Street, signaled and the red light above the lens came on.

"Good evening," said Sir Alistair Saxon from behind a large mahogany desk. "I come to you tonight with news of grave events which, for the moment, have ended in Great Britain's favor."

As the Prime Minister turned and looked into the second camera, the director switched to the prearranged close-up and sixty million screens were filled with the up-thrust chin, the resolute mouth, the uncompromising glare in the eye. Saxon was a showman. He knew how to use his vague resemblance to Churchill, conjuring the ghost.

"Early today, in the dining room of Buckingham Palace, a British Special Forces unit under the command of Major General Jock Cabot intercepted agents of a foreign nation, which must remain nameless for the time being, in a scurrilous attempt to assassinate King Charles, the Third."

The director began his planned move, widening the shot slowly as Saxon continued. "I know you join me in thanking providence that His Royal Highness was unharmed and wishing the assassins a speedy descent into hell." The pull back stopped and the Prime Minister smiled ever so slightly, his lips pressed grimly together. "A journey, which I can confirm they all have begun."

Saxon took his time now, bringing his hands together in front of him at his desk, building a steeple. "Unfortunately, the nation has paid dearly in the process of foiling this unthinkable crime. It is with a heavy heart that I must inform you of the death of one of our most respected entrepreneurs, the Chairman of United Kingdom Communications and founder of the TV3 network, Sir Geoffrey Kitterage. Sir Geoffrey was meeting with His Majesty on a project of vital interest when he was cut down by assassin's fire. History will remember him as a brave and loyal British subject who gave his life defending his sovereign.

"It is also my unpleasant duty tonight to expose a near fatal flaw in the defenses which protect the British monarch. It has been established that two of the provocateurs in this incident were double agents working for Scotland Yard as royal bodyguards. The third was an employee of the Royal Family itself."

Saxon paused for a moment, then picked up the pace slightly, shifting to his take-charge persona. "This is a completely unacceptable situation. Because of it, at my suggestion, and with the agreement and by the authority of His Royal Highness, two unprecedented actions have been taken. First, I have this afternoon ordered a full scale investigation of all British security services to be conducted by a special commission appointed by

Parliament, with myself as acting chairman. Second, pending the completion of this investigation and the identification of all individuals who may have been involved in this assassination attempt, King Charles and the entire Royal Family have sequestered themselves in a location known only to myself and a handful of trusted security personnel."

The television director switched back to the original camera, angled so that the flags of Great Britain and the Commonwealth countries fanned out behind the Prime Minister were clearly visible. Saxon turned to the camera and began again.

"And now I come to my final reason for speaking to you this evening. For tonight is not only about the events of today, however unsettling they may be, but also about the future. The future of our United Kingdom."

He looked down to open a leather-bound folder on the desk in front of him, revealing a thick sheaf of printed pages. "We are all sorely aware of the wide range of problems faced by this nation as we struggle with the trials of this new century. You need only try to use the telephone or take a motor trip to the countryside, apply for a loan, or even purchase a plate of fish and chips to feel the effect. Labor unrest, shortages of petrol and other supplies, double-digit inflation. The list is long.

"However, the news is not all negative. After months of debate and study, seeking the advice of experts from every corner, Parliament has proposed declaring war on these public burdens with the Emergency Powers Act."

Saxon lifted a corner of the document on his desk and thumbed through the pages. "It is a remarkable piece of legislation which will create a power base from which even our most vexing problems can be attacked and overcome. Legislation that has passed both Houses of Parliament and only awaits royal assent."

He closed the leather folder and looked into the camera, as the director had the cameraman move in for a closer shot, losing the flags. "I am honored tonight to be a messenger," the Prime Minister said as he reached into the inside pocket of his suit coat and drew out a single sheet of paper, folded lengthwise. "Earlier today His Majesty wrote this note in his own hand. He personally instructed me to read it to you this evening, and to present it to the Speaker of the House of Commons Monday morning."

Carefully unfolding the paper, he began to read. "In my untimely absence, I have requested Sir Alistair Saxon, Prime Minister of Great Britain and Northern Ireland, to inform the Members of Parliament and the people of the United Kingdom of my assent to the legislation known as the Emergency Powers Act."

Saxon smiled openly, the first time since the broadcast had begun. "And now, I believe we all have had quite enough of a day. So I will leave you to the quiet surrounds of family and home. Goodnight, and God save the King."

The Prime Minister's face faded and was replaced by a static shot of the outside of Ten Downing Street.

"We're out!" someone shouted and the office filled with the clatter and buzz of technicians striking the shoot.

Anxious to get out of the glare and the heat from the lights, Saxon removed the tiny microphone clipped to his tie and pushed his bulk up from the chair. General Ian Baker-Smythe was waiting at the corner of the desk.

"Well?" said the Prime Minister.

"I thought it went well. Very well," the General answered, nodding.

Saxon gave him a sour look. "I don't need your opinion, Ian. I meant Prince Harry. Have you spoken with Nigel? Do they have him yet?"

The General's face flushed slightly, but he controlled a flare of anger by delaying his response while they walked several steps together. "Not as of fifteen minutes ago. I'll contact him again now."

"The agent hit by the taxi, has he said anything?"

Baker-Smythe shook his head. "Not expected to regain consciousness."

They stepped out into the hallway and crossed to the stair railing overlooking the entrance foyer to the Prime Minister's residence. Below, a technician was expertly coiling television cable. In the noisy comings and goings of the rest of the TV3 crew they were alone.

"When you reach Nigel again tell him he has one hour and then your people are taking over," Saxon said.

The General looked at him sharply. "The regular military? On the streets of London?"

"We've had a full day of his sneaking around, with no result. I don't care if it takes ten thousand men, just find the lad."

"I thought anything of that nature would have to wait until the EPA was official."

"We can't wait any longer," the Prime Minister said tiredly.

"What about the media?"

Saxon thought for a moment. "If it comes to that, tell them we've just unearthed new information that there was an assassin who got away. Two, if you need it."

16

Prince Harry awoke with a start. Someone had pushed against his shoulder. He jerked back, twisting away.

The museum guard threw up both hands, stepping back. "Keep your bloomin' knickers on," he said. He cocked his head and squinted at Harry.

Instinctively, Harry tugged down on the ski cap.

"You homeless or just pissed?" the guard asked.

After a moment, Harry said, "A little of both."

The guard shook his head, muttered something under his breath, and pointed toward an archway with an exit sign over it. "You can't sleep it off here. The museum is closing."

So, Prince Harry was shooed out of the British Museum into the cold with the rest of the visitors at seven o'clock, the regular closing time on weeknights. He'd hidden nearly the whole day in one room or another of the museum, dodging groups of school children, sliding away from tourists. It had given him a chance to rest and think, but he still had no idea what he was going to do. He'd counted the money Camilla stuffed into his pocket more than once. It wasn't enough to buy a disposable phone. Besides, who would he call? He knew now that Camilla was right; they were watching everyone he knew. He might already have been responsible for something terrible happening to one of his best friends.

Harry was angry with himself and, he had to admit, frightened at the same time. The thing that bothered him most was realizing how much he'd always counted on other people to solve his problems.

His windbreaker had long ago dried while he was in the museum, but it offered little protection against the cold night coming on. And even with the ski cap pulled down over them, his ears were quickly beginning to feel like chunks of ice. However, that wasn't the worst of his troubles. It was his stomach. He was starving.

It was nearly dark now. That, at least, was one positive; he felt less exposed. Harry glanced around and didn't see anyone looking his way. He hefted his bag and set off, determined to find a place where he could get something to eat with the little money he had.

By 7:30 the news anchors and their talking head experts had started their second analysis of the speech. Vivian Warwick turned off the portable telly in her cubical at McDonald's. Good news, bad news, she thought. The King is out of danger; the country isn't.

She wondered if Tom had been watching. She hoped so. It might make him feel a little better. Who knows, maybe his father actually had a premonition. Vivian promised herself not to question it if Tom brought it up. She already had enough questions about this Emergency Powers Act, starting with how it would affect business at McDonald's unit 1209, 810 Oxford Street. She decided to check the dinner crowd before Tom called.

At first she thought he looked familiar for the same reason all young men his age looked familiar; his mouth was full and his hat was on. She could tell from the paper remains crumpled on the table that he was working on a Big Mac, with a large order of fries and a medium Coke. The hat was a dreadful, drab ski cap, pulled down over his ears.

She might have passed him by with a roll of her eyes, but something was wrong. When it didn't come to her automatically, she let her eyes drift to the next table where a fat woman sat spooning a chocolate sundae into her mouth non-stop. Her four or five year-old daughter, a pear shaped miniature of her mother, was struggling with a double dip soft yogurt cone. Vivian watched the cone drip a mess on the table, then turned back to the ski cap.

She took a studied, second look. It produced a shiver. Suddenly she knew what was wrong. Unless she was blind or crazy, this particular young man shouldn't be here at all. He was . . . what had the Prime Minister said? Sequestered in a location known only to a handful of trusted security personnel?

Vivian was still trying to decide what she should do, if anything, when a young woman slid into the chair opposite the ski cap. She was pretty and sexy. Polished. Out of place. He reacted as if it was a snake.

Without thinking, Vivian stepped out from behind the serving area and quickly approached the table. She had no idea what she was going to say until the words came out of her mouth.

"Freddie, I'm not going to tell you this again," Vivian said sharply. "Employees eat in the break room in the back."

Harry spun around to look at Vivian. "What?" he mumbled through a mouthful of hamburger. His eyes, already wide in surprise, grew into saucers.

"You don't have time to eat at any rate," Vivian added. "You're already late for your shift."

Up close, the woman wasn't so young. Or pretty. There was something hard around the eyes and mouth. She definitely wasn't happy about Vivian's sudden appearance. Vivian didn't wait to find out what she might do about it.

Leaning into her face she said, "I guess you're the girlfriend. I am sorry, but we don't encourage friends stopping in during working hours. Tends to distract them. I'm sure you understand."

The woman wasn't impressed. She murmured something, but made no move to leave. Vivian smiled and straightened up as if that was an affirmative. The young man seemed frozen to his chair, his eyes still saucers.

"Well, Freddie?" Vivian pressed. *What if he didn't move, if she was wrong?* She pointed in the general direction of the French fryer and the corridor through the preparation area to the back. "I suggest you get back there and get changed, young man." She glanced at her watch. "Your shift started five minutes ago."

Harry looked from one female to the other. He made a decision and stood. Vivian breathed.

"That's a good Freddie," she said patronizingly. She turned to the young woman with her manager's smile. "Sorry, again. You're welcome anytime he's not on shift." Then, stepping behind Harry, she put her hand in the small of his back and firmly applied pressure. He headed off toward the back of the restaurant, and Vivian tried to appear calm as she moved back behind the serving area again.

However, her façade crumbled when she turned around. The young woman, her eyes fixed on the corridor where ski cap disappeared, had taken out her mobile phone and was dialing someone. The woman started to talk. Vivian felt her face flush, her heart begin to thump in her chest.

Then a tall, thin man dressed in a long black coat sat at the table next to the woman. With a start, the woman suddenly held the phone away from her ear. She shook it, then tried again. The static was so loud Vivian could hear it in the serving area.

"Bloody hell!" the woman exclaimed and got up and hurried outside. When it was clear through the window that she was still having trouble with the phone, Vivian quickly moved down the corridor to the back of the McDonald's.

Harry was waiting, sitting uncomfortably in a chair in her office. She closed the door and moved to her desk. "Why did you do that? Who are you?" he said.

"Well, that's not a question we have to ask you, is it?"

"You know?" He looked like he was ready to run.

Just then there was a knock on the office door. Before either could say anything or move, the door opened and the tall man in the black coat stepped inside.

17

"I'm sorry to interrupt," said Merlyn. He glanced back down the hall the way they had come. "But don't you think we should be going?"

For a moment, both Vivian Warwick and Prince Harry were speechless. Then Vivian said, "Who are you?"

"A friend," said the Wizard. "An advisor to the King." Harry was staring at him. At first Merlyn reasoned it was the raincoat. "Don't worry, Prince," he said. "The raincoat is only, what is it called . . . a cover? I borrowed it from one of their men. He won't need it anymore."

Harry shook his head. "You're not an advisor to my father," he said with a gritty look. "I would know."

A stout heart, Merlyn thought. Excellent. We'll need it. Then he took the young Prince's feet out from under him. "Did you know your father refused assent to the Emergency Powers Act? Did you know you'd have to run?"

Harry frowned, but was silent.

"I think your knowledge could use some updating," suggested the Wizard.

"The King *refused* assent?" Vivian said. "*Their* men? I don't understand." She nodded toward the front of the restaurant. "Did you do that to the woman out there, to her mobile phone?"

Merlyn smiled. "I believe it is called interference. She won't be a problem now."

Vivian looked from the Wizard to Harry and back again. Shaking her head, she said, "I don't understand any of this."

"There will be time for explanations on the way," said Merlyn.

"To where?" Harry asked. He appeared unprepared to go anywhere.

"Camelford, I believe," Merlyn said to Harry, then turned to Vivian. "Isn't that where you were going?"

She hesitated, but only for a moment. "Yes." She scooped her purse out of the drawer and came around the desk. "Come with me," she said to Harry. "The car is out back."

Before he could get up, the phone rang. Vivian gave Harry a sign to sit tight and answered it. It was Tom.

"How's your father?" she asked.

"No change. The doctor says he's unconscious, but stable."

"Well, at least he's stable. That's good," said Vivian, and Merlyn gave a small satisfied grunt.

"Did you see the Prime Minister on the telly?" Tom said. "It has to be a coincidence, but it's bloody unbelievable."

She didn't give him time to get into it. "I'm coming to Camelford. Tonight. We can talk then."

"What?" he said. "Why?"

Merlyn raised a hand, then placed a silencing finger across his lips.

Vivian acknowledged it with a nod. "I think your father could be right. You know, about you helping that . . . *person*? Things are not always the way we hear in the media."

"What are you talking about, Viv?" Tom asked.

She pushed ahead, cutting him off, ending the conversation. "I'll explain when I get there. Anyway, see if you can get a room for us somewhere. Love you. Bye."

Vivian hung up and turned to Harry. "All right, let's go."

Harry pointed at Merlyn. "What about him?"

"I'll be going with you," said Merlyn. "And with a little help from providence, we'll be joined by another on the way."

Vivian hesitated. "Another?"

"Another friend," Merlyn added as he moved aside to make room for her at the door.

Vivian looked at him a moment, then shook her head in exasperation. "What am I getting myself into?" she asked under her breath as she stepped into the hallway.

Merlyn beckoned Harry to join her, then followed them both out the back door of the restaurant and to the Warwick's Mini Cooper.

18

They saw the first military vehicles on the streets within twenty minutes, while they were still threading through London traffic. Harry pointed them out, and after that they were all silent, as if any noise might be heard and give them away. Finally, after she had maneuvered onto the M3 headed southwest, Vivian Warwick glanced in the rear view mirror at Harry, who was sardined in, sitting diagonally across the back seat.

"Why aren't you with the rest of the Royal Family?" she asked.

Harry leaned forward, and the lights of a passing car illuminated his face. He looked young. "Are they all right?" he said.

She nodded. "According to the Prime Minister. He said on the telly tonight that they've sequestered themselves in a place known only to him and a few guards."

Harry fell back into the darkness of the back seat. "That's codswallop!" he muttered. "My father was taken prisoner this morning in the palace dining room."

Merlyn turned in the passenger seat. "How do you know?"

Harry looked at him, then back at Vivian. He took a breath and let it out before he spoke. "Camilla told me. She saw it. We were in the kitchen getting ready to . . . we were going to Jamaica."

"She told you to run?" said Vivian.

"Yes," said Harry. After a moment, he went on. "It was the black tale my father always told us, the one about royal assassinations, the French, the Russians. She said not to try to reach anyone I know. They'd be watching. When I looked back, I saw her go into the dining room where my father was."

Now Vivian turned to Merlyn. "You said there would be time for explanations. The time has come. What the bloody hell is going on?"

"The same old thing, I'm afraid," Merlyn said. He knew it could only cloud his answers, but he couldn't resist asking, "Is it true that the Prime Minister's name is Saxon?"

"What kind of question is that?"

He shook his head and smiled to himself. "Sorry." He took a moment, then said, "It's just ironic. Saxons have always sought to wield power over Britain."

"You mean the Prime Minister is behind this?"

"As I said, Charles refused assent on the Emergency Powers Act," Merlyn said quietly.

"He kidnapped the Royals? So he can use that to take over?"

Merlyn stared out into the darkness beyond the passenger window. "They're in no danger," he said. "At least, for now."

"How would you know?" the Prince said sullenly.

"You'll have to take my word for it. At any rate, there's nothing that can be done tonight. Nothing until we can get organized."

"Speaking of getting organized," said Vivian, "who and where is this *other* friend you said we'd pick up? Now would be a good time to talk about that."

Merlyn smiled. "He's waiting in Glastonbury."

"*Glastonbury*?" Vivian said with a surprised look. She glanced over at Merlyn. "Tonight?"

"It's not far out of the way," he said.

"I know where it is," Vivian assured him. "But it will be the middle of the night by the time we get there, maybe later in this car."

"He won't mind," said the Wizard. "He's been waiting a good long time already."

From the back seat Harry said, "A friend in Glastonbury?" The tone was dubious. "I'm sure we don't know anyone in Glastonbury. I know I don't." After a moment, he added, "You still haven't told us who *you* are."

Merlyn looked into the darkened back seat. "As I said, I am an advisor to the King."

"Why haven't I ever seen you at the palace? Or at any of my father's other offices?"

"I'm afraid that's as much as I can tell you right now, Prince." Merlyn turned to Vivian. "And you also."

They rode on in silence after that exchange.

19

The Sea King M4 helicopter, its rotors drooping like a forlorn dog's ears, sat on a concrete slab a short distance from a huge fortress-like stone and mortar house. During the flight from London, the windows had been covered and a circuitous route had been taken so the passengers would have no idea of their destination. As an added measure, they were separated as soon as they landed to limit the opportunity for them to speculate among themselves.

The Queen Consort, Camilla, had been locked in a bedroom suite on the third floor at the north end of the stone house. Sarah Ferguson and her daughters were secured in a larger suite at the opposite end of the same floor. Prince William and Catherine and Prince Andrew were placed in separate rooms on the second floor. King Charles was taken some distance away and locked in the stables house.

None had been fed anything since the helicopter landed in mid-morning, and no one had visited any of them. The isolation was part of the plan.

Finally, at 8:30 in the evening, Major Rhys Mallory unlocked the door to Camilla's room. "You will come with me, madam," he said.

Camilla had been sitting on the bed. She stood and crossed her arms over her chest in a defiant gesture. "I will *not!*" she declared.

Mallory shrugged. "Bring her," he said and turned on his heel.

When two of his khaki clad men entered the bedroom, Camilla had second thoughts. "Come with you where?" she said.

"To the King," the major said. "He insisted on seeing that you're safe."

"You'll never get away with this, you know?" Camilla said. "The British people will not put up with it."

Mallory shook his head and sighed. "You still don't understand, do you? The reason this is happening is because the British people are finally tired of putting up with you Royals."

"Then why aren't we all dead?"

He just stared at her.

"They wouldn't put up with *that* would they?"

"You're asking the wrong person," the major said. "I carry out orders, not give them."

"I see," Camilla said. "You mean I should ask the Prime Minister?"

Grim-faced, Mallory said, "What you should do is control yourself, madam. Before that order is given. And carried out."

They rode the short distance to the stables house in a pick-up truck, with the Queen Consort squeezed between Mallory and one of his men armed with an automatic weapon. Once there, she was escorted to the door of a stone cottage. The guard stationed there opened it. Camilla was pushed inside and the door was closed and locked.

The cottages were small; a bedroom and an area that served as a cramped kitchen and living room. Charles had just come out of the bedroom.

"Camilla?" he said, obviously surprised to see her.

"Reporting as ordered, Your Majesty," she said with a slight curtsy. Then she smiled the tough wry smile he knew so well. "They said you demanded to see me."

He moved to her and they embraced perfunctorily. "I didn't think they'd allow us to see each other," Charles said. "Are you all right?"

Camilla glanced over her shoulder at the locked door. "As well as can be expected with these brutes. Their commander as much as told me they would kill us all if ordered to do so."

"He didn't mention Harry, did he?"

"No." She suddenly was blinking away tears. "Poor Harry."

Charles took her in his arms again, this time with warmth. "He's a bright lad, Milla," he said. "He'll find his way out of this, and do something to put an end to it. And failing to grab Harry is not the only mistake they've made."

She pushed out of his embrace and looked up at him. "What do you mean?"

"I know where we are. I've been here before; when I was young, on holiday from school."

"Are you sure?"

Charles nodded. "We're on Tresco in the Isles of Scilly. This is the Tresco Abbey. It's private, the entire island is private."

Camilla frowned. "How could that be?"

"Augustus Smith, a merchant banker and politician, leased it from the Duchy of Cornwall in the early 1800s when there was nothing here. The Smith family still controls it."

Before either could say anything more, the door to the cottage opened and Major Rhys Mallory entered. "Thank you, Your Majesty," he said. "We were fairly certain you would remember, but your confirmation dispels any question of mixing you, and now the Queen Consort as well, with any of our other *guests*. You may or may not consider it a positive result that we have decided to house you together."

"What have you done with the others?" Charles demanded.

"They are no concern of yours, so long as you don't try anything stupid. Then, I'm afraid there would be consequences."

Charles glanced around the cottage. "You have a recording device in here."

"You sound as if you think it unfair," Mallory said.

"Why are you doing this? And for whom?" demanded Charles.

"I'm sure you remember, Your Majesty. Duty? It's what you commit to do."

"Duty to whom?" Charles asked.

The Major let a moment pass. "To the people of Great Britain," he said. "The people *you* swore to protect."

"It's Saxon, isn't it?" Charles said. "What is he telling the people?"

"Have a good night's sleep, Your Majesty, Queen Consort," Mallory said. He closed the door and walked away, leaving them in the dark.

After the Major's footsteps had died, the King moved to a small wooden bench sitting against one of the walls. He reached under the seat, felt around a moment, then jerked something loose. He put the something on the floor and stepped on it. It made a small crunching sound. "I thought he might look at it," he said.

"Look at what?" said Camilla.

Charles smiled. "The microphone."

"But they'll just–"

"I know," the King interrupted. "We don't have much time to talk. I remember these stables. They're nowhere near the water, and that's the only way to escape. But I have a plan."

20

They came upon Glastonbury shrouded in fog, tendrils of vapor slowly rising. Vivian Warwick took a breath, slowed the car, and then stopped. "I see what they mean," she whispered. "The mists of Avalon."

"Once it was an island in the middle of a vast lake," Merlyn said, then added, "At least that's what they say."

She shivered slightly. "Creepy." Turning to him, she asked, "Where do we go? I've never actually been here."

"It is a while since I've been here myself," Merlyn said with a wry smile. He closed his eyes. After a moment he said, "There are the remains of an abbey; nearby is a well, the Chalice Well." He opened his eyes. "At the base of the Tor. We'll find him there somewhere."

Just then the lights of a lorry appeared in the fog behind them. The vehicle came up close and stopped, waiting. Merlyn reached out and laid his hand on Vivian's arm. She looked at him strangely. "Perhaps you could ask them where the Chalice Well is," he said quietly. "Better a fair maiden in distress than a lost old man?"

She glanced in the back. Harry was asleep. "I guess we can't send him," Vivian said." She got out of the car and went back to the lorry. In a minute she returned.

"There's a bakery on the way," she chirped, the tiredness gone from her face. Merlyn gave an askance look. "Well, I'm hungry," she said, grinning.

He considered only a moment, then nodded. "Take me first. Then go to your bakery, and get enough for four."

From the back seat, Harry said, "You think they'll have American donuts?"

Vivian rolled her eyes. "I thought you were asleep."

"I like American donuts."

Shaking his head in mild exasperation, Merlyn pointed out the windscreen. "Drive, woman."

They passed the bakery on the way. It was open, an island of light in the fog. The abbey ruins, when they found them, were still floating in mist, an eerie ghost.

Vivian made no move to get out the car. That was as Merlyn had hoped. "I don't see anyone," she said, the pitch of her voice sliding upwards slightly.

Merlyn smiled. "He's here. Waiting for us."

Shivering again, she said, "If you say so. How long will you need?"

"I'm not sure," he answered truthfully.

"Where is this Chalice Well?" she said. "Maybe one of us should go with you that far." She glanced back at Harry. He was asleep again, or at least appeared to be.

"In the abbey garden," Merlyn said. He pointed toward two stone columns rising through the mist like arms beseeching the heavens. "Through there. You can watch me from the car. When I reach the columns, I'll signal and you can go back to the bakery to get breakfast."

She sat there a moment, then inhaled a deep breath and let it out. "All right. I'll come back as soon as I can. We'll be waiting right here."

Merlyn got out of the car and walked through the mist to the stone columns. Once there, he turned and waved his arm. He waited until he saw the car lights begin to move away, then started across the garden. When he reached the stairs to the Chalice Well, he moved past them and out of the abbey garden. That had never been his destination. He crossed a deserted street; Chilkwell, the street sign read. There was a small building shielding it, but he had little trouble finding what he was looking for–the White Spring.

For thousands of years legend held that its waters rose from under the Tor and flowed through caverns that once were the entrance to the Otherworld hidden beneath the sacred Celtic mound. With a glance around him to make sure he was alone, the Wizard stripped off his clothes and stepped into the water.

21

Much of the fog had dissipated, leaving only dense patches in the low areas. Vivian Warwick was concerned. They'd been back at the abbey nearly half an hour and there was no sign of their benefactor in the black coat or anyone else. The two big scones with currants she bought for herself and Harry were gone. The loaves of Irish soda and muffin bread were growing stone cold.

After a while, Harry stirred in the back seat and said, "Maybe he isn't coming back. Maybe he was just looking for a ride."

She turned and looked at him. "You proved you can be impertinent with that Nazi cock up. You don't need to do it again. Without him, heaven knows where you'd be."

The reprimand didn't set well with Harry. "All right, all right, I'll go find him," he said sullenly. He sat up straight and reached to open the passenger-side door.

"I don't think so," said Vivian, catching his arm. "You have no idea where he is."

"He said the well was in the abbey garden. It can't be that hard to find." Harry pointed out the windscreen. "Look, the fog is almost gone. It'll be light soon." Then he winked at her and grinned. "And, in case you haven't noticed, I'm a big boy now."

She stared at him a moment, then looked out the windscreen at the thinning fog. Finally, she let go of his arm with a shake of her head. "And a cheeky one," she said. "Don't be long."

Harry was nearly to the stairs leading down to the Chalice Well when he realized he wasn't alone. There were two men sitting on the ground near one of the crumbling walls of the abbey. He couldn't see them well through the fog, but their voices told him as much as he needed to know. He stood still for a few moments and listened to them laughing and whispering in drunken slurs to one another. Too late, he felt the third man.

"Well now, what do we got here?" asked a voice from slightly behind him and to his right.

Harry swiveled slowly to look at the man. He wasn't large, but was thick through the body, and well muscled. He had the face of a mean spirit; heavy-lidded eyes and a mouth twisted slightly, ready to snarl. Like the other two, he was drunk. Harry could smell the alcohol from two meters away.

The man spent a few seconds appraising Harry, then gave a guttural laugh. "The abbey don't open for tourists until daylight, laddie boy. I think you made a mistake you'll be sorry for."

In a sudden move he produced a five-inch knife from somewhere. "Don't you move," he said. "Or I'll slice your young gullet." Keeping his eyes on Harry, he called to the other two men near the abbey wall, "Here, you chappies! Come look what I found in the loo."

One of the drunks hollered, "It bloody well better be beer!"

Harry could hear them scuffling to get up. "Where's the man in the black coat?" he said, managing to keep the tremor in his voice under control.

As if on cue, Merlyn stepped out of a swirl of mist behind the drunk. He grasped the man in the curvature between his neck and right shoulder and squeezed with his thumb and fingers.

"I'm right here," the Wizard said softly.

The drunk started to turn his head, but half way around his eyes rolled back in his head and he collapsed on the ground.

Harry was stunned. He looked down at the drunk, then up at Merlyn. "How did you do that?" he whispered.

Merlyn shrugged. "It's an old trick, popularized recently by a scientist named Spook, I believe."

"Spock?" Harry said incredulously.

"Where the bloody hell are you, Charley?" one of the drunk's friends called through the fog. He wasn't far away.

"This isn't the time for nitpicking," Merlyn said as he disappeared back into the mist. A moment later he reappeared, supporting a man. "Or meeting *Charley's* friends. Now, give me a hand here."

Vivian saw them as they came through the lingering mist near the columns. They each had an arm around the bent form of the man, helping him walk, moving slowly toward the car. It looked like the man was in pain. She got out of the car and started off to help them, but Merlyn held up a hand. "Open the rear door," he called softly, as if not to draw attention. "Then get back in."

She did as he asked. In a few moments they reached the car. Merlyn and Harry helped the other man into the back seat and Harry squeezed in with him. Their new passenger was draped in a long cloak that smelled musty. Vivian felt a chill raise the hair on her arms. Before she could get a good look at the face, Merlyn got into the front next to her. He took the soda bread from its bag, tore off half of the loaf and handed it into the back seat.

"Give him some of this, and some privacy," Merlyn said to Harry, then turned back to Vivian. "Now, let us go."

She glanced over her shoulder into the back. "He looks like he's drugged."

"Smells like it, too. Disgusting," said Harry.

"A herbal mixture," said Merlyn. "To keep him comfortable during the trip. Once we get to Camlann it will subside."

Vivian gave the Wizard a quizzical look. "Camlann?" she queried. "This car is going to Camelford."

Merlyn's head bobbed up. *Senile old wizard,* he thought. "Yes, Camelford," he corrected, "that's what I said."

"Then you'll introduce us to our new friend in the back?" Vivian said.

"And yourself?" Harry added from the back seat.

Merlyn nodded. "As I said, there will be time for introductions later." Then, deflecting the conversation, he said, "Now, Prince, why don't you tell us about the man you met in the abbey garden?"

"What man?" Vivian said, glancing back at Harry with a parental frown.

As Harry fumbled through an explanation trying not to expose too much of what really happened, Merlyn settled back in his seat and calmed himself. Soon they would all be where it was destined, and the games would begin.

22

"Well, Nigel?" the Prime Minister said as he settled his bulk into the chair at the head of the conference table in his study on the second floor of Ten Downing Street.

Nigel Gibbon, Director General of MI-5, stubbed out his Players in an overflowing ashtray and shook his head. "The news is not good," he said. "Agent Blevins never recovered from the taxi accident. We had several possible sightings reported after that, but they all proved negative."

Saxon stared out the windows. It was raining again. He couldn't see it falling in the dark, but he could hear the staccato spatter against the glass panes. He felt a chill and rubbed his arms. After a moment, he turned to General Baker-Smythe. "What about your people, Ian? You've taken over, right?" As an afterthought Saxon turned back to Gibbon. "And for God's sake, Nigel, empty that ashtray. Sorry, Ian."

"Yes sir," the General said. "We have the responsibility now."

"How many men do you have out there?"

"Almost two thousand," the General said, then he also shook his head. "But timing is the problem. The young bastard had time to go to ground before we were called in."

Gibbon moved in his chair, but Saxon himself reacted to the slap from Baker-Smythe. "I'm not looking for finger pointing, Ian," he said sharply. "Or excuses. We need results!"

"Yes, sir. I understand that," said the General.

The Prime Minister frowned. "He couldn't be out in this rain. You say he's gone to ground. Where? Do we have any idea? Does he have any friends in London proper?"

Nigel Gibbon interrupted to answer. "Several. But he won't be contacting any of them now. That's how we nearly caught him early on. He used his mobile phone to reach a young chap, Michael Christian. We were able to trace the call and intercept their meeting, but the bloody sod, Christian, wrestled with my agents long enough for the Prince to make off."

"Where is he now, this Christian?" said Major General Jock Cabot from his chair next to Baker-Smythe. "It won't take water boarding to make him talk."

Gibbon finished lighting another Player's, exhaled, then shook his head. "In the hospital," he said. "Gunshot wound to the stomach. Unlikely to regain consciousness, the doctor reports."

The Major General, who had leaned forward, sat back in his chair. "It probably doesn't make any difference. Prince Harry may be young, but he's had several years of military training. He's not stupid either. He wouldn't have told Christian much. And Nigel's right; now he'll steer clear of any other friends he has, expecting us to be watching."

"So what does that leave?" Saxon said.

Now it was Cabot shaking his head. "There are hundreds of possibilities. Retail shops, motion picture theaters, museums."

The Prime Minister looked at his watch. "They'd all be closed, long ago."

"And that much the better for hiding," Cabot said.

Saxon now joined the others, shaking his head. "It's one thing to have them on the streets, but we can't have armed military personnel probing our theaters and shopping centers," he said. "The media will set up a howl of invasion of privacy."

The Prime Minister turned to the fourth man at the table. Michael Lyme, the Home Secretary, was texting on a Blackberry, apparently not listening. Saxon sighed. "Michael, we've placed the Royal Family in custody and taken over the government of Great Britain. Do you have a moment for us?"

Lyme looked up from the Blackberry. "What?" He blinked several times and glanced around the table. "Oh, I'm sorry! I was–"

"Put a sock in it, Michael," Saxon said flatly. He took a breath, let it out slowly, and rubbed the back of his neck. "How do you feel about your Bobbies inspecting every theater and shop and other place we can think of in which young Harry might be holed up? Do you have enough men?"

Lyme's shake of his head made it unanimous. The night *was not* going well. "I'm sorry, Prime Minister. We can barely handle the criminal cases we're getting."

"Perhaps it's time for one or even two of those *additional* assassins," General Baker-Smythe said to Saxon. "That would cover us searching the theaters and other potentials."

The Prime Minister looked at him tiredly. "I intended that as a worse case scenario when I suggested it. How long ago was that?"

"A few hours," said the General.

Saxon leaned back in his chair and massaged his temples. "By now, I thought I'd be on Tresco convincing Charles that it's hopeless to resist; his best strategy is to go along with us. I can't do that with this young pillock thumbing his nose at all our efforts to find him, out there ready to throw a spanner in the works at any minute."

He got up tiredly from his chair and went to the window and stared through the rain-spattered glass into the darkness below. "There must be *something* we've overlooked."

"There is one thing," Cabot suggested. "His stomach."

"What the bloody hell are you talking about, Jock?" Saxon said, turning around, frowning at the Marine Commandant. "Make sense, man. His *stomach*?"

Cabot smiled. "Harry may be a prince, but he is still a young man." He rubbed a hand over his own stomach. "And after sex, food is the center of the world."

Suddenly Nigel Gibbon came to life. "One of the possible sightings was at a McDonald's."

"I'd like to see that report," said Cabot.

23

It was not yet dawn, but Trevor Warwick had a visitor. Commander Clive Kay had risen early and crept quietly into the ICU. He was there on a mission. Kay was determined to expose the Major. The doctors could call Warwick's sudden recovery *remarkable* and blather on about there being no lingering signs of his stroke. The nurses could murmur about miracles. But Kay knew better.

"Don't think you can pull the wool over my eyes," he whispered as he moved close to the bed in the darkened room. "I know the truth."

His accusation elicited only a soft snore.

Kay poked the lump under the blanket with a boney finger. "Wake up, you old fool."

The lump gave a grunt and changed shape. A moment later, there was another snore.

Kay poked again, this time harder.

Trevor Warwick grunted again and squinted up through the darkness.

Kay leaned down from his towering height close to the Sergeant Major's face. "Faker," he said, blowing out a lungful of sour morning breath laced with smoked kipper and onions.

"What the . . ." Warwick mumbled. Then he recognized his assailant. "You!" he shouted. "Get out of here!" He shoved Kay away with what strength he could muster.

"I thought so! You've been faking from the beginning," declared Clive Kay at the top of his voice. "To make people feel sorry for you; to get your own way!" He turned, took two of his long crane steps to the wall, and flipped on the lights, momentarily blinding the Sergeant Major.

"Help!" Warwick yelled. "In here! He's gone bloody mad!"

Tom Warwick who was sleeping in a vacant room close to his father's was the first on the scene. He managed to get between the two old men, then slipped and fell on something spilled from the bedpan. The intern on duty arrived seconds later. While helping Tom up off the floor, he was kicked in both shins and forced into a limping retreat. Finally, Nurse Harriet Claiborne put an end to the skirmish, threatening both of the old men with enemas.

As Merlyn had foreseen, the foursome in Vivian Warwick's Mini arrived at the Camelford Veteran's Home not long afterward. The timing was fortunate from the Wizard's point of view. The reverberations from the scrap between Clive Kay and Trevor Warwick were still rattling along the halls of the Veteran's Home, keeping most of the staff in gossip mode and less than on their toes.

At Merlyn's request, Vivian parked as close as she could to the front door. The Wizard also suggested that Harry stay in the car until Vivian could find out where Tom had arranged rooms for them.

Harry wrinkled his nose. "I'm not staying with him," he said, jerking a thumb at the man from Glastonbury. "He smells."

"You won't have to," said Merlyn. "He's coming with us."

Vivian had started to get out of the Mini. She stopped and looked at the Wizard. "What?"

"Didn't I tell you?" Merlyn said with a dry smile. "He's a war veteran. I made arrangements for him to stay here while he recovers. A few days at most, I would judge."

"When did you do that?" Vivian said.

"Oh . . . some time ago," said the Wizard with another wry look. "Would you mind helping me get him inside?"

Vivian shook her head and mumbled something, but came around to the back door of the car. Together, they helped the man in the long, musty cloak into the lobby and settled him in an armchair.

Then Merlyn said, "I think I can take it from here. Why don't you go look for Tom? I believe you'll find him in one of the treatment rooms."

Suddenly alarmed, Vivian said, "Treatment rooms?"

Merlyn smiled and shook his head. "Don't worry. It's minor. Only a bump on the head from a spill he took." He pointed to a spot on the back of his own head. "Rather aromatic, though."

Vivian stared at Merlyn, then glanced at the man in the armchair and back to the Wizard. She inhaled slowly, deeply, and let it out. "All right, that's it," she said. "I'm going to find Tom. And then you are going to tell all of us what the bloody hell is going on here. Is that understood?"

Merlyn put a hand to his chin. "Yes," he said thoughtfully. "I suppose now is the time. Why don't we plan to meet in Tom's father's room? I think our friend will be checked into the one next door."

"Tom told me his father was in Intensive Care."

Merlyn smiled his wry smile. "He's had a remarkable recovery. I believe they're moving him back to his normal room even now."

"You're impossible," Vivian said, shaking her head. She turned and started down the hall.

Merlyn cleared his throat. She stopped and looked at him. He shook his head and pointed down the hall in the opposite direction.

Once she was gone, Merlyn approached the front desk, which was empty. He rang a small bell by tapping it on the top. The sound produced a clerk from a room in the back; a pleasant looking middle-aged woman with a full figure and mouse brown hair.

"May I help you?" she said.

"I made arrangements for my friend," said Merlyn, pointing off toward the armchair. "But I heard all the commotion; yelling and so forth. Perhaps this is not the place for him?"

The clerk seemed a bit flustered; afraid the commotion would lose a new customer. "You can rest assured that kind of disturbance is certainly not normal," she said. "By no means."

Merlyn took a moment, glancing over at the man in the armchair, then finally said, "Well, how long would it take to get him a room?"

"No time at all, as soon as I find his registration papers," the clerk said. She looked through some papers on her desk, then looked up at Merlyn. "I'm sorry, I can't find the papers, but we'll just fill out new ones." As she pulled a registration form out of a drawer, she said, "There are just a few items to complete right now. Normally we have the new resident take a physical, but the doctor is busy at the moment. That can wait until later."

"Well . . . all right," Merlyn said.

The clerk smiled. "This shouldn't take long," she said, readying her pen over the form. "Name of the patient?"

"Art," said Merlyn. "Arthur Penn." He glanced at the armchair again. "Poor chap." He shook his head, then tapped the side of it with a finger.

"Oh," the clerk said, dropping her eyes to the form.

"Thinks he's the King," said the Wizard.

The clerk nodded and checked a box on the form. "I see." She gave the man slouched in the armchair a pitying glance. "How long has he been . . . the King?"

"Oh, a good long time," said Merlyn.

"I see," the clerk said again. "It can be a burden for friends and loved ones."

"Indeed," the Wizard agreed. As she opened her mouth to speak again, he leaned across and placed his hand on the clerk's arm. She looked down at her arm, then up to his face. "Yes, indeed," Merlyn said, staring into her eyes." After a moment he nodded and took his hand away.

"What insurance does–" the clerk began as if nothing had happened, then stopped. She frowned and her eyes glazed slightly. She looked down at the form and back up at Merlyn and smiled.

"We need to assign him a room," Merlyn said. "Room 127, next to Sergeant Major Trevor Warwick is available."

"Room 127 is available," she repeated.

"This is all taken care of now," said Merlyn.

"Yes," she agreed in a reedy voice. "It's all taken care of now." She filed the nearly empty sheet of paper in a cabinet and turned back to Merlyn as if she was waiting for him to say something else.

Just then, at no surprise to the Wizard, a young nurse came down the hall and started across the lobby, her uniform whispering. The clerk watched her a moment, then seemed struck with an idea. "Harriet," she called softly to her. "Could you give us some help here?"

Harriet came over to the counter and smiled at Merlyn. "How can I help?"

The clerk told Harriet that Merlyn's *friend* was being checked into the room next to Sergeant Major Warwick and asked if she would assist him to his room. While she explained, Merlyn enjoyed a surreptitious look at the young woman. She was a true beauty; slim and sculptured, with striking dark eyes that matched her lustrous black hair.

The clerk turned to Merlyn and said, "Harriet is one of the nurses for that area of the first floor. I know she'll take excellent care of your friend."

"Yes, I'm sure she will," Merlyn said with a melancholy smile, for he knew where it would lead.

24

The morning was warm in the Isles of Scilly. If the King's plan was successful, it would soon be warmer, even scorching. Last night, when Charles had smashed the eavesdropping bug, he only had time to give Camilla a sketchy description.

With raised eyebrows, the Queen Consort had uttered one word: "Bully!"

The King smiled. Thank God Milla had a deep down toughness, he thought. It was one of the qualities that drew him to her in the first place, and they would both need a strong measure of it to bring this off.

There were two keys to the escape plan. The first was the horses. As Charles recalled from his visit to Tresco years ago, the Smith family kept a string of Arabians on the island. With the cottage this close to the stables, it was clear they still did. Now, shortly after 6 a.m., with a gray mist still shrouding the stables and the wooded area surrounding them, several lads had arrived and began to feed and exercise a group of the magnificent animals.

However, the second key was still in question. Could the Monarch of the United Kingdom, by the Grace of God, King of Great Britain and His other Realms and Territories, Head of the Commonwealth, Defender of the Faith, start a fire without matches? It had taken some head scratching to come up with a way to accomplish it.

The marine commandos had stripped the cottage of anything they thought might be used in an escape attempt, including all of the matches, if there had been any. That was problematic because there was no stove and the fireplace looked as if it hadn't been used in the last century.

From the lines of grime on the kitchen counter, it appeared that there had been a small microwave, but it was gone now. There was no toaster, griddle, coffee maker, or any other appliances for that matter.

The silverware drawers were empty, not only of knives, but all utensils. The lamps and anything else that might have been used as a club had also been packed up and carried off.

The beds had been stripped, the closets cleaned out. They'd left nothing in the bathroom except toilet paper, some cotton balls, and, undoubtedly as a rude joke, a jar of Vaseline.

It was a thorough job. Charles gave them that much. However, in their attention to details, the Commandos had missed the big picture. The stable cottage still had power. The King planned to use that oversight to create a smoke screen, literally, to help him and Camilla escape. He was pleased that, in the process, he would be using their rude joke *against* his captors. For, apparently, they had also missed the proper military training in basic science.

Royal Marines should have known that Vaseline was a brand name of petroleum jelly–petroleum, as in *petrol*. Charles couldn't remember where, but he was certain he'd read that cotton balls saturated with Vaseline made an effective fire starter. Once ignited, they could be used to start the toilet paper and that to start strips of his torn shirt, and those to touch off the curtains, and that was all they would need.

"Bully," Milla had declared last night when he explained his plan. Yes, quite smashing, Charles thought. And perhaps completely boneheaded. A raging fire in a stables area full of high strung and highly valuable horses, to say nothing of the King and Queen Consort of Great Britain, would likely cause a panic. That should give two expert equestrians such as Camilla and him a chance at escape. However, it could also lead to a conflagration in which they might both die. But what was the alternative? Sit and wait while Alistair Saxon established himself as dictator of Great Britain?

On that thought, Camilla squeezed his hand and smiled. She gave him the button she'd popped from the remnants of his shirt. Charles smiled back a bit grimly and turned his attention to an electrical outlet in the wall of the bedroom, the one closest to the window with its curtains. On a chair near the outlet was a stack of Vaseline sticky cotton balls and a pile of toilet paper.

Using the shirt button as a screwdriver, Charles removed the plastic cover and pulled the electric receptacle out as far as the coiled wires inside the wall would allow. It was just enough to reach the chair. They exchanged silent smiles again. Then he loosened the two wires and pulled them off the receptacle, careful not to touch the bare copper himself or let the wires touch each other. Finally, holding one 240-volt wire in each hand, the King braced himself, reached out over the cotton balls, and brought the live ends together.

25

The horses were first to sense danger. A gray Arabian mare flared its nostrils, the whites of its eyes showing, and suddenly reared, giving a frightened scream. The stable lad walking the mare tried to calm the animal.

"Here, here, lady. You see to your knittin'," he cooed, shortening the lead and tightening his grip on it. Busy with the mare, he failed to see a wide-eyed black stallion that had taken the bit from his rider and was nearly trampled by it. As the stallion careened past, the gray mare reared again and broke away.

"Arsehole! What you bloody doin'?" the lad yelled at the stallion's rider.

"Up yours!" the rider hollered back as he struggled to control his mount.

The clatter of hoofs and shrill voices of the men alarmed several of the other already skittish Arabians, and they began pulling at their leads and neighing. Within seconds two more horses had broken away.

Finally, one of the stable lads with a sensitive nose detected the cause of the commotion.

"Smoke," he called, turning to look around for the source.

Another lad had already found it. Pointing toward the stable cottage, he shouted, "Fire! The cottage is on fire!"

It wasn't until then that the marine commando standing guard outside the cottage realized he had a problem. Later, he would claim that the wind was blowing the wrong direction and he couldn't smell the smoke, but it was more likely that he was tired at the end of his six-hour watch, and he'd been distracted by the horses.

At any rate, now he was totally unnerved, aware that he'd made a major mistake. His second miscue followed immediately when he failed to take time to alert his superior. Instead, he charged the door to the cottage and yanked on the doorknob, momentarily forgetting that it was locked. Now the smoke was obvious, and he began coughing himself. He dug the key out of his pocket and opened the door. Black smoke billowed out.

"Bloody idiots!" the marine shouted. He took a deep breath and, keeping low to avoid as much smoke as possible, moved into the cottage.

He found them in the bedroom. They were both down. He couldn't tell whether or not either was still breathing. The Queen Consort was half on and half off the bed. The King was on the floor near what was left of a chair. It looked as though he'd tried to open the window to get out. Instinctively, the marine went to Camilla, the female in distress. Leaning his automatic weapon against the dresser, he started to lift her off the bed. Then he stopped. Squinting through the smoke at Charles, he had a second thought.

"Bloody *Royal* idiot," he said. Shaking his head, he left Camilla where she was to see to the King of Great Britain.

It quickly became apparent that the marine wouldn't be carrying the fourteen stone Charles anywhere. If he was going to get him out of the house, he'd have to drag him. Despite the situation, the marine smiled to himself. This will be a story to tell, he thought. He rolled the King onto his back, took hold of his ankles, and began to tug.

Head down, sucking in sooty air, he struggled with Charles' inert form, pulling him out of the bedroom and halfway across the main room. There, he stopped a moment to catch his breath.

"That will be quite far enough," a voice said.

The marine looked up and realized he'd made another mistake. The Queen Consort was standing a couple of meters away. She had his weapon, and she looked like she knew how to use it.

He put up an open palm as if to hold her off. "Madam, you can't do this," he said, gasping for air.

"Hands on top of your head," Camilla said bluntly, sliding the safety to the off position on the silenced SA80 9mm assault rifle.

That was the end of the conversation. Charles got to his feet, and the three of them made their way outside as fast as they could, coughing and stumbling through the blinding, acrid smoke. It was well timed, if fortuitous. Just as they cleared the doorway to the cottage, the roof and ceiling over the bedroom collapsed with a rumble, spewing a cloud of ash into the air.

The scene in front of the cottage wasn't what Charles had anticipated. The chaos he'd counted on was limited to a single chestnut stallion dragging a smallish stable lad across the yard. The King had the presence of mind to shout, "Where are the horses?"

"In the woods!" the lad yelled back.

"I'll take the gun now," Charles told Camilla, holding out his hand.

Keeping the weapon pointed at the marine, she passed it to the King. "The safety is off," she said.

"Turn around," Charles said once he had the assault rifle. "Start walking toward the woods."

The marine did as he was told. "Are you going to shoot me?"

"If you don't shut up!" the King said. "Get going!"

With the marine a few steps in front, the three of them moved quickly away from the cottage and into the wooded area surrounding the stables. Once in the cover of the trees, Charles ordered the marine to stop. "You go ahead," he said to Camilla, pointing deeper into the woods. "I'll catch up."

The Queen Consort frowned. She glanced at the marine and back to her husband. "Charles?"

He shook his head. "This has to be done."

She took a moment, then nodded. "Don't be long," she said grimly, and walked away.

"You're not going to get away, you know that," the marine said with a tremor in his voice. He started to turn around.

"Get your back to me, both arms out to the side," ordered Charles. When the Commando complied, he said, "What is your name, Marine?"

"Dennis," he said. "Corporal Dennis Clark."

The King took a step closer to the Commando. "Well, Corporal Dennis Clark, I have a message for you and all of the others involved in this. Don't *screw* with the bloody *Royal* idiot!" On the last word he hit him with a roundhouse blow using the butt of the assault rife. The Marine crumpled to the ground, unconscious.

Minutes later, the King came upon Camilla standing near the edge of a steam. She wasn't alone. A white-haired old man with a scraggly beard was there, holding the leads of two Arabians. The horses seemed remarkably quiet based upon what had happened, calmly grazing on a patch of grass. From the ill-fitting clothes he was wearing, Charles assumed the old man was a tramp. He tightened his grip on the SA80.

As Charles approached them with the weapon at the ready, the old man seemed not to notice it. He smiled broadly at Charles. "The lady tells me you're looking for these," he said, raising the horse's leads.

The King couldn't remember the last time he'd been completely speechless. Finally, he managed a terse, "Yes."

The old man leaned over, said something to the Queen Consort that Charles couldn't catch, and gave her the leads. She nodded, then walked the horses over to the King. He frowned and she shrugged.

"He said to tell you the other horses were skittish and ran off. He conjured these up for us," she said.

Charles rolled his eyes and shook his head. "Barmy old codger," he said. He hooked the assault rife over his shoulder. Cupping his hands, he gave her a lift onto one of the Arabians.

She settled herself, then, looking down at her husband, Camilla said, "He said something else too, Charles."

The King ignored her. Using the mane, he scrambled aboard the other horse.

"Head south," Camilla said. "He said, 'Head south.'"

Charles looked at her a moment, then shook his head again. "Just as crazy," he muttered. "There's nothing but cliffs to the south. The boat docks are on the *west* end of the island." Jerking on the mane of his horse, he started in that direction. "Follow me," he called to Camilla.

As an afterthought, the King turned to give the old tramp a digital expression of his contempt and felt a chill run down his arms. There was no one there.

26

It was nearly 7:00 a.m. and Cabot still had seen no specific information on the reported sighting of Prince Harry at a McDonald's in SoHo. He finally called MI-5 Director Gibbon directly and was fended off by a protective administrative assistant for nearly fifteen seconds.

"I'm here, Commandant," Gibbon said with a tired, haughty tone as he came on the line. "You don't have to take people's heads off, you know?"

"You've been stonewalling me, Nigel," said Cabot. "This isn't cricket. It's England's future."

Gibbon's Dunhill lighter rasped on the line followed by an exhalation of smoke Cabot could almost smell. "I'm sorry, Commandant," the MI-5 Director said. "I assumed you'd want to speak directly to the agent who reported the sighting and I've had trouble getting in touch with her. I should have called you."

"And now you've reached her?" Cabot said cynically.

"Only moments ago," said Gibbon. He took time for another drag on his cigarette, then said, "Special Agent Rebecca Donovan. I have her on the line now."

Obviously reading from a dossier, he quickly filled in the agent's background. "She grew up in Liverpool, went to University at Newcastle, north of Sydney, Australia on a mathematics scholarship. Twenty-nine years old and single. She's been with the service for five years. I'm transferring you now."

Cabot went straight to the night in question and asked Donovan to describe what happened. She sounded professional enough, but seemed combative about the reported sighting.

"You sound like you're not convinced it was a negative sighting," he said.

"I didn't say that. It's just that . . ."

"Just what?" said Cabot.

"The restaurant manager."

"What about him?"

"Her," she corrected. "It was a woman, about my age."

Cabot waited. Donovan apparently wasn't sure of herself, or her facts. "We don't have time for twenty questions, agent Donovan," he said finally. "Spit it out."

"I don't know. The manager acted like she knew the bloke, but I didn't believe it. I got the feeling she thought he might jump up and run."

"Why didn't you report that at the time?"

"I tried to, but my mobile phone went berserk, started blaring out static. I stepped outside to see if I could get through, but it was no good. When I went back into the restaurant, the manager and the young man were nowhere to be seen. He must have left. Or they were somewhere in the back, I guess."

"Did you get the manager's name?"

"Not until later. We were under pressure to find the Prince, and I moved on. Her name is Vivian Warwick. She's been a manager at that location for about a year. Married, no children."

"What did you say?"

"I said, she's married, no children."

"No, the name; what was the name?"

"Warwick. Vivian Warwick."

Cabot absently felt the whiskers on his jaw line. They were standing up. "So, you did a follow-up with her later?"

"I tried to, but she was gone."

"Home, you mean?"

"The assistant manager said he didn't know where she'd gone. I got the home address from him, a flat on Beak Street in SoHo, and stopped by, but no one was there." After a moment of silence she added, "There still isn't."

"And that makes you think what?" said Cabot.

"I'm not sure."

At that point, Cabot's aide entered the Major General's room interrupting the conversation. "Sir," he whispered. "You have a priority call on line two. It's Major Mallory."

Cabot put agent Donovan on hold and took the call. "Cabot."

"We've had an incident, sir. A fire at the stables cottage."

"Are the *guests* all right?"

Mallory hesitated. "We're not sure. We don't know where they are."

"You mean they got away?"

The Major hesitated again, then softly said, "Yes, sir."

Cabot punched line one. "We'll have to get into this later, Donovan," he said. "In the meantime, I want you personally to follow this lead. Go back to the McDonald's; talk to the employees, see if you can find anything in the manager's office. Track down the husband, talk to him."

"But Director Gibbon said—"

Cabot cut her off. "The military is now in charge of this investigation," he said. "This is an order, Agent Donovan. You understand?"

After a gulped silence, Donovan said, "Yes sir!"

"Report anything you find directly to me," Cabot said. He hung up the phone and had his aide order a car to take him to the heliport.

Had he known what was happening in Camelford even then, he would have ordered help for Donovan.

27

Arthur Pendragon, High King of all Britain, opened his eyes. "Merlyn?" he whispered, his voice raw and hoarse.

There was no answer.

Arthur struggled to sit up, but grimaced in pain and fell back. Even his beard hurt. He tried to remember the lessons the Wizard taught him long ago in Sir Ector's forests, when he was just a lad called Wart. *How does a wounded deer recover? How does a frightened bird still fly?* He closed his eyes and breathed deeply, slowly. After a few moments, he called out again. "Merlyn?"

He was about to try once more when the door opened. It was the young woman from before, the one who brought him to this room, who couldn't speak the language. She was the brazen wench who poked and prodded him until he ordered her out of the room, the one who didn't pay any attention.

"You!" he exclaimed as she swept into the room. "What are you doing back here?"

Harriet Claiborne smiled and moved to the bed. He jerked his blanket up higher and pointed a finger at her. "Don't you know I am the King?"

"Of course I know, Your Majesty," she said. He opened his mouth to speak and she stuck a thermometer in it. "Hold that under your tongue with your mouth closed," she instructed him. Without waiting for a reaction, she took his arm and wrapped the blood pressure band around it. Then she put her stethoscope in place, and began pumping the rubber bulb.

He put up with it, but in frustration. "At least you're learning the language," he mumbled through the thermometer.

"No talking," Harriet said, shushing him with a finger across her lips. When she was done, the young nurse took the thermometer and read it, then put the King's arm under the blanket and patted it. "No fever and a BP of one forty over eighty. That's good for a person your age," she told him with a beautiful smile.

"Who *are* you?" he demanded.

She leaned in closer and smiled again. "I'm Harriet, your nurse."

He stared at her face for a long moment, tilting his head slightly as if he were admiring a painting. Finally, he caught himself and sputtered, "How did you learn our language so quickly? Are you a spy?"

Harriet giggled. "I'm sorry, Your Majesty. But *you* are speaking *my* language."

He frowned and looked around the room. "What is this place?" he said.

Harriet moved to the window and opened the blinds. Light flooded the room, revealing a corner of the brick building and the fields surrounding it.

Arthur squinted, wincing in pain.

"This is the Camelford Veterans Home," she said.

The squint was suddenly gone. "Camlann?" he said.

Harriet smiled and shook her head. "That's what it was once called, according to legend. Now it's Camelford." She put the blood pressure band back on its hook. Then she added, "But Slaughter Bridge is still there. They haven't changed that."

Arthur took in a breath and turned toward the window, staring off into the distance. "I was there," he said, a husk in his voice. His face had lost what little color it had. He seemed shaken.

"Are you all right?" said Harriet. She stepped close, taking his wrist to check his pulse.

He recoiled from her touch, jerking his hand away. "I am the King," he said.

Harriet relaxed. His cheeks had turned ruddy.

"Yes, I know," she said. "And that is why we give you this royal device." She reached over and picked up the remote, which had controls for the lights and television, and the nursing call button. Pointing to the call button, she said, "If you need assistance, you simply push this button and a nurse will appear."

He glanced at the remote and looked back at her. "Just like that?" he said, snapping his fingers.

"Well, nearly so," said Harriet.

He took the remote from her hand, looked it over, then pushed the call button. A moment later, to his utter surprise, a disembodied voice said, "May I help you?"

Harriet snatched the remote back and said, "Just testing. Thanks."

"No problem," said the disembodied voice.

In the silence that followed, they both could hear the ticking of the clock on the wall. He looked up at it. Another mystery.

"Who was–" the King started, but Harriet just shook her head and handed back the remote.

"If you need assistance," she repeated with a fleeting glimpse of that beautiful smile. Then she started toward the door.

"Veterans of what?" Arthur said.

Harriet stopped and turned around. Arthur was titling his head slightly, staring at her. He tipped his head back up and smiled.

She sighed, gave a small shake of her head, then moved back to the bed. "The War," Harriet said. "You remember that, don't you?"

Arthur nodded enthusiastically. "Against the dreadful Saxons."

Harriet smiled and patted his hand. "You mean the Nazis, Your Majesty."

The King frowned. He seemed confused. "Navies?"

"The Germans; they nearly destroyed London, threatened to over-run all of England. They might have if it weren't for the Americans. More than three million of them came here to help us in the fight."

Arthur was quiet for a long moment. "When was this?" he said finally.

"From 1939 until 1946," said Harriet. "We won, I'm sure you know that." She smiled and patted his hand again.

As she turned to go, she said, "Now, I have other patients to see. I'll be back later." Then she was gone, whisking away with a crinkling of her uniform.

Arthur lay there watching the door she had disappeared through. "Harriet," he murmured to himself and nodded with satisfaction. "A fine name." Then he put the young nurse and his thoughts about her aside.

Where was Merlyn? Why had that damned Wizard brought him here? After more than a thousand years? And what was that contraption on the wall that ticked? How did that voice spring from the magic wand she gave him?

He held up the remote and looked at it closely. There were several other buttons on it besides the one that produced the voice. He pushed one of them.

There was a click. Then he could hear a woman's voice. He looked toward the sound and an image began to fade in on the black box hanging on the wall opposite his bed. It was a beautiful young wench in a revealing dress. She was standing next to a carriage without horses, like the one he rode in from Avalon. This one was blood red and had no top. She called it a B and W. The wench was praising the carriage, claiming it was green. Just as he thought to speak to her, to tell her of her mistake, she disappeared, replaced by a man at a scribe's table. As the man started to speak, words began to crawl across the front of the table.

"A wizard," Arthur murmured, "just as Merlyn." He couldn't read the words, but he heard the man. The Saxons were searching for another man who would assassinate the King. He had to find his old advisor and friend.

Arthur pushed the button again and the image on the wall disappeared. He turned and looked out the window, seeing the blood-drenched fields that once surrounded this place.

"Everything has changed, and nothing," he said to himself.

He took some deep breaths the way Merlyn had taught him and made another attempt to sit up. This time he made it, despite the pain. After a few more deep breaths he managed to slide his legs off the bed and stand up.

"Merlyn?" he whispered as he inched forward. "Where are you?"

28

The two marine commandos stationed at the boat docks were at a picnic table having a breakfast of pre-packaged rations and instant coffee when they heard the first alert. It mentioned the fire, but nothing about an escape. It was another mistake. By the time the second report was on the air, the marines were looking down the barrel of a 9mm assault rifle in the firm hands of the King of Great Britain.

"Take out your weapons and drop them on the ground," Charles said.

The two men glanced at each other.

"Carefully," the King added, slightly adjusting the 9mm in his hands.

It was enough of a threat. Both men removed the handguns from the holsters on their belts and dropped them.

"Who has the radio?"

One of the men couldn't resist a glance, giving away the other one.

"Drop it with the guns," said Charles.

After a frustrated sigh, the man took it out of a jacket pocket and dropped it.

"Now, get me the keys to the fastest boat," Charles said.

The taller commando, the one who had the radio, shook his head. "You can't get away, Your Majesty."

Charles fired a burst over the man's left shoulder.

"Bloody hell!" the other commando shouted. "Get him the keys, Freddie."

Freddie had spilled his coffee down the front of his uniform. He didn't try to wipe it off. He kept his hands at chest height in front of him. They were shaking. "They're in the boathouse," he said to Charles.

"Let's go," Charles said, giving him a motion with the submachine gun. He glanced at the shorter commando. "You, too. Keep your hands out where I can see them; both of you." Without looking at her, Charles said, "Camilla, pick up the weapons and the radio and follow along."

The commandos did as ordered, walking in front of the King to the boathouse, their arms out, hands visible. When they got there, Charles told them to turn around. They were both ashen-faced.

"I don't want to kill you. But be certain that I will," said the King. "Do you understand?"

They nodded.

"Very well," said Charles. "Camilla, you guard the short one. I'm going into the boat house with . . . Freddie, isn't it?"

"Yes, sir," said the commando. He turned and walked into the boat-house and Charles followed. The King didn't have to look back. He knew Camilla had one of the commando's guns trained on the other man and she would use it if need be.

Inside, Freddie went to a wooden box on the wall and opened it. There were two rows of hooks with keys hanging on several of them. He selected one and proffered it to Charles. "This one is to the Sunseeker Tomahawk. We don't have anything faster, not even close."

Charles took the key. "Stand clear," he said, motioning him away from the box with his gun. The commando stepped back, and Charles took all of the other keys off their hooks and put them in his pocket. The King allowed himself a small smile. "Just in case," he said. On the way out, Charles picked up two coils of what appeared to be docking rope.

Outside, with Camilla holding a gun on both commandos, Charles made the larger of the two men take off his shirt and give it to him. The

King slipped the shirt on, then the Royals marched the two commandos a short way into the woods. They sat them down with their backs against two trees that were several meters apart and tied them up with the rope.

Once he'd checked to make sure both men were secured, Charles said, "It won't be too long. Even Major Mallory should be able to find you. When you see him, tell him for me that he will regret striking the Queen Consort of England. Very much."

Ten minutes later Charles and Camilla were aboard the sleek, Sunseeker Tomahawk heading out to sea. The Queen Consort shouted over the roar of the 425-horse power engine, "I have a question!"

Charles nodded.

"Where the bloody hell are we going?"

Charles yelled back, "Land's End! It's the closest–" He stopped and looked at her. Then he shook his head and trimmed the throttle back so they could hear over the engine.

"What's wrong?" Camilla asked.

"That's where they'll be looking," said Charles. "North of the island."

Camilla gave an impish grin. "You mean the old *barmy codger* in the woods was right?"

Without answering her, the King pushed the Sunseeker back to full throttle and headed south.

29

"This is *your* muck up!" General Ian Baker-Smythe said angrily into his mobile phone. "I told you Mallory couldn't be counted on."

"He has the situation under control," said Cabot.

"Does he even know where the bloody hell they are?"

Cabot took a breath before he answered. "On the island."

"That won't do, Commandant. We have to get them locked down."

"I've spoken with the Major. He assures me it's only a matter of time," said Cabot. "He has men at the main house, the heliport, and the boat dock. There's a crew of six commandos searching the woods. The Royals have no chance of escape."

"I think you should get down there, and take control," the General said.

It was a moment before Cabot said, "I'm calling from the car, on my way to the heliport."

The General cleared his throat. "You should have said that to begin with."

"Yes, sir."

"I want a report on your personal assessment of the situation when you land."

"As soon as I can," said Cabot.

Baker-Smythe clicked off, ending the conversation. He put his phone in the pocket of his crisp, ironed shirt and turned to the man sitting in front of his desk. "Put that damned thing out!"

Nigel Gibbon stubbed out his Player's and exhaled. "A situation, I take it?" he said with a smile. There was a wisp of smoke still floating up from his nostrils.

"Don't try to be funny with me, you pipsqueak," said the General.

"Sorry," said the MI-5 Director. "Not my intention. Not at all." He made a move to take out another cigarette and cut it off midway. "I might be able to help. What exactly . . ." He paused, playing the waiting game at which he was so practiced.

And Baker-Smythe obliged him. "There was a fire in the stables cottage where Charles and Camilla were housed. In the commotion of putting it out, they escaped."

"Charles intentionally set the fire?" said Gibbon.

"That's the assumption. It happened just as the grooms were taking the Arabians out for morning exercise."

Gibbon smiled, started to fish out another Player's, caught himself again, and said, "And both of the Royals are expert equestrians."

"With no place to ride," said the General.

He waited for Baker-Smythe's conclusion to sink in, then Gibbon said, "Except the boat docks."

The General shook his head. "Cabot said Mallory has two commandos there."

The MI-5 Director stood. "Well, I'm sure Jock Cabot will see to it that they're scooped up and put back under lock and key." He took out his package of Player's. "Let me know if there's anything–"

"Put those fags back and sit down," said Baker-Smythe. He waited until Gibbon was back in his seat. "Did Cabot get the background on that potential sighting of the Prince at McDonald's?"

"Not until this morning," Gibbon said. "It was after 7:00 when he finally called."

Weren't you to call him?"

Gibbon nodded. "Didn't answer."

The General frowned. "Why did he wait so long?"

Gibbon shrugged. "I have no idea. Busy possibly."

"Do you think there's something wrong with Major General Cabot? Is he distracted, slipping?"

"I'm afraid I couldn't say. There are things even Bond didn't know," Gibbon said. He smiled at his own quip, exposing a row of nicotine stains. "At any rate, I don't think the delay is important. The agent didn't even report the McDonald's sighting until an hour later. Excuse was a mobile phone malfunction. More likely a Big Mac attack." He huffed a smoke-smelling chuckle.

Baker-Smythe remained straight-faced. "You keep an ear on that one. Now get back to it." He summarily turned to some paperwork on his desk.

"Yes sir," Gibbon said and got up and left.

In the hallway outside the General's office, the MI-5 Director lit a cigarette and took a deep drag. Then he took his mobile phone out of his jacket pocket and turned off the record function.

30

Tom and Vivian Warwick had only just arrived in the Sergeant Major's room when the knock came at the door. The old man, Trevor, was sitting up in his raised bed. The doctors had assured them his 'stroke' was a false alarm, but Tom wasn't so sure. He thought his father looked a little gray, washed out.

"Who can that be?" Tom said. "I don't think he's ready for visitors."

"We're expecting someone," said Vivian.

Tom frowned and went to the door. He'd never seen the man standing there.

"I'm glad you all could come," Merlyn said with a smile. He stepped aside and guided Harry into the room. "I believe we all know who this young chap is."

"My God," Tom whispered. He looked at Vivian, then back at Harry. "I thought they were all sequestered."

"That's what I was trying to tell you on the phone," Vivian said.

The Sergeant Major leaned forward and squinted. "That's young Prince Harry. I know him from the telly. But who are you?" he said to Merlyn. He turned to Tom and Vivian. "Who is that?"

Tom glanced at Vivian. She raised her eyebrows and shrugged. "That's why we're here."

"Actually, *I'm* here to seek your help," said Merlyn.

"Help with what?" Trevor said, sitting up straighter. The gray, washed out look Tom thought he'd seen was gone and the Sergeant Major's eyes were bright with interest.

Harry had moved away from the others and was slouched against the kitchen sink in the corner of the room. He sighed sullenly. "I knew it," he said. "You're not a friend or an advisor to my father. You're just trying to help that drug addict we brought here."

Merlyn turned suddenly and eyed Harry. "Where *is* your father, Prince?" he said, a sharp edge in his voice. "Do you know?"

Just as suddenly, the slouch was gone. Ramrod straight, Harry glared back at Merlyn, his cheeks crimson with emotion. "He's . . . somewhere! Being held against his will, with Camilla and William and Catherine and the others. They're all being held. I'm the only one who got away."

"Kidnapped?" said Trevor.

"My God," Tom repeated. "Is that true?"

Merlyn looked at the faces turned to him. This was the band of brave warriors he had gathered to save the kingdom? It could be a long campaign, he thought. Finally, he nodded. "The Prince is right. They're on Tresco in the Isles of Scilly, being held by Royal Marine Commandos at the order of Prime Minister Saxon. We need your help to free them. To help them regain their rightful place."

"Why should we believe you?" challenged Harry. "How would you know they're on Tresco?"

Merlyn stared at his feet for a moment. "I was just there," he said.

"That's ridiculous! You've been with us the whole time," Harry insisted.

Trying to bring some order to the moment, Vivian interrupted. "This isn't getting us anywhere. Can we back up for a minute? You said '*we* need your help.' I take it that means there are others involved?"

"For the moment only one; the man we brought here from Glastonbury," said Merlyn.

Vivian rolled her eyes. "Oh, grand," she said.

"You still haven't even told us who that old sot is," Harry said, back to his sullen tone.

"You brought someone here from Glastonbury?" Tom asked.

"You promised, remember?" Vivian said to Merlyn. "Now is the time. Who is he? Who are *you*?"

Merlyn took a moment, then sighed and nodded. "This isn't going to be easy."

"Try us. You might be surprised," Vivian said. She smiled weakly and waited.

The Wizard looked at Tom. "Your main study at University is history?"

"Yes, I plan to teach."

"What do they say in your classes about England in the Dark Ages, during the Sixth Century?"

"You mean actual history or the Arthurian legends?"

"They're not the same?"

Tom chuckled. "We English are full of our legends. Robin Hood and his Merry Men, King Arthur, but that's all they are–legends."

"And places like Camelot and Avalon? They don't exist, never did?" said Merlyn.

"Oh, you always have so-called researchers digging up something. They say they can prove Camelot was at Cadbury or here in Camelford. Others insist it's somewhere in Scotland. But they're not serious historians."

"Where do they say Avalon was?" said Merlyn. "The isle where Arthur was taken by the Ladies of the Lake to recover from his wounds?"

Tom frowned. He glanced at Vivian. "Glastonbury."

"I don't think I like where this is going," Vivian said. "What are you trying to say?"

Merlyn smiled tightly. "I know it may be difficult to accept at first."

Harry couldn't contain himself. "At first?" He groaned and shook his head. "This is hopeless! He's trying to get us to believe that the old sot from the car is King Arthur."

That started everyone talking.

"Maybe he is," said Trevor excitedly.

"I think I need to sit down," Tom said, gingerly touching the bandage on the back of his head. He moved to one of the chairs near the bed.

Vivian held her hands up for quiet. "Wait! Just wait a moment. Let me get this straight. The man from Glastonbury–who is he?"

Merlyn glanced at the floor, then looked up at Vivian. He smiled his wry smile. "Arthur Pendragon, High King of All Britain."

She closed her eyes, nodding her head. "I see. Arthur Pendragon," she said. Then she opened her eyes. "And that would make you?"

"Some call me Emrys Myrddin. Others know me as–"

"Merlyn, the enchanter," Tom finished for him.

Before anyone could react, there was a hard rapping on the door, and Nurse Harriet Claiborne pushed into the room, nearly banging the door against the wall. She was out of breath, her face flushed. "He's gone," she exclaimed. "Your friend in 127 is gone."

31

Arthur had only managed to make it down the hall and around the corner. His legs were rubbery, and he was short of breath. Leaning against the wall, he called out the Wizard's name one more time.

"Merlyn?"

To his surprise, a door opened. Standing there was a giant, a gaunt tower of a man. "There's no one here by that name," he said. He started to close the door, then, after an appraisal of Arthur, he sighed and shook his head. "Sod of the week," he said to himself. To Arthur, he said, "Can I be of assistance? I'm Commander Kay."

Suddenly Arthur's face lit up. He cocked his head quizzically and squinted at the tall man. "Kay?" he said. "Is that surely you? You look old."

The Commander was obviously annoyed. "If you're going to insult me, you can help yourself." He turned and started back inside his room.

"No! Wait!" Arthur blurted before the door closed. "It's Wart, your brother."

"I don't have a brother," Kay said and closed the door.

Arthur teetered over and rapped on it. "Sir Kay," he called. "I need your help."

The door opened almost immediately. "What did you call me?" Clive Kay demanded.

Arthur stood there in stunned silence for a moment. "Sir Kay, your rightful title," he said finally. "I'm sorry I didn't recognize you at first. I'm older myself."

Kay frowned. "Who the bloody hell are you?" he said.

Arthur glanced down at the hospital gown he was wearing, tried to straighten it. Clearly, he was embarrassed. "The one you hunted with in Sir Ector's forests," he said.

Kay rolled his eyes. Caustic bullies and so-called friends had been trying to play him his whole life, making fun of his effeminate last name or its supposed place in medieval history. He wasn't about to let a perfect stranger score at this late date.

"You can do better than that, can't you?" the Commander said derisively. "Why not try the sword in the stone story? How I was the one who actually drew it out? That's a jolly good one."

Arthur appeared confused and worn out. He looked off down the hallway. After a long moment, his gaze drifted back to Kay.

"I am the King you swore allegiance to, the one you sat on the right hand of at the Round Table," he said.

This caused an eyebrow to rise. He didn't know why, but Clive Kay felt a vague connection with this poor wretch. Something made him think the man actually believed what he was saying. "When was this?" Kay asked.

Arthur thought for a moment. "Long ago," he said.

The Commander stepped out into the hallway. "You're either a blithering idiot or a shade. But my forbearers would expect me to find out before turning my back," he said. He took Arthur by the arm and headed him toward his room. "Come in here while I fix some tea."

Kay sat Arthur in the only armchair in the room and covered him with a blanket, as much to hide the skimpy hospital gown as to keep him warm. While the water heated, he busied himself preparing the kettle.

"Where are you from?" the Commander asked Arthur.

"As I told you, I grew up with you at Sir Ector's castle in the Forest Sauvage," Arthur said. "After that came the years with Guinevere and the knights at Camlann. Then I was . . ." He seemed to drift off, staring into the distance. When the steaming tea splashed into their cups, he turned and looked at Kay. "Mordred is dead, isn't he?"

Without answering, Clive Kay brought Arthur a cup and took the other to a small table with a single straight-backed chair. Once they had both sipped at the tea, he said, "Why are you here?"

Arthur set his cup on his lap. "I'm not sure," he said. "Merlyn brought me from Avalon; in the woman's horseless carriage. There was a lad with us."

He turned and looked Kay in the eye. "The Saxon have returned and assassins are after the King. Is that true?"

Kay had been keeping up with the news alerts, including the latest one. "You mean the Prime Minister?" he said, then nodded. "Saxon just announced they're searching for another man."

"I must have Excalibur!" Arthur declared. He suddenly threw the blanket off and started to get up, spilling his tea onto the floor.

Adding to the commotion, there was a knock at the door and someone called, "Arthur?"

"Keep your knickers on!" Kay yelled.

He moved swiftly to the small kitchen area and grabbed a towel. When he turned back to mop up the mess, he was taken aback. An old man with white hair was helping Arthur back into his chair, whispering something to him.

"How did you get in here?" Kay said.

"I'm sorry. I thought I heard you invite me," said Merlyn. "Commander Kay, isn't it? A veteran of World War II; wounded in North Africa."

Clive Kay nodded. "That is correct, but–"

Merlyn interrupted. "Your great grandfather was in the British Expeditionary Force that helped save Paris from the Germans in the Great War and died near the River Marne?"

The Commander frowned. "Yes, but–"

"And *his* grandfather fought under the Duke of Wellington at Waterloo in June of 1815? In fact, men with the sir name of Kay have been standing strong for Britain as long as these isles have existed."

"I don't know what you're–" Kay started.

Merlyn raised a hand and stopped him in mid sentence. "My friend was wrong," Merlyn said. "You are not the man he thought you were. But you are a direct descendant. And Britain needs the help of a Kay again. Now."

The Commander huffed a guttural laugh, then bent down, and began wiping the floor. "To clean up the mess," he said.

"I'm sorry," the Wizard said. He indicated Arthur. "Has he been trouble to you?"

"Some spilled tea; that's about all, but he's a bit of a nutter."

"How's that?"

Kay glanced at Arthur, then turned to Merlyn. "This chap actually thinks he's King Arthur."

Merlyn smiled slightly. "I'm afraid it's worse than that. He *is* King Arthur."

32

Commander Clive Kay would have none of it. "Preposterous!" he declared.

Merlyn had anticipated this, of course. "Perhaps you'd like to meet the reason the High King has returned?" the Wizard said.

That drew a sharp, "When Hades freezes over." The Commander dropped the towel he'd been using to wipe up the spilled tea, walked stiffly to the door and threw it open with a bang. "Your drama is over, gentlemen. I get the joke. Now leave."

"As you desire," said Merlyn. He helped Arthur up. At the door they hesitated long enough for him to add, "Should you change your mind, we will be in Sergeant Major Warwick's room, at least for a time."

Kay didn't react, except to close the door behind them.

"He didn't *look* like Kay, either," Arthur muttered as they walked down the hall. Merlyn smiled and took Arthur's arm to stop him. They both turned as they heard the door reopen.

Commander Kay had slipped on a navy sport coat and tied a gray cravat loosely around his neck. He started toward them. "I want to make it perfectly clear that my only interest in this is to see just how bloody insane–" His eyes widened and he went silent even before the small squeal sounded from behind Arthur and Merlyn.

It was Nurse Harriet Claiborne. She hurried up to the trio in the hall. "Here you are," she said to Arthur, smiling and patting him on the arm. "Thank heavens."

She turned to Merlyn. "And thank you for finding him." Then, as if she'd just noticed him, she turned to Kay and said, "Commander Kay, what are you doing here?"

Kay didn't take it well. "Thank you for even recognizing me," he offered acidly. "I'm the one who took this slacker in and served him tea. Then he and this other tramp tried to make a fool of me."

"Shame on you, Commander," Harriet said. "You shouldn't insult people you don't even know."

Kay sighed. "Very well, you tell me, who is he?"

The nurse looked at Arthur, and he glanced at her. Then she turned back to Kay. "The King," she said. "This is the King."

Kay shook his head and moaned slightly. He pointed at Merlyn. "I suppose this is his Wizard, Merlyn?"

Harriet giggled, thinking Kay had joined in the charade. "Of course," she said.

Merlyn smiled and gave him a nod in acknowledgement just as Vivian Warwick came around the corner. Vivian smiled brightly at the sight of Arthur and Merlyn. "What is this, a party?" she said.

"We found him!" said Harriet with her own bright smile.

Commander Kay sighed again. "I beg your pardon, madam, but *I* found him."

As Vivian joined the group that now nearly filled the hallway, she eyed Merlyn closely, and he winked at her. Counting on her fingers, she said, "My, we're getting to be quite an army. I count eight people now."

"Excuse me?" Kay said, glancing at the fingers of his own hand. "I count only five individuals, although that may be rather propitious for one of them." He offered his hand to Vivian. "Allow me to introduce myself. I'm Commander Clive Kay."

She took his hand and smiled. "Hello. I'm Vivian Warwick," she said, then pointed over her shoulder. "There are three more back in Trevor's room."

"Three more Warwicks?" said Kay. His face looked as if they were talking about roaches.

At this point, Merlyn cut in. "I've been thinking about that," he said. "With this many people, perhaps it would be better if we gather somewhere else. Say . . ." He turned to Harriet. "The Recreation Lounge?"

She looked at her watch. "It should be empty, at least until after lunchtime."

"Very good. You lead the way with Vivian and the Commander, if you will, Harriet. Arthur needs to change into something more suitable. I'll bring him and the other three." He took Arthur by the arm, turned on his heel, and the two of them started down the hall.

"Wait!" Kay said. You mean to bring that conniver Warwick into this?"

"Two more of them," Merlyn called. "And the man who is the reason we're all here."

Once they were out of earshot, Arthur said, "We need to talk."

"What is it, Your Majesty?" said Merlyn.

Arthur hesitated. "I am the High King, correct?"

"Of course."

"Ruler of all Britain?" said Arthur, spreading his arms to take in the entire hallway.

Merlyn nodded. "Yes, My Liege."

"Then, why don't I know anything?"

The Wizard grinned. "I've been waiting for your inquiry," he said.

Arthur smiled kindly. "You remind me of the lessons in Sir Ector's forest, noble teacher. Now answer me this; everyone wonders who I am, but I have my own wonderings. Who are they? And what are we doing here? Do you know it has been more than one thousand years since we last spoke?"

"Do you remember that last conversation, King?" said Merlyn. "Before Nimue trapped me in my cave? I told you then that it would be many years, but we both would return."

"When England needs us most," Arthur said, hushed, under his breath. He stopped and turned to Merlyn. "Is it true then, the Saxons have also returned?"

The Wizard shook his head. "No, Your Majesty," he said. "It is one man named Saxon, the Prime Minister of Great Britain. With a group of his henchmen he seeks to supplant the rightful rulers of these isles, the people and their King, and to rule by force."

"Is the lad who came with us their King?" said Arthur.

Merlyn shook his head again. "No, Your Majesty. He is a Prince, second in line to the throne, and the only member of the Royal Family who has not been captured and secluded on an island in the sea."

"Call out the Knights!" Arthur commanded. "We must protect him. And free the others."

Merlyn smiled softly. "I'm afraid there aren't any Knights, Your Majesty."

"Then find some!"

"I believe, with some modest good fortune, that is what we are doing," said the Wizard.

Arthur turned to Merlyn. He frowned, tilting his head slightly. Then, after a moment, the frown disappeared and he said, "Very good."

Merlyn took him by the arm. "Shall we go then?"

Arthur held up a finger. "One more thing. You said I must change into something more . . . suitable. Where shall we get these garments?"

The Wizard smiled again. "You already have them on, Your Majesty," he said.

Arthur looked down and was surprised to see it was so.

33

Major Rhys Mallory saluted smartly as Cabot stepped off the helicopter in Tresco. The Major General waved the salute off and, crouching slightly, moved toward him through the roiling air from the blades of the AW159 Lynx Wildcat.

When they were close enough to hear over the din, Cabot's first words were, "Do we have them?"

Mallory was forced to shout, "No, sir!"

"Where is the MK4?" Cabot asked, looking for the huge Sea King helicopter.

Again, Mallory was forced to shout a negative. "We sent it back to Base Chivenor."

Major General Cabot nodded with a sour smile. "Because this could never happen," he said.

After that, neither spoke until they reached the pick-up truck parked at the edge of the heliport. Mallory opened the door for Cabot. The Major had lost the authoritative air he'd had with the Royals and actually looked deflated.

"Sorry about the transportation, sir," Mallory said. "Cars are not allowed on Tresco Island. We only have this truck and a fire engine."

"Is that your excuse for why this is taking so long?" Cabot said. Without waiting for an answer, he got into the truck.

Mallory went around the front of the pick-up and slid in the driver's side. Before he started the engine he said, "While you were in the air we had a break in the search. We found two men in the wooded area near the boat docks."

"Marine commandos?" said Cabot.

"Yes, sir. The two men assigned to guard the boats. They were tied to trees with ropes. I haven't had a chance to talk with them yet. That's where we're going."

"Is the site of the fire on the way?" Cabot asked.

Mallory turned and looked at him. "There's not much left of the cottage, sir," he said.

Cabot leaned back in his seat, put his head back, and closed his eyes. "We already know they're in a boat, Major. I assume you have people looking for them. I want to see the cottage."

"Yes, sir," Mallory said.

"And talk with the guard who was on duty," said the Major General. He opened his eyes and looked at Mallory. "He's alive, I take it. You haven't executed him?"

Mallory didn't know whether or not to smile. "No sir. Not yet. Corporal Clark was knocked unconscious by the King, but he's been cleared by medical and returned to duty." After a moment's pause, he added, "Guarding the burned out cottage." He chuckled at what he thought was his own bit of humor.

Cabot closed his eyes and leaned back again. "You can punish him later, Major. We need every hand we have now."

"Yes, sir," Mallory said. "I'll add him to one of the search teams."

Mallory stopped the pick-up in front of what had been the cottage, and they both got out. Cabot walked past Corporal Dennis Clark without even looking at him and proceeded to scuff around in the charred remains. Mallory followed him, staying a couple of scuffs behind. After a few minutes, Cabot squatted to look closer at something. He stood with a partially melted piece of copper wire in his hand.

"Electrical. Charles started the fire by touching the bare wires from a lamp or appliance," the Major General said.

Mallory shook his head. "All the lamps and electrical appliances had been removed."

Cabot thought for just a moment. "But the electricity was on?"

Almost immediately Mallory said, "Crap! He took the panel off an outlet."

Cabot moved on, scuffing through the debris. It wasn't long before he knelt again. This time he came up with a melted plastic container. He put it to his nose, but only for a second. "What is *this* doing here?" he said and offered it to Mallory. "Somebody have chapped lips?"

A few minutes later it was Mallory, with Cabot by his side, who asked the same question of Corporal Clark.

Clark couldn't help but glance at Cabot, trying to judge how much trouble he was in. Enormous, he decided.

"Well?" said the Major.

"It was . . . it was just supposed to be a joke," the Corporal said. "You know, them *getting together*."

"What is Vaseline made of, Corporal?" Cabot asked.

"I don't know, sir. It's old stuff. We never had it at home," Clark said.

"Did Charles say anything to you, Corporal?" said Cabot.

"It was mostly the Queen Consort," Clark answered. "They were both down in the bedroom. She was on the bed and he was on the floor. They appeared to be out from smoke inhalation. I put down my weapon so I could drag Charles out of the cottage. I was halfway to the door when she came up behind me with my gun. She looked like she could handle it. The King got up, and she ordered me outside.

"Charles took the gun then. We walked into the woods, and he made me turn around. I thought he was going to kill me, but he asked me my name. Then he leaned in close and said he had a message for me and all the others involved in this."

Cabot gave him a moment, then said, "Well, Corporal?"

"He whispered it, right in my ear; 'Don't *screw* with the bloody *Royal* idiot!' That's when he hit me."

"I'll be in the pick-up," Cabot said to Major Mallory. "Before you reassign him, tell him what petroleum jelly is." Then he walked away.

The boat docks were only a few minutes away. When they got there, Mallory introduced Cabot to the team leader for the area, Sergeant Henry Parke. Parke explained that they had two boats in the water searching for the Royals; a Crownline 250 with a cruising speed of twenty-five knots on its way for Land's End, the logical place they'd head, and a Targa 27 that makes eighteen knots heading more northeast.

"What did the Royals take?" Cabot asked.

"The Sunseeker Tomahawk," Parke said. "Lance Corporal Fred Stockdill recommended it."

Mallory cut in immediately. "What the bloody hell was he thinking?" He looked around. "Where is he?"

"In the boathouse, having breakfast," Parke said.

The Major pointed his finger at Parke. "You're in trouble, Sergeant!" he said. "Get Stockdill out here."

Parke headed for the boathouse, and Cabot said to Mallory, "What's the top speed of the Sunseeker?"

Mallory's gaze followed Parke for a moment, and then he turned to Cabot. "Forty knots," he said.

Lance Corporal Fred Stockdill wasn't quite running when he approached, but he was out of breath. His hand flew to his forehead where he'd forgotten to put on his hat.

"Sir! Lance Corporal Fredrick Stockdill reporting," he said to Mallory.

The Major gave him time to let the fear bubble. Then he said, "Tell Major General Cabot about your meeting with the King of England."

Stockdill turned slowly to face Cabot. "Sir!" He saluted again, and then began. "The King got the advantage on us because we were eating. He took our guns and the radio. He made me go inside the boathouse with him, ordered me to give him the keys to the fastest boat. I knew that we'd screwed the pooch. I had to do something."

The pregnant pause was too long for Cabot. "Well? Are you going to tell me?" he said.

"You gave him the keys to the Sunseeker, the fastest boat we have?" Mallory pressed.

Stockdill glanced at the Major, then closed his eyes. "Yes, sir, I did." He looked as if he was struggling to stop a smile from appearing.

After a moment, Cabot said, "Why?"

The Lance Corporal opened his eyes. "Because it has a problem with the petrol gage. We worked on it all day yesterday, but we couldn't solve it. It indicates it's full even though it has less than half a tank."

34

Wing Commander Simon Firth was not pleased. He was missing an episode of Lion Man for this bloody exercise class, and no one was here. He was about to walk out of the Recreation Lounge when Eliza Jackson, the physical therapist, pushed through the double doors from the kitchen. The men argued about Eliza's age, but Firth was sure in his own mind that she was not yet thirty. She looked her normal self this morning; glossy auburn ponytail, short shorts and tank top, both filled nicely to capacity. She had a glass of water in one hand and a tall plastic container in the other.

"Hello, Simon," Eliza burbled though a mouthful of water. Then she spit the water into the plastic container and gave him a pained smile. "I'm glad you could make it. Sorry about re-scheduling the class for this morning, but I have a dentist's appointment at our normal time this afternoon."

The Wing Commander pointed at the glass. "Salt water?"

Eliza nodded, took another mouthful, and began swishing it around.

He gave her an approving smile and, using a forefinger and a thumb, smoothed his meticulously trimmed pencil moustache. "My great grand mum Beddy's prescription."

From behind Firth someone said, "Bugger! Are we going to have to live with old Beddy again today?"

Firth swung around. It was Captain Colin Mackenzie. The Scot was a squat, fireplug of a man with an unruly mop of graying blond curls and what the Wing Commander called a Scotch-ish complexion.

Eliza spit her water out in the container. "Welcome, Colin," she said. "Up early today, I see. Bright and pleasant as usual."

"Sir Colin to you, lovely," he said.

Wing Commander Firth harrumphed. "Charles is more likely to lay his sword on my great grand mum's shoulder than your stuffed shirt. Even though the dear is years in the ground."

At that point, a fourth voice joined the fray from behind Mackenzie. "Did you hear?" said Warrant Officer Evan Gray. "It's on the telly. There's another assassin on the loose." He swiveled around, looking this way and that, his eyes wide in mock fear. "And he could be me!"

The other men moaned, as they usually did at Gray's antics, and Eliza Jackson gingerly massaged her cheek. The pain was getting worse. She wanted to cancel the class, but felt she couldn't. There were five more veterans on the way if they all got the message about the re-scheduling. However, she had an idea.

"While we wait for the others to join us, why don't we turn on the telly here?" she said. That would at least let her gargle more salt water instead of talking.

"Excellent idea," said Wing Commander Firth. As ranking officer, and the oldest as well at seventy-eight, he was practiced at taking control. He commandeered the remote, switched on the set, and selected a channel only to be shouted down when Lion Man faded in. Under protest, Firth finally switched to Sky News.

The missing assassin was still leading the news cycle, with reports coming in from locations scattered around the British Isles. The video was mostly of uniformed soldiers smashing doors, stopping and questioning drivers, and generally harassing people.

"Ghastly," Firth said after one rather graphic clip.

Captain Mackenzie shook his head and sighed. "Bugger all! If you've no stomach for it, why don't you get me some tea?" he said.

By then, three of the other men in the exercise class had joined the group and one of them, Chief Petty Officer Nathan Grimsley, said, "A spot of tea sounds golly good. I'll go get us both some, Captain."

Major Guy Samson, who was just sitting down, said, "Add me to that list, with milk instead of cream. I'm on a diet."

Another of the newcomers, Lieutenant Michael Mitchell, chimed in, "Make it a large pot, Nate. I'll give you a hand, and we'll see if we can uncover some scones."

As Grimsley and Mitchell got up and headed for the kitchen, one of the doors to the lounge opened and someone came in. Expecting more exercise class members, no one paid much attention.

Then a woman said softy, "Oh dear."

They turned in time to see the towering frame of Commander Clive Kay come through the doorway behind two women.

Eliza Jackson, who was sitting at one of the empty tables swishing salt water, spit it into her plastic container. "I'm sorry, but this is a re-scheduled exercise class."

"Eliza, it's Harriet Claiborne," said Nurse Harriet.

"*And* Commander Clive Kay," Kay added, pushing past her and Vivian Warwick.

"Hello, Harriet, Commander. Can I help you?" said Eliza.

As if on cue, the other door to the lounge opened and Merlyn stepped into the room. "In fact, that is why we are here," he said and, for the slightest moment, his words seemed to echo.

Captain Colin Mackenzie stood. "What the bloody hell is going on here?"

"This is all my fault," said Harriet. "I've been running around and . . . well, I didn't see the notice about the class change." She looked across the room at Merlyn. "We'll have to find another place to meet."

He smiled warmly at her, but then shook his head. "No, my dear, I'm afraid we won't. The time has come." He motioned her into the room. "Why don't you three sit at one of the tables over there?"

"I said, 'What the bloody hell is going on here?'" Captain Mackenzie demanded.

There was a shuffling behind Merlyn, and Sergeant Major Trevor Warwick stepped out. "You remember me, Colin?" he asked.

Mackenzie sighed, glanced down at the floor, then looked back up at the Sergeant Major. "The wee lad who got his arse kicked last night by that nancy over there?" He pointed at Clive Kay, who was trying to find room for his legs under a table in the middle of the room.

Trevor stared hard at Mackenzie a moment, then said, "We can fight that battle later. Now, I'd like to introduce my son, Thomas Warwick."

Tom stepped forward and gave a small wave. "Hi! My wife Vivian is over there with the other intruders," he said and pointed toward her.

"Hello," Vivian said. She raised her hand for everyone to see.

Now Eliza Jackson cut in. "I don't understand this. Do you need our help?" she asked Merlyn. Then she chuckled. "It looks like you have your own army."

He smiled and nodded. "The beginning of one, but it's not yet strong enough. We can use more recruits."

Wing Commander Firth looked at Eliza. "Are these people from one of your classes?"

She shook her head. "I don't think so," she said.

"Then, who are they?"

Commander Kay struggled to untangle his legs and stand. He finally made it when the chair next to the one he'd been sitting in fell over backwards with a crash.

The room was silent except for the television, which someone had turned down.

"I will tell everyone who *two* of them are," said Kay. "You there, the twit behind Trevor." He pointed at Arthur. "Step out here."

Arthur did as requested and the Commander said, "This one is completely barmy and thinks he is King Arthur." He paused for effect, then added, "You heard me correctly. I said *King Arthur!*"

With all eyes on him, Arthur looked around the room, acknowledged the claim with a slight nod, and smiled at those present. He was clearly and rapidly coming out of the life-saving fog Merlyn had put him into so long ago, once again taking on the commanding, charismatic presence that had made him a legend.

No one said anything. The television babbled on.

Kay then turned and pointed to Merlyn. "And let me also introduce *Merlyn, the magician*. This is the sod who uses his friend, the poor nutter, to diddle people out of God knows–"

At that point, Merlyn reached out toward Kay. The Commander's eyes widened, and he grabbed his throat. He voice was reduced to a guttural cough.

"Thank you, Commander," Merlyn said. "That will be enough."

This produced an undertow of muted explicatives during which the Wizard whispered something to Trevor Warwick and the Sergeant Major and Tom moved to a table. Then Merlyn stepped forward, making room for the man behind him.

"I, too, have an introduction to make," he said. As Prince Harry removed the ski cap he had been wearing, Merlyn said, "It gives me great pleasure to present Henry Charles Albert David Mountbatten-Windsor."

There was a general intake of breath, then a hushed, "Bugger."

35

Camilla had fashioned two towels she found in the cabin of the Sun-seeker into Arab type head wraps for them. The canvas top above the cockpit also offered some cover. However, both she and Charles were burned from the sun as well as the salt spray and the wind. The Queen Consort was worried about a particularly red area on the side of Charles' neck.

"I should have brought it with us," she yelled into the wind and the roar of the dual 200 horsepower engines.

"What?" Charles yelled back.

She gave him what he called her *devilish* grin. "The Vaseline."

He rolled his eyes. "One more comment like that, you brazen tramp, and I'll stop the boat right here," he yelled. Charles pointed toward the cabin. "You're looking like a lobster. Get out of the sun for a while."

Camilla shook her head and started to speak, but he jabbed his finger at the cabin again.

She scowled, and obeyed the King.

However, she'd barely reached the third step down into the cabin when the Sunseeker suddenly slowed. That crazy man, Camilla thought. As she turned to come back up the stairs, the engines coughed, and she lost her balance and fell. The crack she heard as she hit the floor of the cabin was ominous because she'd heard it before. There wasn't any pain, at least not yet, but the Queen Consort remembered the fall she'd taken on a hill walk at the Balmoral Estate in Scotland not so long ago. She was certain she'd broken her left leg–again.

Charles was there to help her up within a moment or two.

Camilla gave him a cheeky grin. "Sorry, Your *Horney* Majesty," she said. "The Vaseline was burned up in the fire."

"What happened? Are you all right?" Charles said. He had on his troubled face.

"You didn't know I fell, did you?" Camilla said.

Charles put her arm over his shoulder and helped her move to the curved couch in the bow of the boat.

"Keep your weight off your legs," he said. Then he headed back up the stairs into the cockpit. "I have to check on something."

"What's wrong, Charles?" she asked.

He stopped and looked at her a moment. "I didn't cut the throttles back," he said. Then he was gone.

In the cockpit, the King checked the fuel gauge again. It still indicated that the tanks were full, 172 gallons.

"Bloody *stupid* Royal!" he yelled, and banged the dash with the heel of his hand. The needle in the gauge bounced a tiny laugh at him, and returned to full.

Charles grimaced and looked at his hand. It wasn't broken, but he'd have a hell of a bruise. He shook his head in irritation with himself. He had been pointing out their captors' mistakes all day, and he'd made the biggest one himself. He thought he was smart, checking the fuel before they left Tresco. He should have questioned why that young commando gave up the key to this boat so easily. Now it was clear. There was something wrong with the fuel gauge. The petrol tanks weren't full. Not even close.

As if to put a period on that thought, the engines stopped their coughing and went silent. The boat immediately began to slew with the waves.

Back in the cabin, Charles explained the situation to Camilla.

"You couldn't have known," she said. "You checked the gauge."

He nodded with a rueful smile. "Yes, but only once. Not since then. I shouldn't have been in such a hurry, should have thought it through."

Camilla smiled her tough girl smile. "And that's what we're doing now." She pointed to a panel on the wall. "Is that what I think it is?"

"VHF radio," said Charles.

"Can we use that?"

"If we want them to pick us up. They'll be listening on channel sixteen, the one everyone has to use for emergencies."

An hour later there was a short burst of static on the Sunseeker's VHF channel sixteen and a voice said, "If in trouble, go to channel nine." It was a young female, and she was speaking French.

36

Prince Harry surprised everyone by moving among them and warmly shaking hands with each one, including Grimsley and Mitchell who, hearing the commotion, had returned from the kitchen sans tea or scones. That done, Harry smiled and said, "I suppose you have some questions."

Most of the veterans expected Wing Commander Simon Firth to take the lead, as usual, but he seemed lost in thought, at least for the moment.

Clive Kay had regained his voice and took advantage of the void. "We were told that your father and all of the Royals are sequestered," Kay said. "Are they?"

"As far as I know, I'm the only one who escaped," said Harry.

Evan Gray moved in his seat. "You're saying they were detained?" he said. "The Royal Family?"

"Kidnapped," Harry said bluntly.

"Bugger!" exploded Captain Colin Mackenzie. He leaned forward in his chair. "By whom? They will bloody well pay for this!"

"I'm . . . not sure," Harry said. The others in the room could see he was struggling to control his emotions and most of them glanced away or looked down.

Merlyn stepped in to give him some time. "Perhaps I can add some light to this subject," he said. "We all know that this is not the first time. Men who seek power, who believe they know better than the common man, have sought to take advantage of times of crisis as far back as Caesar. You know the names in your time: Stalin, Hitler–"

Nodding, Chief Grimsley offered, "Mao Zedong."

Guy Samson carried the list on with, "Castro, Pol Pot, Kim Jung Il."

"You should also know the name Santayana," said Merlyn.

Tom Warwick started to raise his hand, stopped, then quietly said, "George Santayana. The philosopher who wrote, 'those who cannot remember the past are condemned to repeat it.'"

"That bloody *Emergency* Act!" said Colin Mackenzie with a snarl. "It was Saxon, wasn't it? He's behind all of this."

Merlyn nodded. "With a cadre of men he has convinced it's the right thing, at least for now."

After a moment, Evan Gray said, "Do you know where they've been taken? The Royal Family, I mean?"

The Prince tried to resist a glance at Merlyn, without success. "I'm not sure," he said again.

The room was silent except for the telly in the background. Then Lieutenant Michael Mitchell said, "How did you get here?"

The question produced a weak smile from Harry. "After being on the run all day, I got hungry," he said. "I took a chance and went into a McDonald's in SoHo. That's when I got lucky."

He turned and looked across at Vivian. "That's when she found me."

Vivian returned his smile, but then immediately countered with, "I'm not so sure it was all luck. Don't forget the woman who sat next to you. And the man in the black rain coat." She glanced at Merlyn.

"Aha! The thick plottens," Evan Gray said to a round of groans.

When Harry didn't pick up the story, Vivian did. "I manage that restaurant and I've seen thousands of young men gulp down Quarter Pounders, but something made me take a second look at this one with his ski cap pulled down about his ears. He didn't just look hungry, he looked . . . well, scared."

"It wasn't *that* bad," Harry protested.

"I'm sorry, Prince," said Vivian. "But when that woman sat next to you, every drop of color drained from your face. And when she took out her mobile phone, I thought for sure you were going to run."

She got up and walked to the table where Harry, Merlyn, Arthur and the Warwick men were sitting. She stood behind Merlyn and put her hand on his shoulder. "Then our new friend here came in wearing a black rain coat."

"The men chasing me were wearing black rain coats," Harry volunteered.

Merlyn looked up at Vivian and smiled mildly. "A disguise," he said. "Borrowed from one of the villains of the piece."

"The woman was one of those looking for Harry, wasn't she?" Vivian said to Merlyn.

He nodded slightly. "I believe so," he said.

"What did you do to her mobile phone when she tried to use it?"

The Wizard smiled again. "I interrupted it," he said. Then he reached out toward the television set, and it suddenly blared with static. When he drew his hand back, the screen went blank and the set silent.

Clive Kay was the first to react. "What did I tell you?" he exclaimed. "The man is a charlatan!"

"I wouldn't know about that," said Evan Gray. "But I'm glad he's on our side."

No one laughed.

In the silence that followed, Wing Commander Simon Firth finally found his voice. "Beddy," he said.

Colin Mackenzie sighed and shook his head. He turned around to Firth. "What the bloody hell does she have to do with this?"

"It's the legend," Firth said. "The one Beddy always spoke of."

Lieutenant Mitchell still wasn't ready to give up. "Wait," he said. "We need to hear the rest of it." He swept his hand around the room taking in the newcomers. "How did all of you get here in Camelford? And why?"

"That was my doing," said an unfamiliar voice.

Everyone turned to look at Arthur as he stood.

"The result of decisions made long ago, I'm afraid," Arthur said.

"Oh yes, long ago," Clive Kay said, mocking Arthur. Before anyone else could speak up, he added, "When you were *High King* of all Great Britain."

Arthur nodded. "Quite so," he said. He began to move toward Commander Kay as he continued, "When I chose to face Mordred at Slaughter Bridge here in Camlann."

Kay was a much taller man, but he seemed to shrink as Arthur drew closer and continued to speak directly to him. "When I could, and would, order you tied to the rack and lashed until you bled to death!"

By the time Arthur reached him, Commander Clive Kay had backed up as far as he could and was squatting down into his chair. "This is ridiculous," Kay sputtered.

He turned to Vivian. "I'm told you are the one who brought the Prince and these other two vermin here. Where did you find this one, Bedlam?"

It was Tom Warwick who answered. "Glastonbury."

The word seemed to change everything in the room. Suddenly the air was thicker, the light dimmer, the silence deeper, for all of them knew something of the stories of Glastonbury.

Finally, Harriet Claiborne said, "The place they say is Avalon?"

"Yes," Tom said. "According to some historians."

His answer produced a general murmur with one exception. For a moment, it seemed that Harry was going to argue the point. Then, he sighed and simply shook his head.

"Beddy is your great grandmother?" Merlyn asked Simon Firth.

"Was," Colin Mackenzie said. "But we still have to hear about her at every bloody exercise class."

"Why don't you have a scotch?" Firth said to Mackenzie.

"Gentlemen," Merlyn said before anything could develop.

Then he asked the Wing Commander, "Was that her given name? Beddy?"

Simon Firth shook his head. "Everyone called her Beddy because of her surname." He smiled at some memory. "She was Beatrice Bedevere."

Into the momentary silence, Tom Warwick whispered a hushed, "Bede-bloody-vere."

"Tom, where are your manners?" scolded Vivian.

Merlyn actually chuckled. "Don't be too harsh on him, my dear. It could be his studies at university," he said. "Something he read about one of Beddy's relatives from long ago. Sir Bedevere, the only survivor of the battle at Slaughter Bridge."

Now Arthur added, "He was a Knight of the Round Table, the one I made swear to me that he would return Excalibur to the Lady of the Lake."

It was some time before anyone ventured anything. Then it was Simon Firth. "So, Beddy was right?"

"What did she tell you?" Merlyn said.

Firth took a breath before he answered, then it was quiet and subdued. "She always said that when England needs him most, King Arthur will return."

"Is it true?" someone whispered.

Merlyn nodded. "That is the legend," he said. "I know something else that is true. Those who are holding the Royal Family are searching for Prince Harry. And they are coming here."

Colin Mackenzie skidded back his chair and practically leaped to his feet. "They'll be bloody sorry if they do!" he declared. "We'll take them on. We're all veterans here."

"More than veterans," said Arthur Pendragon. "Knights. Not of The Round Table, but just as valiant. The Knights of Camelford."

The room was silent as the veterans looked at each other. After a moment, Simon Firth stood. "I'm not sure who he is, but if he's here to protect the Prince, I'm with Arthur," he said. "I have a parade sword somewhere in my closet, and I'm not afraid to use it."

Another moment passed, and then the veterans rose one by one, pledged to stand with Arthur, and offered an arsenal of weapons: a cane, a tennis racket, two cricket bats, a pair of field glasses, a Luftwaffe compass, an umbrella.

The last one to stand was Commander Clive Kay. "Perhaps I was wrong," he said. "Like the Wing Commander, I too have an ancestor that once stood with King Arthur, and I will do it again now."

He glanced around almost furtively. "I also must admit to breaking the law. I have a Colt 45 Revolver locked in a trunk in my room, with two boxes of ammunition."

Now, hesitantly, Nurse Harriet Claiborne moved to stand next to Arthur. "There are knives and a cleaver in a locked drawer in the kitchen. I think I can get the key."

She smiled nervously.

"You'll give that key to me," said Colin Mackenzie.

"And *you* will give it to me," Wing Commander Simon Firth said. He smiled for the first time since he'd arrived in the Recreation Lounge. "Chain of Command."

Eliza Jackson spit some salt water into her plastic container and stood. "Then you may want to use the scheduling program on my computer," she said.

"I'm pleased you mentioned that," said Merlyn. "There is a good deal of planning to be done, as quickly as possible. Battle strategy, weapons inspection, guard duty schedule."

"I'll work with Eliza on that," Simon Firth said.

"Very good," said Merlyn. "To give you time, Arthur and I will stand the first watch, protecting the Prince until morning."

"What are the rest of us to do?" said Evan Gray.

"You will require strength and energy for this quest," Arthur said. "Fortunately, that is what you are all here for." He pointed to Eliza. "To train with this young woman."

All three of the women in the room giggled.

"Bugger," said Colin Mackenzie.

37

It was late afternoon. Major General Jock Cabot had spent the day making certain the other Royals were secured and directing the search for Charles and Camilla. In addition to putting two more boats into the water, he'd ordered the pilot of his Lynx Wildcat helicopter to make several sweeps around the other Isles of Scilly, all to no avail. There had been no contacts, not even a false alarm.

Now, with the weather beginning to deteriorate and night coming on, the boats had been ordered to return to Tresco. The Lynx Wildcat was on the ground and refueled. For the same reasons, the MK4 Sea King, which had been on a training assignment in Scotland most of the day, was rescheduled for arrival in the morning.

"I trust I won't have to come back down here, Major," Cabot said as he got out of the pick-up truck at the edge of the heliport.

"No sir," said Mallory. He saluted.

Cabot returned it. "Tell Stockdill when we get the King and Queen Consort, the steak is on me," he said.

He turned and walked toward the AW 159 Lynx Wildcat sitting like a deadly spider on the asphalt. The rotor blades had started to slowly turn.

"You would be welcome, of course," said the Major.

Cabot kept walking. When he reached the Wildcat, he stopped. His mobile phone was ringing. He reached into the pocket of his flight jacket and took it out. According to the caller ID, it was Agent Rebecca Donovan. Cabot signaled the pilot to hold on and the blades wound down.

"What is it, Donovan?" Cabot said.

"I'm sorry to interrupt, sir, but—"

Cabot cut her off. "Have you got something for me or not?"

"Yes sir. According to some scribbled notes in her office, Vivian Warwick, the McDonald's manager, made train reservations yesterday morning from Paddington Station to Bodmin Parkway. I checked with the station, and it was for one person."

"Our target?" said Cabot.

"I don't think so. According to the assistant manager, Warwick's husband, Tom, was in the restaurant early yesterday. He looked up tight. He and his wife went back to her office. After a while he left in a hurry," Donovan said.

"So, you think it was the husband?" said Cabot. He was beginning to sound annoyed. "Why would he be going to Bodmin Parkway?"

"His father, Sergeant Major Trevor Warwick, is in the Camelford Veterans Home, not far from Bodmin Parkway," she said.

More Warwicks, thought Cabot. He was angry without knowing why. "And what the bloody hell does all of this have to do with anything?" he demanded.

"Sorry, Major General," Donovan said. "It's . . . well, there's more."

Cabot was silent.

She finally picked up on the cue. "The Warwick's have a yellow Mini Cooper, plates MFR 1620. It was picked up on the traffic cameras on the A4, heading west at 9:42 a.m. yesterday. There were three occupants; a female driving, two male passengers."

"Vivian Warwick, our target, and who else?" Cabot said.

"I'm not sure," said Donovan. "The traffic system's images are—"

"Crap, right?" Cabot said.

"Yes sir."

"Did you notice anyone while you were in the restaurant? Anyone who could have been a friend of the target?"

"I didn't have a chance. The minute I got close to him, the manager came over and dragged him off; said he was an employee who was late for his shift."

Cabot was silent a moment, obviously thinking. "You said you got out your mobile to call it in as a possible contact," he said.

"Yes sir, that's correct. But then an old man sat down next to me and the phone went ballistic. Nothing but static."

After another moment of silence, Cabot said, "What did he look like?"

"Twenty-four or five and about–" Donovan started.

"No, no!" said Cabot. "The old man; what did he look like?"

Now it was Agent Donovan who was silent, remembering. "The white hair," she said finally. "He might have been the other man in the Mini."

"Good work, Donovan," the Major General said. "Stay available." Then he hung up and gave the pilot thumbs up. As the helicopter blades started to rotate again, Cabot shook off a vague memory of the old man at the war memorial and punched in a number on his mobile.

General Ian Baker-Smythe was angry. "Why haven't you reported?" he demanded.

Cabot considered telling him the truth; that he was a miserable pain in the ass. Instead, he said, "There has been little worth reporting, General. Your time is valuable."

It had the desired affect. "You have the situation under control?" said Baker-Smythe.

"Yes, sir," said Cabot.

The connection was silent for a moment.

"Are they in custody?" the General said.

"They will be soon. You might say their escape is out of petrol," said Cabot.

"For God's sake, Jock," said Baker-Smythe, "this is no time for jokes."

Cabot took a breath before he said, "Yes, sir."

"How long before you can wrap this up and get back to London?" said the General.

Cabot paused, then said, "That's the second reason for my call; to inform you that I'm going to Camelford."

"What?"

"It will do us no good to keep the King sequestered if Prince Harry starts talking."

Cabot could hear the general draw in a breath. "You mean you've found him?"

"I think I may know where he's gone to ground."

"Camelford? Get some men down there, now!" said Baker-Smythe.

"That was my first thought," said Cabot. "But I don't want to scare our rabbit into another hidey hole. With a bit of stealth, I think I can catch him before he knows he's been discovered."

The General's cynicism was clear in his tone. "And if you can't?"

"I've already put a platoon of marines on alert at Base Chivenor in Devon. They can be at Camelford in less than an hour and a half."

38

It was an audacious and possibly dangerous trick to try, but Charles couldn't think of anything better. They had to get off this boat now, before the marines from Tresco found them.

The King switched the VHF radio to channel nine. "This is Edward and Emma Scott. We have a small problem," he managed in somewhat butchered French.

The response was immediate.

"I am Josie Glissant, Captain of the Sailfish, out of Fort-de-France in Martinique," said the young woman, switching to English when she heard Charles' accent. "It is luck we see you drifting. What is your trouble?"

"Thank God, you speak English," Charles said.

"Thank my mother," said Josie. "She was from Dorchester." Then she repeated, "What is your trouble?"

"We rented this boat on Jersey in the Channel Islands," Charles said, making it up as he went along. "We . . ." He paused for an embarrassed chortle, then said, "Well, we got lost. Then ran into some engine trouble. And then my wife fell. I think she may have broken her leg."

After a moment of static, Josie said, "Have you contacted the boat's owner?"

The question caught Charles by surprise. He hadn't thought this through. He looked at Camilla. She didn't know what to say, either.

The King closed his eyes and plunged ahead. "Yes. But the bloody bastards say they can't get to us until late tomorrow."

There was another burst of static, this one longer. Then Josie Glissant said, "We are off your starboard bow. If you will ready for our approach, we will try to help."

Charles took a deep breath and almost smiled. "We'll be here," he said.

Now he had to hope their rescuers wouldn't recognize them. They couldn't afford someone reporting their whereabouts and it getting back to Saxon's people. It was a tall order, especially based on the media circus he imagined had been playing on the world stage in the last twenty-four hours. However, as lame as his ruse seemed, it might possibly work. Camilla was the first to suggest a reason why.

"They're both quite young," she said as the sailboat approached.

Charles knew just enough about sailing to explain to Camilla that it was a ketch, clearly a blue water boat. He guessed it to be over twelve meters long, with a towering mainsail and jib, plus a mizzen and two jennys. The hull was the color of the ocean and the deck cloud white.

Working the sails and tiller were two dark skinned women. The one at the wheel, Charles assumed, was Captain Josie Glissant. The other woman was smaller and athletic.

Once the boats were secured safely together, both of the women came aboard the Sunseeker, and Charles led them down to the cabin where he introduce them to "Emma" who was sitting at the table with her leg elevated.

"This is my crewmate and friend, Franny Azur," Josie Glissant said.

Neither one blinked at seeing Charles and Camilla up close. Charles smiled. "Please to meet you, Franny," he said.

"Francine," Franny corrected with a soft smile.

"Are you from Martinique?" asked Camilla.

Josie smiled. "Yes, both of us. Born there and raised there."

Charles smiled back at her; another reason they might get away with this, he thought. Martinique was a long, long way from Buckingham Palace.

"We are with the Inventory Unit of OceanSailing. It is a charter company operating in marinas around the world," Josie said. "We dead-head sailboats from one marina to another as needed."

"We are mostly in Caribbean. This our first trip to France," Francine said.

"Franny is good with engines," said Josie. She looked around. "Shall we see if she can do something with yours?"

Charles suddenly tensed. If they found out he was simply out of petrol, they might offer to give him some. And that would give Saxon's people another chance to find them.

"I'm worried about Emma," he said. "Even if we get the engine running, I won't be able to take care of her on the trip back." With an embarrassed look, he added, "And we're still lost."

Josie frowned. "What did you have in mind?"

Charles tried what he thought was a pitiful smile. "How about a ride?" he said.

Josie Glissant glanced at her crewmate. Francine shrugged.

Josie thought for a moment. "It's against company rules," she said.

"We don't have any money with us," said Charles. "But we can pay you handsomely. I have a quite lucrative position."

"Yes, quite." Camilla said. She smiled.

Josie glanced at Francine again. This time Francine nodded.

"Well," Josie said. "I think this might be an exception to the rules."

So it was decided. The two women helped Camilla up the ladder to the Sunseeker's cockpit and aboard the ketch. Charles momentarily delayed joining them for two reasons. He needed time to get the Browning 9mm he took from the marine at the cottage out of a drawer in the galley, and to cover for his lie that he would contact the owners and tell them they were safe.

He had no idea how wrong he was.

39

They were packed like sardines in the Warwick's Mini Cooper, Tom and Vivian up front and Prince Harry and Arthur in the back.

"I can't believe you did this," Vivian said, clearly annoyed.

Tom kept his eyes on the road. "You'll like it," he said.

"There are several bed and breakfast inns right in Camelford," said Vivian.

"You asked me to make reservations, and I did," Tom said.

She sighed and turned away, staring out the window at the darkened countryside.

After a moment, Tom said, "I don't get points for suggesting I go back later to pick up Merlyn or whoever he is?"

"He suggested it," said Vivian, still staring out the window.

"But I'll be making the extra trip."

"A whole twenty kilometers."

They rode on in silence for another frigid minute, then, from the back seat, Harry said, "Are we there yet?"

Both Tom and Vivian twisted around to look at him. The Prince sat there with an impish grin. "Sorry," he said. "I thought the conversation could use a bit of humor."

Tom went back to his driving. "Good," he said. "We've got a Royal Comedian with us."

"Tom!" Vivian chided.

"It's funny, actually," said Harry. "I mean, that we're staying at the Jamaica Inn. That's where Camilla and I were going to stay, only the real one in Ocho Rios, Jamaica."

Tom made a huffing sound. "Public school education," he said. "Wetherby followed by Eton, as I recall."

"So?" said Harry.

"Have you ever even heard of du Maurier?" Tom said.

"I don't smoke," said Harry.

Now Vivian turned around to Harry. "Not cigarettes. He's talking about Daphne du Maurier, the author. She wrote a number of famous novels: *Rebecca*, *My Cousin Rachel*, and–*Jamaica Inn*. It's a mystery about smugglers in Cornwall."

"Alfred Hitchcock turned it into a film in 1939 with Charles Laughton and Maureen O'Hara," Tom said. "We Brits had a series on the telly starring Jane Seymour and Patrick McGoohan in 1983."

"And that's where we're going?" asked Harry. "The actual place?"

"Built in 1750 on the edge of Bodmin Moor, a coaching inn for travelers . . . and smugglers," Tom said.

"What did they smuggle?" asked Harry.

"For years, more than half the brandy and a fourth of all the tea smuggled into the United Kingdom came through the Jamaica Inn," said Tom.

"You'll have to forgive him, Prince," Vivian said. "He's practicing to be dry as dust and a somewhat haughty history professor."

They had a small chuckle at that and relaxed, but only for a moment. From the other corner of the back seat Arthur said, "There is more history than that in the moor."

"You're right about that," Tom said. "Did you know that in 1497, a man named Perkin Warbeck, a pretender to the English throne, was declared Richard IV on Bodmin Moor and led a Cornish army of nearly six thousand men against Henry VII?"

"There was no Richard IV, was there?" Harry said.

Tom smiled. "One step at a time."

"Whatever," said Harry. "So, what happened?"

"When Warbeck heard that the King's men had advanced to Glastonbury, he panicked and ran, deserting his army."

"Did he get away?" asked Harry.

Tom shook his head. "Captured and imprisoned in the Tower of London in the company of–you'll love this part–a true claimant to the throne, Edward, Earl of *Warwick.*"

No one said anything.

"*Really*, the Earl of *Warwick,*" Tom tried again.

Vivian sighed. "Does it have an ending part?"

In the moment of silence between them, Arthur said, "Not every story."

Tom glanced over his shoulder at Arthur, shook his head, and ended it. "In 1499 Warbeck attempted to escape, but was captured and hanged at Tyburn."

They rode on in silence for another kilometer. Then Harry turned to Arthur and said, "More history? Like what?"

"You ever hear of Tintagel?" Arthur asked.

Harry showed his impish grin again. "You mean the castle where your father diddled Igraine and you were born?"

Tom glanced in the rear view mirror and saw the look on Arthur's face. "I think I would be careful, Prince, in speaking about a man's mother. Particularly one who claims to be the High King of all Britain."

Before Harry could respond, Arthur smiled wryly and said, "With the crown comes a certain humility, although this Prince may never learn that."

"I didn't mean–" Harry started.

Arthur cut him off. "Do you know what a tiltyard is?"

Harry squinted, thinking. "No idea," he said.

From the front, Tom said, "Isn't that a portmanteau?"

Vivian sighed. "This is getting worse. The King's English, please, professor."

"Portmanteau," Tom repeated. "A word made by putting two other words together. As in tilting and yard–tiltyard."

"Right," said Harry. "And what the bloody hell does *that* mean?"

"A courtyard for tilting or jousting. There is one on the moor." Arthur said. "A field fenced in great stones where the Knights of Tintagel took their pages and squires to train them in battle."

"My God," said Tom.

Vivian looked at him. "Now what?"

"He's talking about a site historians and archeologists have been trying to figure out for decades—King Arthur's Hall."

"The Knights knew it as The Courtyard of Stones," Arthur said.

"Wait a minute," said Tom. "Are you trying to tell me that you or they, built that place?"

Arthur smiled and shook his head. "We only found it and made use of it. The Old Ones built it long, long ago."

"But why? Why did they build it?"

Arthur shook his head again. "We never knew," he said.

Vivian could see that Tom was disappointed and agitated. She tried to make light of the situation with a shrug and a dry chuckle. "What do they say, close but no cigar? At least you know more than before."

Tom slumped a bit in his seat, a sour look on his face. "If you can believe any of this." He glanced in the rear view mirror again. "What about Dozmary?"

Arthur frowned. "Doze Mary? Is that a lady?" he said.

Shaking his head, Tom huffed again. "Dozmary Pool. It's just a small lake, but according to some, shall we say, believers, there's a lady *in* it."

"Oh please!" said Harry. He rolled his eyes. "You mean the *Lady of the Lake*?"

"Stop!" shouted Vivian.

"Don't get so upset, Viv. It's only a conversation," Tom said. He put his hand on her arm, trying to soothe her.

She jerked her arm away. "No! I mean stop the car. We missed the turn into the inn."

That was the end of the conversation, but the surprises and enigma of the day continued. When they finally made it to the Jamaica Inn, Merlyn was waiting for them.

40

Prime Minister Alistair Saxon slammed his fist down on his desktop. "We *have* that young Royal bastard!" he exclaimed.

Sitting in a chair in front of Saxon's desk, General Baker-Smythe allowed a thin smile. "Yes, sir," he said, with a slight nod. "Very nearly."

"Come now, Ian!" Saxon said. "Cabot himself is heading this mission, isn't he?" He got up from his desk and moved to the bar as he continued. "There is no one better to lead it." He poured a splash of Hennessy into a snifter. Turning to the General, he said, "Ian?"

Baker-Smythe shook his head. "Not on duty."

The Prime Minister shrugged and started back to his desk with his cognac. "How many men is Jock taking with him?"

Baker-Smythe hesitated, then stood. "I don't approve of this situation," he said, with a hard edge in his voice.

Saxon was completely baffled. "What are you talking about?"

"Cabot wants to sneak up on the Prince, by himself."

The Prime Minister nearly dropped his drink. "He's going to Camelford alone? With no troops?"

"Says he's afraid of scaring the lad into another *hidey hole,*" General Baker-Smythe said, giving full vent to his disdain.

Saxon sat down. He had a gulp of the Hennessy, then looked at the snifter and wrinkled his nose in disgust. "Damn!" he said. "This is that limited edition VS released in honor of Obama's inauguration; about as rank as his presidency."

He had another sip, shook his head, and sat the cognac down. "I thought I instructed Thorne to get rid of this when the Americans gave Barack the boot."

At that moment, a red light blinked on the intercom system and, as if he'd been summoned, Saxon's aide, Richard Thorne, said, "Excuse me, Prime Minister?"

Saxon pushed a button. "Yes, Richard?"

"Director General Gibbon has arrived," said Thorne.

The Prime Minister glanced at the massive Geochron World Clock framed in black oak on the wall. From its glowing map of the world he could tell the time zone, local time, sunrise and sunset, latitude and longitude of any place on earth.

"Tell him he's late," Saxon said. "Too late."

A few seconds later, MI-5 General Director Nigel Gibbon came through the door, a cigarette dangling from the corner of his mouth, crossed to the Prime Minister's desk, and sat in an empty chair next to General Baker-Smythe.

"Reporting as requested," he said around the Player's.

Baker-Smythe recoiled from the cigarette. "Put that bloody thing out!"

"And turn off the recorder on your phone," Saxon added.

The MI-5 Director complied with both demands, then said, "Thorne reports there is news. We've found the Prince?"

Saxon muttered something under his breath. "Richard didn't tell you that," he said.

"It's my job," said Gibbon. He smiled, exposing his nicotine stains.

"Was it Major General Cabot?" Baker-Smythe asked.

Gibbon took his time. "Indirectly," he said finally. "An agent who has been reporting to him."

"Is he with Cabot now?" said Baker-Smythe.

178

"She," said Gibbon. "Agent Rebecca Donovan, a twenty-nine year-old from Liverpool. Is she with him *now*? Not at the moment, but they've been in contact since the Prince went missing. Donovan is MI-5. However, the Major General, you might say, commandeered her." He smiled through the rest of it. "If you know what I mean?"

The Prime Minister, who had been leaning back in his chair, suddenly sat up. "What the hell is going on here?" he demanded. "That's not Jock Cabot at all!"

"That's what I'm concerned about," said Baker-Smythe.

"I don't believe it," Saxon said. "Do you, Ian? Some daft plan to grab the Prince by himself? Bonking some child in the middle of an emergency?" He shook his head. "Not the Cabot I know."

It was a moment before Nigel Gibbon said, "Men change. Especially under pressure."

General Ian Baker-Smythe turned and looked at the MI-5 Director, then shifted his gaze to Saxon. "Perhaps he has had too much of it in his life," he said.

The Prime Minister returned the stare for a few seconds, then picked up the snifter of Hennessy. He tipped it up, took a mouthful, swished it around and swallowed. Then Saxon turned in his chair, looking out the window into the empty night.

"This is not about a British military hero," he said. "It is about the future of Great Britain herself."

He swiveled back and spoke to the MI-5 Director. "Nigel, I appreciate your information. Continue to collect it."

Gibbon smiled. "Of course, Prime Minister."

"Goodnight."

The MI-5 Director blinked several times, but he showed no tension as he rose from his chair and exited Saxon's office.

Once Gibbon was gone, the Prime Minister got up from his desk and crossed to the bar again. He selected another bottle of cognac, poured a generous inch into a snifter, and had some of it. Then he turned to the General.

Rather stiffly, he said, "General Ian Baker-Smythe, this is an order from your Commander-In-Chief, Sir Alistair Saxon, Prime Minister of Great Britain, and Chairman of the Emergency Powers Council."

Baker-Smythe stood. "Yes sir," he said.

"You are personally to take complete control of the effort to find and subdue any and all persons thought to stand in the way of the recovery of this United Kingdom, including any member of the Royal Family who presents that potential."

The General took a breath. "What about Cabot?" he said.

"You have your orders," said Saxon.

"Yes sir!" Baker-Smythe said again. He picked up his coat from the back of one of the chairs and started for the door.

The Prime Minister downed the rest of the inch of cognac. "And Ian," he said, "use however many men and whatever means you need to make sure that little bastard doesn't talk."

Baker-Smythe looked surprised to find Nigel Gibbon still hovering in the Prime Minister's outer office. Gibbon stubbed out his Player's and joined the General as he walked out into the hall and down the steps.

As he lit another cigarette, Gibbon said, "I take it you haven't told him about Charles and Camilla?"

Baker-Smythe took another two steps down before he said, "His time is valuable."

"True," said Gibbon.

"There is nothing he can personally do about it. The men on Tresco are on top of it. And one negative at a time is enough."

The MI-5 Director smiled. "That should be enough reasons."

The General stopped and looked at Gibbon with a steel hard eye. "I didn't tell you, either," he said.

"Of course."

41

Merlyn slipped past the question of how he arrived before they did with a dry smile, a shrug, and one of his wriggles. "A friend was heading this way," he said. "I took advantage."

Harry rolled his eyes. "Uh huh, a friend. That would be the wind?" he said cynically. But everyone else let it go with a simple shake of the head.

Tom Warwick took care of checking them in, while the others waited in a corner of the lobby. He'd already reserved a separate room for Prince Harry and was able to arrange for Merlyn and Arthur to stay in the room next to it. Tom and Vivian were down the hall.

Once that was done, like dominoes falling, they admitted they were exhausted and trundled off to their rooms. Vivian was first, followed by Prince Harry. Then Arthur excused himself, saying he would take the first watch on the Prince.

That left only Tom and Merlyn and, at the Wizard's suggestion, they too decided to retire–to the Smuggler's Bar.

The fireplace was crackling against the chill that night often brings to the moor, especially when it rains as it was tonight. The leather covered couches and chairs near the fire were taken, so they sat at the long oaken bar.

The bartender came over, put two coasters down, and said, "Gentlemen?"

"Do you have Boodles?" said Tom.

The bartender leaned in close to Tom, raising one suspicious eyebrow. "Are you a Tory?" he said.

Taken aback, Tom frowned. "What the–" he started, but then stopped and smiled broadly. "And I suppose your given name is Edward?"

The bartender chuckled. "Very good, sir!" he said. "I usually get people with that one."

Merlyn looked from Tom to the man behind the bar and back again. "What one?"

"It's a great story from London's history," said Tom and immediately launched into it.

"In 1762 Lord Shelburne, a dyed in the wool Tory who later became Prime Minister, founded a gentlemen's club in St. James for Tories to discuss politics and play cards. It became known as Boodle's Gentleman's Club after the name of its headwaiter, Edward Boodle. Later, the gin was named for the club, and they claim it was the favorite of a long list of famous people, including Winston Churchill."

"Beau Brummel and Ian Fleming, as well," said the bartender.

His comment snapped Tom out of his lecture mode. "Sorry," he said to Merlyn. "I'm prattling on again. Why don't you order?"

Merlyn cleared his throat. "*You* haven't ordered yet."

"Oh, you're right." Tom turned to the bartender. "A Boodles gin and tonic, with lime."

"And you, sir?" the bartender said to Merlyn.

Merlyn scanned the array of bottles behind the bar. He furled his brow, rubbed his chin, then said, "I think I'll have a cup of mead."

"Very good!" said the bartender. He turned away to make the drinks.

"Mead?" said Tom. "You can get that?"

Merlyn smiled. "Since about 7000 BC. Quite a bit of history there too. I believe Beowulf drank it. The Cornish Mead Company in Penzance and others make it now."

When the drinks came, Tom was fascinated. Merlyn's mead was actually in a wooden cup. It was golden honey colored, and almost glowed.

"Marvelous!" Tom said. "I'll have to try that someday."

Merlyn smiled. "Carefully," he suggested. "This is the Cornish Liqueur Mead. Seventeen percent alcohol by volume can sneak up on you."

They each had a taste of their drink, toasted the day, and had a second swallow. Then Merlyn set his mead down. "I need to tell you what happened in Camelford after you left," he said.

When he was finished, Tom was stunned.

"All of them?" Tom said.

Merlyn nodded. "Except the bed-ridden."

"My God," Tom murmured. "They've all sworn allegiance to Arthur? That must be twenty or thirty men."

"Thirty-two, actually," Merlyn said. "But four of them are in wheelchairs. And six others haven't come up with their weapon yet."

Tom had some more of his drink. "Do you know what you're asking of these men?"

"It was not me asking, or Arthur," said the Wizard, shaking his head. "As I explained, Wing Commander Firth and Commander Kay recruited them. They went room to room together, talking to every man, encouraging each to join the *army*, but also warning them of the dangers."

"And they all agreed?" said Tom. "To stand against whatever force Saxon sends for Prince Harry?"

"Yes," said Merlyn. Then the Wizard tilted his head as if he was listening to something. He turned and stared into the fire.

"They're coming, aren't they?" Tom said.

Merlyn turned to him. "Not quite yet, but soon. Perhaps it's time for you to retire, to get some rest."

Tom finished his drink and started to get up, then hesitated and sat back down. "Firth and Kay," he said. "You talked of their connections to the past, their ancestors with ties to the Arthurian legend; Sir Kay, Arthur's brother, Sir Bedevere, and Excalibur. But you never mentioned the Warwick name. Why?"

A gentle smile softened the Wizard's weathered face. "I've been waiting for you to bring it up," he said.

After a moment, Tom asked, "Was there a Warwick at Slaughter Bridge?"

Merlyn's smile broadened as if recalling a pleasant memory. He nodded. "A lad of nearly thirteen; a young page to the King named Tom Warwick."

"Was he killed in the battle?"

"No. Arthur himself made sure of that. In the small hours of the night before the battle, he commanded the page not to fight, but to run. The King had a much more important task for Sir Thomas of Warwick, as he dubbed the young boy."

"Run?" said Tom.

"To stay alive and to live a long life," explained Merlyn. "So he could tell everyone he met of the King's idea, the idea that brought Camelot and all that it stood for into being. A simple thought really; that force should be used, if it were used at all, on behalf of justice, not on its own account."

Now Tom Warwick smiled. "Not might *is* right, might *for* right," he said.

"Ironic, isn't it?" said the Wizard.

"What do you mean?"

"You might say it is your ancestor who is responsible for the legends you don't believe." Merlyn chuckled, raised his glass to Tom, and said, "Goodnight, Sir Thomas."

42

The helicopter pilot keyed his mike. "Rain and turbulence intensifying, sir," he said. "Going to be a bumpy ride."

Major General Cabot tightened his seat belt. Looking out the window, he saw the pilot's point. Visibility was a half notch above zero.

"Just get us there, Lieutenant. As soon as possible," Cabot said. "I have a date."

The pilot smiled dryly and edged the throttle forward.

As he felt the thrust increase, Cabot leaned back, closed his eyes, and asked the same question he'd been pondering since the beginning of this SNAFU. He could thank the Americans for coming up with that description, but armies and governments the world over had been living up to it forever. Where were they screwing up this time? Why, at every turn, did something seem to be going wrong?

Thirty minutes later they were on the ground at Base Chivenor, on the northern shore of the Taw estuary in Devon, and an hour and a half from Camelford by car. Cabot changed into civvies; worn jeans, a faded blue Oxford button down with the shirt tail out to cover the Glock on his hip, black Converse tennis shoes, and a black Nike zippered jacket. He added a baseball cap and put the glasses he rarely wore in the jacket pocket as a feeble covert touch. He never thought of himself as a recognizable public figure, but with the military, even retired, it might be prudent.

Rather than signing out one of the base vehicles, he had a duty sergeant drive him to a local rental car operator where he picked up a Ford Fiesta. It was one of the least expensive hires and he could slip under any radar as common folk with the unremarkable, small hatch back.

In the rain, it took him longer than he planned to reach Camelford, almost two hours. By then, much of the town had gone to bed. He found the Camelford Veterans Home without any trouble, and the lobby lights were still on. Cabot parked in front of the main building and sat there, just watching. He saw a couple of people inside moving past windows, but no one came or left. After a while, he put his glasses on, got out of the Fiesta, and went inside.

The lobby had a long, leather couch with matching armchairs on either end. Two old men were sitting in the chairs, reading newspapers. They both glanced his way when he came in, then went back to their papers. An aging, plump blonde in a bright pink nurse's uniform at the front desk looked up and smiled. "May I help you?" she said.

Cabot waited to respond until he had crossed to the desk. Then he spoke quietly. "Yes, I hope you can," he said. "I believe an old friend is staying here. His name is Trevor Warwick. I wondered if I might visit with him."

The blonde smiled again, this time sadly, and Cabot heard the rustle of a newspaper behind him. "I'm sorry, but visiting hours are over," she glanced up at a clock on the wall, "at nine o'clock. It's nearly nine-thirty."

Cabot checked his own watch, then pursed his lips. "I've traveled a long way," he said.

Behind Cabot a voice said, "Edna, why don't I check on Trevor? See if he's still up?"

Cabot turned to see a tall rail of a man. "Commander Clive Kay," the man said and extended his hand.

Cabot took it. "That would be kind of you."

"No trouble. Who can I say is calling?" Kay said.

Without hesitation Cabot said, "Westland. Craig Westland." His confidence came from his staff's research. Westland was a distant cousin Trevor Warwick had never met.

"Very well," Clive Kay said and walked off down the hall.

The Major General busied himself for a few moments, looking at some of the framed photos on the wall, then sat down on the couch. When he did, the man in the other armchair closed his newspaper and turned to him. "I couldn't help overhearing," he said. "You've traveled a long way? Where are you from?"

Cabot smiled. "London, actually."

"I have a nephew in Cricklewood, south of the city," said Evan Gray.

Jock Cabot frowned. "Cricklewood? I believe that's northwest. Quite a way, in fact. But it has an excellent train to central London."

Gray was ready with his depreciating chuckle. He'd found out what he wanted. The man seemed to know London. Shaking his head, he said, "I always make that mistake."

At that moment, Clive Kay came back into the lobby. Jock Cabot got up from the couch.

"Were you aware Trevor had a medical situation yesterday?" Kay said to Cabot.

The Major General tried to look mildly stunned. It came off well for, in fact, he had no idea. "My heavens, no," he said. "What was the problem?"

Kay looked to the nurse at the front desk and she shook her head. "It's confidential," Kay said. "But confidentially, he's fine now." He smiled. "Just a bit washed out. I'm afraid he's sound asleep."

"You could come back tomorrow," the nurse said, nodding encouragingly. "Any time between eight in the morning and nine at night."

Cabot looked at the nurse and back to Clive Kay. "Thank you all very much," he said. He turned and started to walk away, then hesitated and turned back. "Could you tell me if his son Thomas and his daughter-in-law have been here?"

"They left some time ago," said Clive Kay.

The nurse added, "I'm sure they'll be back tomorrow."

Cabot smiled. "Perhaps we'll meet then," he said and walked across the lobby and out the door.

When he was gone, neither Commander Kay nor Warrant Officer Gray said anything. They simply looked at each other and nodded. It was left to Captain Colin Mackenzie sitting in the office in front of the monitor for the lobby camera to make a comment.

"Cabot," he said under his breath. "Bugger!"

43

Something was wrong.

They'd left the drifting Sunseeker behind some time ago. The weather, which had turned rough, sending them down into the main saloon of the ketch, had finally improved. And Camilla was able to convince Charles to help her back up onto the deck using a crutch they'd fashioned from a mop handle. Now it was a rather pleasant evening, with the ketch plunging into reasonably calm seas and a warm wind under a clear, star infested sky.

Camilla was sitting in a deck chair with her left leg propped up on an overturned bucket. Charles was leaning on a gunwale nearby. "Can you see it?" he said. He pointed a vague finger up into the dark.

She rolled her eyes. "Which one, Galileo?"

"Ursa Major," he said.

They had played this game before. Charles was a Rear Admiral in the British Navy and prided himself in knowing the finer points of navigation. Perhaps more pride than knowing, she thought, but that was the least of his faults. He enjoyed proving his prowess, and she enjoyed helping him.

"Is that a lady friend of yours?" she said, smiling.

Charles didn't return the smile. Instead, he gave a faint shake of his head.

"The Big Dipper, right?" said Camilla. She looked up and squinted into the night.

"Below it is Ursa Minor, the Little Dipper," Charles said. "And on the tip of the Little Dipper's handle?"

She smiled again. "I'm sure you're going to tell me."

He was silent for a moment, then quietly said, "The North Star."

Charles turned to his left, facing into the wind. What little hair he had left fluffed around his rather large ears. He had that look on his face, the one she'd seen so many times in the last year.

"What's wrong, Charles?" Camilla said.

He glanced at her, then turned back into the wind. "We're not on our way to France," he said. "We're sailing west. Actually, a bit southwest."

"What?" she said "But I thought they said—"

Charles interrupted, shaking his head. "No, Milla. In fact, they didn't." He closed his eyes, remembering. "Francine said this was *their* first trip to France. That's all." After a moment, he added, "They're on their way back to Martinique."

"But why wouldn't they tell us?"

"Exactly," said Charles. "I'm going to find out." He moved to Camilla and started to help her up. "You can't stay out here without me. We need to get you below."

She didn't argue.

Josie and Francine were at the table in the galley playing some sort of board game. They looked up when Charles and Camilla came down the ladder.

"How are you doing?" said Josie.

"Very well, but Emma is quite tired," Charles said. "She's off to bed."

Camilla offered a weak smile and said, "Thank you so much for all your help. Goodnight."

Charles helped Camilla into the starboard aft cabin, the one Josie had shown them to when they first came aboard the ketch. He sat her down on the bed, took her hands in his, and looked into her face.

"Are you all right, Milla?" he said.

"That depends on what you're planning to do," said Camilla.

He held up both hands in surrender. "I'm simply going to ask why."

"I don't like it."

"Neither do I, but I can hardly demand they answer the King of England."

"Thank heavens they apparently don't know who you are," she said.

"I'm not sure I do anymore," said Charles.

Camilla huffed at him. "Charles Philip Arthur George, be gone," she said and shooed him out of the room.

Charles returned to the galley. The women were still at the table, playing their game. "Would you like to join us?" Josie asked.

He shook his head.

Josie said something in French to Francine, vernacular Charles didn't understand. They both grinned as if it was a joke.

Then Francine said, "It is a good way to pass time on a long trip."

"You're not on your way to France," Charles said. "You're on your way to Martinique, aren't you? Why didn't you tell us?"

He glanced from one of them to the other, looking for a reaction. Josie smiled, but not like he'd seen her before. This was a different woman altogether, sly and almost sinister.

"It can be dangerous at sea, can it not, Edward?" she said. "What with the weather and sharks, and—even worse? To be returned safely to land after being lost on an ocean voyage must be extremely valuable to you, to your family and friends."

Charles frowned. "What is this? Do you know who we are?"

"We know you have a *lucrative* position. And I'm certain those who surround you are not living on the British dole."

The King was speechless. They had no idea who he was, and it didn't make any difference. Finally, he found his voice. "This is absurd!"

Josie let out a snigger. Her eyes were bright, glassy. "You think the only pirates are in the Gulf of Aden? The Somali? Pirates have been plundering the Caribbean for four hundred years."

"Are you telling me you're pirates?"

Now Francine giggled. "We didn't plan it," she said. "It is just, how you say? Opportunity?"

Bloody hell, Charles thought. They're both on marijuana, or something worse. He slowly, calmly reached his right hand down to his hip where the Glock was stuffed in his pants under his shirt.

"So, you're holding us hostage?" he said.

Josie tried a cunning smile. "Only until we get to Fort-de-France in Martinique," she said. "Until 100,000 British pounds are transferred to a bank account we will give you."

Charles drew the 9mm Browning from his waist and pointed it at them. "I'm afraid you are mistaken," he said.

Josie continued to smile her cunning smile, her olive eyes awash in some drug martini. "I think not," she said.

The blow came from behind and to the left of Charles. He made a huffing sound, and his knees buckled. He fell forward, banging his forehead into the table, then slumped to the deck and lay there, motionless.

44

Cabot's plan to stay overnight in Camelford was frustrated by the late hour. The lights were out at both of the bed and breakfast inns he drove past. The Countryman Hotel was booked. Then the memory of a long ago stay in Cornwall intruded and he used his mobile phone to conjure up that time again for at least part of one night. There was a room at the Jamaica Inn.

How long had it been? Twenty years? It was the last time he saw Victoria alive, the Major General thought. They'd spent a weekend at the Inn doing nothing special and enjoying every wonderful minute. But duty called. He'd had to leave Sunday evening to make it to London for an early Monday morning meeting. The Monday morning his wife died in the crash of a light aircraft; a flight he had arranged for her.

It was nearly 10:30 by the time Cabot reached the turn off for the Jamaica Inn at Bolventor. He checked in at the lobby desk and got his key. The clerk asked if he needed help with luggage, but all he had was the shoulder bag he carried. Cabot asked if the bar was still open and, when the young man nodded, he said he knew his way.

The fire had been newly rekindled and crackled its glow into even the dark corners. The room was nearly empty. A couple in close conversation sat on the leather chairs near the fireplace. A solitary man was at the far end of the aged oak bar. Cabot took a spot several stools down from him, and the bartender came over.

"What can I get you, sir?" he said.

"Scotch, a single malt," said Cabot.

"Do you have a preference?" the bartender asked.

Before the Major General could answer, the man at the end of the bar said, "Glenmorangie, I believe. The eighteen year-old, if you have it."

Cabot turned to look at him and felt the stubble on his face roughen. He hadn't noticed before, but he knew this man. It was the old man from the memorial. "Yes, the Glenmorangie will be fine," he said to the bartender.

When the young man had busied himself getting the single malt, the Major General turned again to the old man. "What are you doing here?" said Cabot.

Merlyn smiled faintly. "Waiting for you," he said.

Suddenly Cabot was angry. "Who the bloody hell are you?" he demanded, a low, angry growl in his voice.

"Like you, a friend to England," said the Wizard.

Cabot stared silently at him for a moment. "Don't compare yourself to me. You know nothing about me," he said.

Merlyn gave him a cheerless smile. "I know why you're here."

The Major General tensed. He glanced into the nearly empty room, then back to Merlyn.

"She was a beautiful woman," the Wizard said.

Cabot frowned. "What?"

Just then, the bartender placed the glass of scotch in front of Cabot. "Glenmorangie, the eighteen year-old," he said. "Will there be anything else, sir?"

Without taking his eyes off Merlyn, the Major General shook his head.

Merlyn raised his cup of mead. "To England," he said. He smiled faintly again, then had a swallow of his drink.

Cabot continued to stare at him. Finally, he lifted his glass slightly. "What's left of it," he said and drank some of the scotch.

"That's for you to decide?" asked Merlyn. "How much is left?"

The Major General gulped the remaining scotch in his glass, and turned on his stool to face the Wizard. "I told you at the fountain that I will do my duty. I will do what is right."

"And when they are not the same?" Merlyn asked.

"Careful, old man, when you challenge me," said Cabot. He reached out to get the bartender's attention. "Another single malt here," he said.

"Yes, sir," said the bartender. He placed another glass on the bar in front of Cabot and poured an inch of Glenmorangie.

For a few moments, neither of the men spoke. The Major General was gazing into his glass of scotch, thoughtfully.

Then Merlyn said, "It wasn't your fault, you know. Victoria, I mean."

"You knew her?" Cabot said as he twisted around to the Wizard, but the old man was gone.

The Major General got the bartender's attention. "Where did he go?"

"Sir?" said the bartender.

"The old man," Cabot said. "What happened to him?"

The bartender frowned. "What old man?" he said.

45

Arthur lay on the bed in his room at the Jamaica Inn and stared at the clock on the bedside table. Timepieces were one of the countless things that fascinated him in this strange, new world. He'd quickly learned how to tell time, but watching it pass was almost addictive for him. He followed the second hand as it slowly crawled around the face of the clock to the top.

Twenty-six after the fourth hour, he thought. First light will be on the moor soon. He looked over at the sleeping form in the other bed. He knew the Wizard would protect their charge in the next room if he were needed.

"Rest well, my old friend," Arthur whispered. "If what you foretell comes to pass, we will both need magic. You have yours and I will soon have mine."

Arthur dressed, then quietly stepped out into the hall and closed the door. He moved swiftly down the hallway and across the lobby of the inn. Once outside the building, he used the fading stars to point him southeast and began walking.

At the edge of the Inn's garden was a wooden gate. He pushed through it and headed into the bleak expanse of Bodmin Moor, a thick mist swirling around his legs as he moved. It was an odd feeling to be where he had spent much time so long ago; as if he'd strayed into a realm that seemed to reverse time, once full of the living and now desolate, an empty wilderness. He was enticed by the stone circles and dark silhouettes of abandoned granite structures he passed, but forced himself to stay clear of them and keep moving toward his destination. As he topped a gaunt rise, he paused a moment, glancing around the horizon, and realized the dawn was near, and something else. He was being followed.

Arthur started downhill looking for cover, and finally found it in a lonely, stunted, and wind-battered Hawthorn. He knelt in the mist, partially hidden behind the tree, and waited. When the follower approached a few minutes later, the King rose from the mist and confronted him.

"Who goes there?" Arthur exclaimed.

There was a sudden scuffling, a gulping sound, then Prince Harry rasped, "Holy crap! You scared the bloody hell out of me!"

Arthur sighed. "You're fortunate I didn't do something much worse. What are you doing here?"

"I couldn't sleep," said Harry.

"You couldn't sleep? Is that how easily you fool your people?" Arthur asked. "With the first thing that comes to a somewhat limited mind?"

Now Harry sighed. "I was following you," he said. "You don't think you and that white-haired old man have fooled everyone, do you?"

Arthur stood there a moment staring at the Prince through the mounting light and rising mist. Then he turned and walked away. "Well, come if you will," he said over his shoulder.

Harry scowled and followed him into the fog. They walked one behind the other through rough pasture for another ten minutes, neither speaking into the low moan of the wind blowing across the moor. Then Harry realized they had started downhill again. A little farther on, the ground began to feel boggy, the air had a damp feeling. Arthur slowed, then stopped walking. Harry stepped up next to him. They were at the rock-strewn banks of a grim expanse of water. The wind had subsided. The only sound was the soft lapping of the water against the reeds.

"Where are we?" whispered Prince Harry.

Arthur glanced at him, then looked back to the water. "Warwick calls it Dozmary Pool. We had another name for it, but it doesn't matter. It's the same place."

"You mean this is where–" Harry started and then went silent.

The King nodded. "She's waiting for me," he said. "Viviane."

"Tom's wife?" exclaimed Harry with a confused look.

"She of the same name and spirit," said Arthur. "The Lady of the Lake."

Harry frowned. "Vivian? She has the same name?"

Smiling softly, Arthur said, "Close enough. Life is lived in circles." He stepped into the edge of the water and began to walk toward the middle of the pool. "Come with me and you can ask her yourself."

The young Prince looked at the murky water and recoiled at the thought. He shook his head. "This is ridiculous! Stop!" he said. When that had no effect, he yelled, "I don't know who the bloody hell you are, but you're about to embarrass yourself–or drown!"

King Arthur was waist deep into the pool when it began. The water all around him took on an eerie glow as if a door was slowly opening somewhere below. The thin haze on the surface became thicker and began to rise, swirling gradually into a pillar of opaque mist.

"Jesus," Arthur heard Prince Harry murmur from behind him.

The mist faded away, leaving a woman in shimmering, white silken robes standing on the surface of the water. She held a long, silver sword with a golden hilt, and a leather scabbard in her hands. Kneeling, she presented Arthur with the sword and scabbard. Smiling tenderly at him, she said something to the King. Then, as the mist had, she faded silently into the dawn.

King Arthur raised the sword and scabbard above his head and walked back to the shore. Prince Harry was stunned, not just because of what he'd witnessed, or what he now knew to be true, but the grim look on the face of Arthur Pendragon, High King of All Britain.

The only thing the Prince could think of to say was, "I'm sorry." He bowed slightly as Arthur came out the water, and was further unnerved when the King handed him the sword.

"Hold this while I put on the scabbard," said Arthur. "Careful of the blade."

Harry hesitated, then took the sword. He was surprised at the weight of the weapon and couldn't help looking down at it. The glimmering blade had words etched in each side that the Prince couldn't decipher. "What language is this?" he said.

"Of the old ones," said Arthur. He reached out for the sword, and Harry gave it to him. Arthur held the sword up and peered at one side of the blade. "Take me up," he said, then turned the sword over. "Cast me away."

"Excalibur," Harry whispered, a sense of wonder in his voice.

The King slipped the sword into the scabbard, which was positioned across his chest and nodded to Prince Harry. "They will wonder where we are," he said and started back toward the Jamaica Inn.

This time the walk was more leisurely and full of questions: on life in sixth century Britain, Camelot, barbarian invasions, the Knights of the Round Table, and down to earth things such as falconry, hunting boars, and spear fishing.

When they slipped quietly back into their rooms, Merlyn kept his eyes closed, as if he still slept. However, he could see an aircraft with a single passenger making its beginning approach to the airfield at Base Chivenor, less than an hour and a half away. His name was Ian Baker-Smythe.

He could also feel the spell of Excalibur, protecting Arthur, already being cast. For as Arthur and Harry had crossed the garden and entered the Jamaica Inn through a side entrance, Major General Jock Cabot, slightly hung over from an hour of drinking and thinking after his encounter with Merlyn, walked out of the lobby to his rental car.

46

She knew his name only because Josie had just screeched, "*Merde,* Henri! You killed him!"

Now Camilla gave him an angry command. "Turn around, Henri!"

When the young, dark skinned man turned, she was standing a couple of meters away supporting herself with one hand on her mop/crutch. In her other hand was a gun pointed directly at his chest.

Henri smiled guilefully, exposing a mouthful of broken and yellowed teeth. "*Bonjour,* Mad–" was all he got out before the Queen Consort fired a shot over his left shoulder, blowing apart a pitcher of juice in the galley.

Drowning out the gasps and yelps that followed, Camilla screamed, "Shut up and listen to me!"

Slowly swiveling the gun from Henri to the two women and back to him, she waited until the only sound was a whimpering Francine. Then she said, "This is a Royal Marine issued 9mm Browning. It's loaded with thirteen rounds, plus the one I fired. I know how to use it, and I bloody well will if you don't do precisely as I say."

Francine moaned.

"Henri, drop the beer bottle and put your hands out to your side," Camilla said. She made a shooing motion with the pistol. "Then get over there with the women."

He did as he was told.

Pointing the Browning at the three of them, Camilla hobbled over to Charles and knelt down to him. She picked up his gun and put it in the waistband of her slacks. Then she laid her hand on his back. His shoulder moved reflexively, and she let out the breath she'd been holding.

"Charles?" the Queen Consort said. "Charles, are you all right?"

He gave a low groan.

"Charles?" she said again, gently pushing against his shoulder to wake him. "I'm sorry, love, but if you have a concussion, I'm afraid we'll have to postpone it."

The King coughed twice, then rolled over and looked up at her. It took a moment and a few blinks for him to focus. Finally, he murmured, "What happened?"

Camilla glanced up at Henri and the women. They were keeping their distance. She picked up the beer bottle and slowly stood up. "Josie, you get him some water and some aspirin," she said. Using the Browning for emphasis, she added, "And no smart stuff from any of you. Understand?"

They all nodded their heads. Josie got a glass of water, two aspirin from a bottle in a drawer in the galley, and brought them over.

"Help him sit up and take it," said Camilla.

After Charles had struggled up and taken the aspirin, the Queen Consort waved her gun to send Josie back next to Henri and Francine.

Charles felt a spot on the side of his head and winced. "What happened?" he asked again.

"Our new friends, Josie and Francine, forgot to tell us they had another crewmate," Camilla said. She pointed the gun directly at Henri. "Meet Henri, the one who tried to kill you with this." She leaned down and handed the beer bottle to Charles. "I was a bit worried about you, chum."

The King turned the bottle around to the label, then shook his head and winced again. With an ironic smile, he said, "Kronenbourg, France's best. At least he has good taste."

Whether it was relief or the narcotic fog she was swimming in, the comment produced a giggle from Josie. It changed the atmosphere in the cabin, somewhat deflating the tension between them.

"We . . . we meant no harm," offered Josie.

"This is truly," added Francine, in a trembling voice.

Camilla rolled her eyes. "Of course. What's the harm in kidnapping? Demanding ransom? How about you, Henri? I suppose you *accidently* tried to kill Charles?"

"Emma," the King said softly. Without looking at her, he casually put a finger across his lips. But the signal was too late. Josie was already frowning.

"Charles?" Josie said. "I thought his name was Edward."

The Queen Consort flushed slightly. She stared a moment at Josie, then glanced down at Charles. When she finally pushed ahead, her voice had a different tone, flat but not as harsh. Still pointing her Browning at the three across the cabin, she said, "Josie and Francine, you help him to the table in the galley, then both of you take a seat. Henri, you sit at the far end."

"You have a plan, *Emma*, I take it?" Charles whispered.

Camilla shushed him.

When they were seated, the Queen Consort hobbled to the head of the table. What happened next appeared to send a sudden stab of fear through all of them, save the King. He knew his life's love too well and had seen it coming in Camilla's eyes. She stood there looking from one of their attempted captors to the other. After a moment, she sighed and slowly shook her head. Then she turned to Charles and said, "I think it's the only thing to do."

He nodded his agreement.

Camilla took Charles' gun out of the waistband of her slacks and handed it to him. Now they both pointed weapons across the table at the three young people.

"Have you heard what's happened in England?" Camilla asked them.

The color drained from Josie's face. "You mean . . . the terrorists?" she said hesitantly.

Now Henri offered his first words in broken English. "I hear Paris radio. It say try to kill the King."

Francine let out another moan. She covered her eyes with her hands and bowed her head. Her voice was quivering, barely audible, as she said, "You are they?"

The cabin was dead silent for five seconds, as if no one was there. The Queen Consort frowned. "What?"

More silence. Then Josie said, "You are not Edward and Emma? You are the terrorists?"

Francine began to cry. "We are mort," she blubbered.

Smashing, Camilla thought. It's Sod's law. We deceive them about being the Royals and end up terrorists. Before she could decide how to even start, Charles stepped in.

"You're right, Josie," he said. "We are not who we said we were. I'm sorry we misled you, but we had a reason. You have no cause to fear us. We're not the terrorists, we are who they're after."

Josie frowned. "I don't understand."

Camilla gave a frustrated sigh and took over. "It is quite simple. The man you tried to kidnap, the one Henri nearly killed with a beer bottle, is King Charles the third, Monarch of the United Kingdom. And I am Camilla, his wife and the Queen Consort."

"Mon dieu!" Henri said.

Francine peeked out through her hands and saw Charles smiling at her. "It is miracle!" she exclaimed. Smiling back, she started wiping the tears from her eyes.

And what Charles and Camilla had been hoping for came from Josie. "How can we help?" she asked.

47

One of the first orders General Ian Baker-Smythe gave when he assumed command of the British Armed Forces was the modification of a Falcon 50 executive jet for his personal use. Produced by Dassault, a French company well known among jet setters, the Falcon 50 offered a full purse of amenities for up to nine passengers: wooden floors, veneered wood trim around the interior, coffee tables, leather easy chairs and couches, Wi-Fi, HD television, plus lavatories fore and aft and a full galley. Promotion for the plane claimed it was like flying in your living room or the company lounge.

All that remained of these plush features in the General's Falcon was one of the lavatories. It was like flying in a War Room, with a dozen straight backed chairs bolted to a steel floor sitting in front of an array of flat screen monitors and communications gear.

This morning, the General was aboard Command One, as he'd dubbed it. However, there were no military techs hunched over the equipment. Baker-Smythe was alone except for the pilots and his aide, Lieutenant Grayson Cowell, and on a singular mission.

The General's plane was descending, on approach to the airfield at Base Chivenor in Devon, when the light on a red phone began to blink. Lieutenant Cowell answered it and then frowned. He turned to the General.

"It's for you, sir," he said. "A Major Mallory."

The General's first inclination was to refuse the call. Then he changed his mind and took the handset. This was a teaching moment, he thought.

"You're out of bounds, Major!" Baker-Smythe declared. "You report to Major General Cabot! What the bloody hell are you doing calling me?"

"I'm sorry, sir. I can't reach the Major General. We don't know where he is."

"Jesus, Mallory! Call his mobile."

"Our techs say it's turned off."

"What?"

"And this is important, sir."

After a long moment, the General said, "It had better be."

Mallory took a breath before he began. It did little good. His voice was still pinched taut. "We found the Sunseeker Tomahawk, the boat the Royals took."

"So, we have them?" Baker-Smythe interjected.

"It was empty."

The General shook his head and pushed back savagely. "Another cock up! You got the *wrong* damned boat!"

Now Mallory seemed to almost relax. The worst was over. He had a response for this assertion. "I'm sorry, General, but I'm afraid that's not correct," he said. "When we commandeered the boats we put serial numbers on all of them. We checked. This Sunseeker has the right number." He took another breath and let it out before he continued. "And there's something else. We found a shoe, a woman's left shoe, in the cabin. One of the men she held a gun on at the boat docks recognized it. It belongs to the Queen Consort."

The line went silent.

"General?"

"Good lord," Baker-Smythe said finally. "You think they fell overboard? Or jumped? Committed suicide?"

"Or maybe they were picked up by another boat," the Major hesitantly suggested.

The General was quiet again. This time Mallory could almost feel the bile rising over the phone. "Bloody ridiculous!" Baker-Smythe spat. "How could they have planned that?"

"We found the Sunseeker on the edge of a shipping lane. All they needed was a bit of luck."

At that moment the engines on the Falcon 50 roared a warning, and Lieutenant Cowell interrupted. "Seat belts, sir," he prompted. "We're landing."

"This is on your head, Major," the General said. "You find those two. And report through Major General Cabot!"

"Yes, sir! If I can find him," Mallory said, but he'd already been hung up on.

As the plane thudded down on the tarmac, bounced once, and the reverse thrust of the engines began to slow it, Baker-Smythe kept spewing orders.

"Lieutenant, identify the leader of the commando platoon Cabot has on alert for this mission. Order him to meet me in the Base Commander's office–now! And find out where the hell Jock Cabot is hiding!"

"Yes, sir!"

General Ian Baker-Smythe, Chief of the Defense Staff, Supreme Commander of the British Armed Forces had been waiting in the Base Commander's office for thirty minutes when Corporal Ethan Evans finally arrived. Evans was the essence of a British commando, young, muscled, laced up tight. From the look on the Base Commander's face, the Corporal knew he was in trouble, just not how much, or why.

He took two steps into the room and snapped to attention. "I'm frightfully sorry, sir," he began, but was cut off by the Base Commander, Colonel James S. McCray.

"Name and rank!" McCray demanded.

Evans tightened his stance. "Evans, Corporal."

The General took over at that point. "Forget the excuses, Evans, Corporal," he said snidely. "How many men are in your platoon?"

"Thirty, sir."

"Where are they?" Baker-Smythe asked. "Are they ready to ship out?"

Evans was clearly confused. He glanced at the Base Commander, looking for help. There was none. A moment passed. Finally, he answered. "No, sir. We were ordered to stand down."

"*What?*" said Colonel McCray. He turned to Baker-Smythe. "General, I wasn't made aware of this."

Baker-Smythe acted as if the Colonel wasn't even in the room, continuing to stare at Corporal Evans. "Why?" he said.

The Corporal swallowed and stood even straighter. "Major General Cabot said the mission might be changed. He told me to give the men some rest while we can. A group of them went into Barnstable; the rest are in the barracks."

Now, General Ian Baker-Smythe turned to the Base Commander. "I trust more than one of those men carry a radio or mobile phone?"

This time it was Corporal Evans giving the Colonel help. "Yes sir! Several of them!" he said.

"Good," said the General. He looked at his watch. "You are dismissed Evans, Corporal. You have precisely two hours to get all thirty of your men assembled and equipped to push off on the original mission. If there are those who are not present and accounted for they will be dishonorably discharged–along with you."

48

All five of them were sitting at a table in a corner of the Peddler's Food Bar at the Jamaica Inn, with Prince Harry hiding under a baseball cap and sunglasses that Merlyn found somewhere. They were finishing breakfast when Tom offered the first surprise.

"I'd like to get an early start so we can make a stop on the way back to Camelford," he said.

Vivian was sitting next to him. She paused with a last piece of lemon scone halfway to her mouth. "Where?" she said, frowning.

Tom took a furtive glance at Merlyn. The old man was occupied with his tea at the end of the table. "Slaughter Bridge," Tom said. "It's close to the Veterans Home. Only a kilometer or two away. But I'd like to look around, spend some time."

Vivian ate her scone. "What a horrid name," she said. "Why stop at a bridge?"

Tom looked uncomfortable. "It's . . . well, it's the site of an ancient battle," he said. He picked up the bill their waiter had left on the table, examined it briefly, then laid it down. "You have a problem with that?"

This drew a thin smile from Arthur, who was sitting across from Tom. "I thought that was only legend," Arthur said.

Now Merlyn looked up from his tea. "It was," said the Wizard. "Until last night." When Arthur's smile began to spread into a toothy grin, he added, "However, good men can change their minds. And see the truth of something they have doubted."

Merlyn turned to Prince Harry, seated next to him. "Isn't that right, Prince?"

Harry had just put half of a sausage link in his mouth. Turning to Arthur, chewing and talking at the same time, he said, "Have you told them?"

"For heaven's sake!" said Vivian. "What is this, soccer? My neck is getting tired with all this back and forth. Told us what?"

The Prince swallowed his sausage. He pointed at Arthur. "He snuck out of the inn in the middle of the night. Around 4:30."

"How would you know that?" asked Tom.

Harry chuckled. He seemed suddenly buoyed, brighter than any of them had seen him. "I followed him," he said. "You won't believe where he went, and what happened."

At the end of the table, Merlyn cleared his throat. He tipped his head, indicating a nearby table full of other guests. "I think this story might be better told with a bit more privacy." He folded his napkin and laid it on the table next to his plate. "It appears we are all nearly finished. Shall we take Tom's suggestion and get an early start?"

"But what about you?" Vivian said to Merlyn.

Before the Wizard could respond, Harry offered up another surprise; a complete change in his attitude toward the old man. Smiling broadly, the Prince said, "He doesn't need to fly back on the wind. He can come with us. It's not far, and we can squeeze him in."

Then Harry turned to Arthur and gave a theatrical wink. "But we'll have to make room for something else, too. Right, Your Majesty?"

Arthur didn't answer, but pushed back from the table and got up. Harry joined him and, as Arthur started to walk away, Harry followed, saying, "You blokes can take care of the bill, can't you? We have to get something from the room."

When they were gone, Vivian turned to Merlyn with a bewildered look. "What was that all about?" she said.

He smiled. "I'm sure we'll find out."

In the end, it was Vivian who was squeezed in, perched on Harry's lap in the back seat of the Mini Cooper. Arthur sat next to them. Tom was in the driver's seat with Merlyn on the passenger side. The *something else* Prince Harry had mentioned stretched vertically through the cab of the Mini Cooper, from the dashboard nearly to the back window. It was shinning and sharp.

Once they were back on the highway, Vivian delicately touched the sharp edge with a finger and ventured, "I'm sure someone is going to explain this."

Arthur took a breath, but Prince Harry couldn't contain himself. "I take back everything I said about them," he exclaimed.

"Who?" said Tom. He glanced in the rearview mirror.

"Merlyn and King Arthur."

Vivian turned and stared in Harry's face. This close, he could feel her soft breath. "You believe that is who they are, truly?" she asked.

"I know it is." He reached out and tapped the shining steel blade only inches away from them. "And here is the proof. This is Excalibur, King Arthur's sword. I saw the Lady of the Lake give it to Arthur last night."

"My God," murmured Tom.

Vivian chuckled softly. "Teacher, you've been saying that a lot lately."

"Tell us about it," said Tom. "I want to hear the whole story."

So Harry did. And with everyone's attention on the Prince, Merlyn took the opportunity to make something happen in another story. Quietly, he took Tom's mobile phone out of the cup holder where Tom had put it and turned it off. He smiled to himself as he placed it back. His timing was rather good. The first call to the phone wouldn't be made for another five minutes.

Then the Wizard leaned his head back against the seat and closed his eyes. He had another rendezvous to keep.

49

"Bugger!"

Wing Commander Simon Firth sighed. He swiveled his chair away from Eliza's computer and looked over his glasses at Captain Colin Mackenzie. "Is that the only English they teach in Scotland?"

"Bugger you!" Mackenzie threw back at him. "We've got to warn them off, and Tom's mobile keeps going to voice mail."

"It might not be the emergency you're making it," Firth said. "Cabot might not come back."

Mackenzie shook his head in disgust. "Bloody daft! That's what you said last night and he was here when Nurse Harriet unlocked the door this morning." He looked at Harriet, who was collecting the medical charts for her rounds. "Correct, Harriet?"

"I didn't see the man asking after Trevor last night, but there was a man here first thing this morning," Harriet said. She smiled her bright smile. "Actually, he was quite nice."

"For a viper," said Mackenzie.

Simon Firth sighed again, tiredly. "Is that the way you describe the hero of the Falkland Islands? A holder of the Victoria Cross? Commandant of the Royal Marines?"

"All the more reason he should be shot," countered Mackenzie.

Firth turned to Harriet Claiborne. "What precisely did he say to you?"

She closed her eyes and thought for a moment. "Let's see . . . I remember he was calm. He has a deep voice."

"Fine!" said Colin Mackenzie. "We get it. You think he's a bit of all right. Now answer the Wing Commander. What did he say?"

Harriet glared at the Captain. "You seem quite gassy this morning, Captain. Perhaps, before my rounds, I should give you an enema."

Mackenzie took a deep breath and let it out slowly. Rather stiffly he said, "Very well, Nurse Harriet. I apologize," then slipped back into his sardonic voice. "Perhaps I'm taking this too seriously. It's only a matter of sink or swim for all of Great Britain."

Commander Clive Kay had been watching the shouting match from the other side of the office while he sipped a cup of tea. He raised his eyebrows. "The Victoria Cross?" he said. "Really? I didn't know Cabot had the Victoria Cross."

"When he was in Iraq," said Simon Firth. "Pulled an Audie Murphy. Climbed up on an Iraqis tank and dropped in a grenade. Saved a platoon of men."

"And now he thinks he's a King maker," Mackenzie said.

"In reality, we don't know that, Colin," said Commander Kay. His nose in the air, oozing elitism, he added, "It was I who actually spoke with the Major General last night, and I saw no blood in his eye."

Mackenzie gave a sharp bark of a laugh. "You spoke with Craig Westland and didn't know the bloody difference, you wonk!"

"Put a sock in it, both of you!" Simon Firth demanded. He turned again to Harriet. "Now, Harriet dear, what did Jock Cabot say this morning?"

"Thank you, Simon," she said and smiled. "He asked me to tell Trevor not to worry, everything is going to be all right."

"Is that it?" said Mackenzie. "What does that mean?"

Harriet put the medical charts on the nurse's cart. "He also said he was sorry he missed seeing Tom and his wife, and hoped he might meet them during some other visit."

This elicited another raised eyebrow from Clive Kay. "Where is Tom, and the others?" he asked.

"Don't get me started," Mackenzie warned, then plunged into it. "I've been trying to chase him down ever since Cabot came this morning. Called every hotel and rooming house in Camelford. Then our Commanding Officer, the always informative Wing Commander, Simon Firth, finally tells me they booked rooms on the other side of the bloody moor at the Jamaica Inn. So, I called there just in time to hear they've checked out."

Commander Kay rolled his eyes. "I know it's beyond many of our seniors, but there is a new technology called the mobile phone. I suppose you've tried that?"

"How would you like one stuffed up–" the Captain started and then glanced at Harriet and changed his mind. "Tom's mobile is apparently turned off," he said. "Every time I call, it goes to voice mail. We don't have a number for Vivian, and the Prince said he threw his phone away when they were chasing him in London."

Kay nodded. "Smart young man. What about the others? Don't they have phones?"

"Oh, certainly!" said Mackenzie, loading it with sarcasm. "A King from the sixth century and his Wizard." Turning to Firth he said, "Both of them would be likely to have mobiles, don't you think, Wing Commander?"

Simon Firth swiveled his chair away from the desk he'd been sitting at and stood. "I have to finish the guards schedule on Eliza's computer in her office. Is that all, Harriet? About Cabot, I mean?"

Harriet had finished gathering the medical charts she needed and pushed the nurse's cart over to the door leading to the veterans' rooms. Now she stopped.

"There was one more thing. He said it was his first trip to this part of Cornwall and asked if there was anything nearby he should see. You know, historical, that sort of thing. All I could think of was Slaughter Bridge."

She went out door and started down the hall.

50

Charles heard it first: a sound from his years in the Royal Navy. He would never forget the thumping noise of an attack helicopter, and especially if there was reason to fear it might be looking for him.

The King was alone on the deck, acting as lookout. The others were all down in the galley having breakfast. They didn't expect any trouble this far from the Isles of Scilly, but they had all agreed with the old saying, better safe than sorry. Good thing, Charles thought.

He grabbed the binoculars from their pocket in the cockpit and scanned the horizon to the north. It took a moment to find the aircraft. When he did, he cursed out loud. It was still a large bug in the sky, crawling toward them, but he was sure it was a Sea King MK4, the same kind of copter the commandos used to kidnap the Royal Family.

Charles dropped the binoculars on a seat in the cockpit and clambered down into the cabin. Everyone at the table in the galley looked up.

"Trouble on the way," he said, suddenly short of breath. "A military helicopter."

Henri was the first up from the table. "Putain!" he shouted, then switched to his fractured English. "I check out." He started for the stairs, but Charles grabbed his arm.

"No! We shouldn't let them see us," the King insisted. Then he hesitated and turned and looked at the women.

Josie smiled. "You are right," she said as she got up from the table. "It is *better* they see us; Henri and Franny and me on deck. We show our excite at seeing them. Then no questions." She took Francine by the hand and pulled her up from the table.

Now Camilla chimed in, supporting the argument. "I agree, Charles. If no one is on deck it will just make whoever is in the copter curious." Then she grinned. "And, heaven forbid, everyone knows the stuffy King of England wouldn't be fraternizing with a group of . . ." She glanced around the room, "Young people from Martinique."

"Even black ones," Josie added and everyone got a chuckle, punching a hole in the bubble of tension that had enveloped them.

Soon after, when the Sea King MK4 crossed low over the ketch, there were three animated, dark-skinned kids with cheery faces on deck, jumping up and down and waving at it. The copter thrummed by and disappeared on a straight line into the distance.

It was just over an hour later, with Henri on lookout duty, when the boat appeared on the horizon. The others were below, napping or playing scrabble and arguing about how to spell French words. After Henri had spent a minute or two watching the boat through the binoculars, he leaned down the stairs to the galley and shouted, "Something up here. Good you come see."

Camilla stayed in the cabin with her broken leg. The other three came up on deck and found Henri on the port side of the boat looking north through binoculars.

"What is it?" said Josie.

"I fear problem," Henri said. "Far away yet, but could be soldiers."

Charles stepped up close to Henri. "Here, give me the glasses."

Henri took the binoculars down and turned to look at Josie. She nodded and he handed them to Charles.

"Sorry," Charles said. "I didn't mean to be officious."

Henri appeared to have no idea what the word meant, but he smiled
and nodded. Then he pointed where he'd been looking and said, "*Le
bateau* at end of water."

"Got it," said Charles. "A boat on the horizon."

He put the binoculars up to his eyes, adjusted the focus, searched
a moment, then stood there for a minute. When he brought the glasses
down the look on his face told them Henri was right. They had a
problem.

"Dark green," said Charles. "They're wearing dark green, the color
of the Royal Marines' uniforms."

"How many?" Josie said.

Charles shook his head. "I couldn't tell. They're still too far away–
thank God."

"We sure they see us?" asked Francine.

Shrugging, Henri said, "Make straight line here."

Charles had raised the binoculars again. "He's right," he said.
"They're coming our way, moving fast, and it looks like the boats the
commandos had at Tresco."

Josie put out her hand and said, "Please, *des jumelles*."

Charles guessed that meant binoculars and passed them to her.
"Anyone got a plan?" he said with a touch of irony.

He was surprised when Josie answered immediately, even more so
at her answer. "We will handle this one. You get below. Take Queen into
your cabin and stay there."

"But what are you going to do?" said Charles.

Josie put her forefingers at her temples pointing up, and wriggled
them. "Voodoo!" she said with a gorgeous smile.

With no alternative coming to mind, the King followed her directions.

Sergeant Mark Gates was the officer in charge of the Crownline 250,
an ocean going powerboat. He had two corporals with him. All three
had weapons, handguns as well as assault rifles. After the sighting by
the copter, Gates had been told to investigate and stay in touch with their
commander, Major Mallory. Now that they were closing in on the ketch,
he was back in contact with home base on Tresco.

"Did you try to reach them on the shortwave," Mallory asked.

"Yes, sir, we did," said Gates. "We made contact."

Silence.

"Well? Did they identify themselves? Who's on board? Where are they bound?"

"Sorry, sir. It was all in French. I think."

Another moment of silence.

Mallory mumbled something and audibly sighed. "And none of you speak it," he said.

"Sorry, sir." Gates repeated.

This time the Major mumbled loud enough for Gates to make out, "Another muck up!"

"Sir?"

"Close on the ketch and find out who the bloody hell is on the thing!" Mallory said, then broke the connection.

Fifteen minutes later Mark Gates contacted Tresco and asked for Major Mallory. It was another five minutes before the Major came on the line.

"Mallory," he said.

"We are close off the port bow of the ketch, sir," said Gates. He sounded up tight, as if something was wrong.

Mallory paid no attention, figuring it was rookie battle nerves. "Very well! Send one of your men over to reconnoiter. Get back to me when you have information. Who are these people, where are they going?"

"I recommend we do not board, sir," said Gates. "There's no need, actually. We can see them from here. They're out on the deck; two young women and a man."

"Didn't you hear me, Sergeant?" said Mallory. "Send a man over there! If you're worried the big bad French will get him, send two."

"They're all black, natives, I think," Gates said. "They're dancing, waving for us to join them."

"So what's wrong with that?" Mallory said.

"They're all naked," said Sergeant Mark Gates.

There was some mumbling and then Major Mallory said, "Get the hell out of there."

51

General Baker-Smythe had taken over the Base Commander's office, relegating Colonel McCray to a conference room down the hall. While he waited for Corporal Evans to get his platoon together, he placed a call to the Prime Minister, conveniently *forgetting* to report anything about what was happening; the escape and rapidly chilling trail of the Royals, the missing Jock Cabot, or Cabot's order for the Alert Platoon to stand down.

It wasn't difficult to duck those negatives. In fact, they didn't even come up. All Saxon wanted to talk about was the headway he was making on solving the country's problems. In a special session of Parliament, his Emergency Committee had been given the power to ration food and medical services. Legislation was also being written that would retroactively increase taxes on the rich. And the Privy Council had given its nod for the establishment of internment camps should they be needed for unresponsive segments of the population, including Muslims and the unions.

After listening to Saxon spout for nearly half an hour, the General called MI-5 Director, Nigel Gibbon. The Director came on the line coughing. Once he got it under control, Gibbon said, "I take it this means you've recaptured the Royals."

When he was greeted with silence, Gibbon added, "Or perhaps you have Prince Harry under lock and key?"

"If you keep it up, you are not going to live through this, Nigel, one way or the other," said the General.

"Simply trying to keep things light," Gibbon offered.

"Do you hear me laughing?"

"Very well," the Director said tersely. "What can I do for you, General?"

"There are two things, actually. We found the boat the Royals stole on a course that might suggest they were trying to reach France. See what you can do to set up a welcoming party, just in case."

"That shouldn't be difficult. I've worked with my French counterpart several times before," said Gibbon. "She's quite imaginative."

Baker-Smythe sighed. "Keep it in your pants, for once."

"No worries. Sadly, Capucine is all business. What's number two?"

"Alistair tasked you with keeping an eye on Jock Cabot," said Baker-Smythe.

"Yes. In his office, as I recall. Just before he threw me out."

"Spare me the hurt feelings. Where is Cabot now?"

The flick of a cigarette lighter was followed by more coughing.

"Well?" the General prodded.

"Unknown," said Gibbon.

"That's not good enough, Nigel. You must know something."

"We know where he was going."

The rolled eyes were obvious in Baker-Smythe's voice. "He already told us that; Camelford."

"Where in Camelford, I mean. We picked it up on the tap of one of his conversations with our operative, Rebecca Donovan."

"You listen in on your own agents?" asked Baker-Smythe.

"We record them, every call they make," Gibbon said.

"And this conversation?"

The MI-5 Director paused a moment, then said, "Would you like to hear the Cabot/Donovan recording? It's about two minutes long."

After they listened, the General said, "Have you called the Veterans Home?"

"Yes. They've never heard of Jock Cabot. But a Sergeant Major Trevor Warwick is staying there and his son is visiting. Of course, you heard on the recoding that the son's wife, Vivian Warwick, is the manager of the McDonald's where Donovan believes she saw Prince Harry."

Baker-Smythe was quiet, thinking. "Cabot said he'd use stealth. It would be simple to deceive the old fools at a veteran's home," he said. "That's where he is; I know it! And he wouldn't go there unless the Prince is there." After a moment, he asked, "Why isn't he contacting us?"

"Most likely One or The Other," Gibbon said.

The General could hear a nicotine smile in Gibbon's answer. It sparked an angry, "What the bloody hell are you talking about?"

"The rule," said the MI-5 Director, "in the big spy book. You can turn any man with sex or money."

"You're suggesting that Cabot actually has something going with your agent?"

"No, General. I'm reminding you of how much money is available to the Royal Family. Even a young prince."

Baker-Smythe was silent again, thinking. "If you get any new information on Jock Cabot, contact me first," he said. "Understand?"

"Yes, sir," Gibbon said to the dial tone.

"Lieutenant!" the General called to his aide sitting in the corridor.

A chair scooted back, and Grayson Cowell appeared in the door of the General's office. "Yes, sir," he said.

The General waved his aide in and pointed to a chair in front of his desk. As soon as Cowell sat down, Baker-Smythe said, "What do you know about Major General Cabot?"

The Lieutenant was somewhat taken aback. It wasn't the kind of question the General asked of him. He scratched his cheek in thought and frowned. Then he said, "He's the Commandant of the Royal Marines. And holder of the Victoria Cross."

"No, no. I mean more personal things."

The General smiled with a touch of unease and it occurred to Lieutenant Cowell that it was the first time he'd ever seen the man actually smile. Be careful, he thought. "I'm not sure what you mean, sir."

The smile disappeared. "You know, things like, is he in debt? Is he on drugs? Is he having an affair? Have you heard anything like that?"

"Oh! Well, there's plenty of scuttlebutt out there on almost everyone; a good deal of it made up. Facebook stuff. But I've never heard anything about the Major General's financials. Or his sex life. You know his wife died, of course. Most of the chatter is about the incredible things he has done in battle."

Baker-Smythe was gathering himself to ask another question, when his mobile phone rang. Cowell said, "I'll come back," and got up to leave.

The General opened his phone. When he saw the caller ID, he stopped his aide with an urgent, "Wait!"

"Sir?" Cowell said.

The General pointed to the phone. "It's Cabot. Find him. GPS!"

Cowell nodded and rushed out of the room as Baker-Smythe answered the phone.

"Hello, Jock. I've been waiting for you to call." For a moment the General thought he'd lost the connection. There was nothing but static, a low-grade hiss.

Then Jock Cabot said, "Hello, Ian." He sounded flat, nothing like the usual stronghold of energy.

"Where are you?" the General asked.

Ignoring the question, Cabot said, "I was wrong. I couldn't find the target."

Baker-Smythe allowed himself a slim smile. Nigel Gibbon's big spy book, he thought. He pictured Prince Harry sitting next to Cabot.

"Do you want me to send troops? The Alert Platoon you put together?"

"I take it you know I ordered them to stand down."

"Yes. I was wondering why. Corporal Evans said you didn't give a reason."

"I don't need them."

"Why?"

After a few more seconds of static, Cabot said, "I'm going to come in. I need to talk with you and Saxon."

"About what, Jock? You know, we're in the middle of something here; changing an empire, saving it."

"That's what I want to talk about. Changing it into what? Saving it from what, and for whom? As I recall my history, those who seize power to do the right thing do well until the people find out."

The General smiled again. The Prince must be driving a hard bargain, he thought. He not only wants his freedom, but the complete failure of the transformation. Well, he will have neither. And Jock Cabot is likely to get a prison cell instead of a traitor's fortune.

"All right," Baker-Smythe said. "I understand your concerns. Let me arrange some time with the Prime Minister. When I can make room in his schedule, I'll call you."

After what seemed like an hour of hissing static, Cabot said, "Very well."

The General closed his mobile and looked up at Lieutenant Cowell, who had quietly reentered the room toward the end of the conversation. Cowell smiled.

"We found him?" said the General, making it more of a statement than a question.

His aide nodded and said, "Yes, sir. Major General Jock Cabot is in North Cornwell near the hamlet of Slaughter Bridge. It's about four kilometers northwest of Camelford."

Baker-Smythe pushed his chair back from the desk and stood. "Tell Corporal Evans to assemble the Alert Platoon," he said. "Immediately!"

52

As they neared the turn off from the A39 to B3314, Tom Warwick fished his mobile phone out of the cup holder in the console. He started to punch in a number, then frowned.

"When did I do that?" he said to himself.

"What?" said Merlyn.

Tom shrugged. "Nothing," he said, turning on the phone. "I'm going to call the Veterans Home and let them know we're stopping by Slaughter Bridge."

"I thought you might," said the Wizard. "Good idea."

As it came to life, the phone beeped three times. Tom chuckled. "And just in time," he said. "I've got three voice mails." He tapped the voice mail app, and three stars appeared. He touched one to open the message, and they all disappeared.

"Crap," Tom muttered.

Looking out the window, Merlyn smiled faintly. Then he turned to Tom. "Who was it?" he asked.

Tom sighed and shook his head. "Who knows?" He started punching in numbers again. "Probably just adverts. If it was anyone from the Veterans Home, I'll find out now."

On the fourth ring, someone picked up. "Hello?" said a squeaky female voice. "I mean, Camelford Veterans Home."

Tom chuckled. "Are you sure?" he asked.

"Sorry," she said. "How may I help you?"

"This is Tom Warwick, the son of Sergeant Major Trevor Warwick," Tom said.

"Yes, sir. This is Edna Stevens, the lobby clerk. We met yesterday."

"Hi, Edna. I'd like you to do me a favor, if you could."

"I'll certainly try."

She sounded tense to Tom. "Is something wrong?"

"No, no," said Edna. "There's simply a lot going on, people rushing around. Not quite the norm for us."

"Well then, I won't take much of your time. Could you please let my father or Wing Commander Firth know that we'll be somewhat delayed getting back? We've decided to stop and have a look at Slaughter Bridge."

"Will you be long?"

"No, not very. I just didn't want them wondering where we are."

"Very well," said Edna. "I've made a note of it, and I'll inform them as soon as I can."

"Thank you, Edna, and we'll see you soon."

"Cheery bye, then," she said.

As she hung up the phone, Edna turned in her chair to see who was now scuffling across the lobby. It was Captain Colin Mackenzie. He was headed directly for her desk.

Oh dear, Edna thought. This is what trouble looks like. She smiled at him as he stopped in front of her desk. "Good morning, Captain," she said.

"What's so bloody good about it?" Mackenzie snapped.

Edna flinched. "My heavens, Captain, do we have a problem?"

"Problem? It's a bloody disaster!" Mackenzie grumbled. "His *Highness* Firth has used his rank to monopolize Eliza's computer all morning. Doing what? Drawing up a bloody guard schedule! Totally unimportant! And all the while preventing me from doing the serious work–laying out our battle plan!"

As his rant had gone on, the old Scot's face had gone from ruddy to splotchy maroon, and the desk clerk was worried about him. Putting on her serious face, Edna said, "My Heavens! I'm sure he will clear the way for you soon."

The Captain opened his mouth to speak, then shut it. He frowned and looked around the lobby. It was empty. He leaned in toward Edna and said, "Do you know how to use a computer?"

Edna couldn't stop a slight nod, but tried to dampen it with, "Well . . . some."

Mackenzie smiled. He moved close and took her by the arm. "Madam, your country needs you," he said. Then he helped her stand. "Come with me."

"My Heavens," said Edna. She grabbed her purse, and the two of them crossed the lobby and disappeared down a corridor, leaving behind the note she made from Tom Warwick's phone call.

53

"Ten-Shun!" shouted Platoon Leader, Corporal Ethan Evans, as General Baker-Smythe entered the largest classroom at Base Chivenor. The thirty men of the Alert Platoon who were sitting there jumped to their feet and stood ramrod straight, expressionless.

"Is this all of your men, Evans, Corporal?" Baker-Smythe asked.

The Corporal didn't know whether or not to smile at the General's dig. He chose the right response when he snapped a salute and said, "Yes, sir! All present and accounted for!"

The General spent most of a minute looking from face to deadpanned face, staring hard at each man before he said, "Very well. Sit."

More than a few of the men glanced at Evans as they followed orders and took their seats. A number of others winced and turtled into their shells. The room virtually crackled with tension. Baker-Smythe walked to the desk at the front of the room and stood there. He took a small pad from a pocket, opened it, studied it a moment, then laid it on the desk.

"What do you know about your mission?" the General said to the room full of men.

Future King

Corporal Evans who was in the front row quickly stood and answered, "Sir! We were told we'd be briefed before we left."

"By whom?"

"Major General Cabot, sir," said Evans.

"I thought he was the one who told you to stand down."

The Corporal shifted his weight from one foot to the other. "Yes, sir, he did. Early this morning."

Baker-Smythe took his time. He looked at the pad on the table, then back to Evans. "Why?" he asked.

Evans shifted his weight again. "I'm not sure. The Major General said he'd changed his mind. But I don't know why. He didn't say."

"He gave no reason?"

"No, sir."

The General slowly let out the breath he'd been holding. Cabot hadn't poisoned these men with his quixotic nonsense. What was it he said on the phone; doing the right thing is fine until the people find out? Something like that. Bloody pathetic! That's a dreamer's code, not a soldier's, a war hero's. In the real world the power decides what is right, then makes it so. Leaders can't rely on the dumb masses. They have to tell them what to do. When this was all resolved, he would have Jock Cabot's Victoria Cross confiscated, melted down for scrap; and the man as well.

Baker-Smythe allowed himself a small smile. In the middle of this muddle he'd also picked up a bone to trip that sod Gibbon. No doubt Nigel was right; Cabot had been turned by money. But there was something else involved in this idiocy; an overdose of morals.

One of the men in the back row of chairs coughed, and the General dropped out of his reverie. Corporal Evans was still standing at the front of the group, waiting for a response or instruction to sit down.

"Corporal, your platoon is now under my command!" the General declared. "I want every man armed and prepared to depart within thirty minutes. You will arrange transportation for the platoon in civilian vehicles. Your destination will be Slaughter Bridge. Your mission will be to capture or kill an assassin involved in the recent attack on the Royal Family."

For a second, the stunned marines just sat there.

"Go!" Baker-Smythe commanded, shooing the men with both arms, and the room was filled with noise and moving bodies.

54

Charles and Camilla were relaxing on deck as the ketch pushed through moderate, five-foot swells. The weather was fine, and they were upbeat for the first time in days. And for good reason; the coast of France was visible in the distance. With the binoculars they could even make out the harbor entrance at Saint Malo, their destination.

"Well, it's nearly over," said Charles.

The Queen Consort glanced his way. "You mean all the fun we've been having?"

"That, too," he allowed.

They both smiled.

After a moment, Charles said, "Actually, we've a long way to go. I've been thinking about what we'll have to do when we get back to London."

Camilla turned and looked at him. "You've already solved the first problem we face?"

The King frowned and waited to be enlightened.

"Have you looked in the mirror lately?" Camilla asked. "With that scruffy beard, I hardly recognize you myself. I wouldn't be surprised if the French arrest you as a vagrant."

Charles tilted his chin up slightly in a pose. "I think it's rather rakish, bohemian," he said.

With a small mocking smile, Camilla said, "No worry. I've arranged a solution with Josie. More precisely, with her straight razor."

The pose disappeared. "You expect me to shave with a woman's razor?"

Camilla shrugged. "Henri doesn't have one."

Charles made a face. "She shaves her *legs* with that," he said.

Camilla nodded, smiling broader. "And other places."

"Ugh!" he said distastefully. "You *do* remember that I'm the King?"

"Oh yes, My Liege." She bowed broadly. "King Scruffy."

Their playful banter was interrupted when Henri suddenly appeared on deck. He was clearly upset about something.

"You come down!" he shouted. "Come down now!" Then he was gone, back down the stairs to the cabin.

Charles got up and started for the stairs. "I'll find out what this is about," he said. "You relax, get some rest."

Camilla stopped him with a rather sharp, "Wait, Charles!" When he turned to her, she shook her head and said, "That look on his face; I don't like it." Then she put her arms out toward him. "Help me up. I want to hear this, too. Besides," she added with an impish grin, "I'm getting hungry."

With Charles supporting his wife, they managed to get across the deck and down the stairs to the cabin in just a couple of minutes. But it was too late.

"*Fils de salope!*" declared Josie. She crumpled up the cardboard cup she'd been drinking from and threw it across the cabin, nearly hitting Francine in the face.

Francine, who already had tears on her cheeks, moaned and started to cry again.

"What the bloody hell?" Charles demanded.

Josie threw up her hands and shot a glance at the ceiling. "*C'est du bazaar!*" she spat.

At that point, Camilla stepped in. "English, my dear," she said. "If you want us to help, speak English."

Josie took a breath and tried to calm herself. "Son of a bitch, I said. And what a mess!"

"What mess?" asked Camilla.

Pointing at the radio, which was playing music, Josie said, "We were listening to this French station and they interrupted with, how you say, *communiqué*?"

"A news bulletin?" said Charles.

Josie nodded. "Yes, a bulletin of news." She shook her head in exasperation. "*C'est du bazaar!*"

The King pulled out a chair from the table. "Here, sit down," he said. "Try to relax." Once she was sitting, he asked, "Can you remember what they reported in the bulletin?"

"Oh, yes," said Josie. She opened her mouth, but then suddenly closed it and looked at the radio. The music had stopped. There were three short alarm type rings, and an announcer began to speak urgently. "Again, the *communiqué*!" Josie said.

"Try to translate for us," said Camilla.

Josie closed her eyes, frowning, then started talking in starts and stops. "British *les autorites* have asked French National Police and the *Gendarmerie* . . . to help in search for an escapee in the assassination attempt on the British Royal Family. This man who is . . . look alike for King Charles . . . is thought to be on his way to France. The French government has issued a plea to all of its citizens to help capture this criminal, alive or dead. The British have placed a reward of 50,000 pounds on this man . . . and France has added 50,000 French Euros."

By the time Josie finished, the station had reverted to music. For nearly a minute, the only other sound in the cabin was the soft blubbering of Francine.

Then Charles whispered, "What a bloody mess."

55

Commander Clive Kay was half way across the empty lobby of the Veterans Home when he noticed that the clerk, Edna Stevens, wasn't at her desk. He shook his head in disapproval. Impossible to get good help these days, Kay thought. What if someone came in the front door? What if there was a phone call? Others might let this dereliction of duty go without comment, but he wasn't about to. He crossed to the clerk's desk intent on leaving a scathing note and found a pen in the desk drawer. As he started to tear off a page of the note pad by the phone, he noticed some scribbling on it. He took a closer look and then drew in a breath.

"Oh, my God!" the Commander blurted. "They're walking right into Cabot's arms."

With the piece of paper still in his hand, Kay turned and began running stork-like down the hallway leading to the recreation lounge. By the time he got there he was gasping for air and could only stand and wheeze, "Tom . . . Slaughter."

Wing Commander Firth was in the lounge briefing a group of *Knights* on the guard schedule he'd developed. He was the first to reach Kay and caught him as he began to collapse.

"Hold on, man," Firth implored.

Sergeant Major Trevor Warwick was in the group of men listening to Firth. He quickly moved to help. As they half guided, half-dragged the gasping Kay to a chair at one of the tables, Warwick said, "Did he say Tom? If this is something about my son, I need to know."

"Of course, Trevor," the Wing Commander said. "But first we've got to get him calmed down." Then, he turned his attention back to Kay. "Slow down, Commander. Relax. Try to take a deep breath."

Kay nodded and blew in and out through pursed lips, struggling to catch his breath. Still, it was a full two minutes before he was calm enough to answer Firth's first question.

"What's wrong?"

Clive Kay looked around at the stunned faces in the room. They didn't know. Someone had to tell them. In desperation, he gasped, "Where's Edna?"

Firth frowned and shook his head. "I don't know," he said.

Warrant Officer Evan Gray was also among the group of men being briefed. He stepped forward. "I believe Edna is with Captain Mackenzie; in Eliza's office." He gave his here's-the- joke smile. "Battling with the Captain to get our grand strategy down on Eliza's computer."

"I don't think this is funny, Evan!" the Wing Commander snapped. "Go get her. We'll continue with Commander Kay."

Sufficiently chastised, Gray mumbled "Sorry," and did his turtle move with his head and shoulders and hurried off.

At that point, Trevor Warwick noticed the piece of paper in Commander Kay's hand. "What's this?" he said, taking the paper. He turned it over and read the scribbled note: *Tom called– stopping @ Slaughter.*

"Clive, what does this mean?" he said. And then it suddenly hit him. "Bloody Hell!" he exclaimed. He looked at Kay. "Edna took a call from Tom this morning?"

Kay nodded and started to speak, but Edna Stevens who was now standing at the door to the lounge cut him off. With a small tremble in her voice, she said, "I'm sorry. Tom said to tell you, Sergeant Major, and Wing Commander Firth."

She had tears in her eyes, but Firth gave that fact no pass. "Then why the bloody hell didn't you?" he bellowed.

Edna started to cry and another voice entered the fray. "Bugger you! Knock it off, Firth!" Captain Colin Mackenzie yelled back. "It's my bloody fault. I had her helping me with that bloody computer in Eliza's office."

It was Evan Gray who brought things back to earth. He was standing with Edna and Captain Mackenzie. "I don't get it," he said. "What is so awful about Edna taking a phone call from Tom Warwick?"

Edna sniffed. "He told me they, Tom, Harry, and the others, were stopping at Slaughter Bridge on the way back here. He said they would only be a little while."

"So?" said Gray. "It's a nice place; historical, you know."

"That's where Nurse Harriet sent that traitor Jock Cabot this morning," said Colin Mackenzie.

Wing Commander Firth had to raise his voice to be heard over the invective bouncing around the room. "How long ago did Tom call?"

Edna sniffed more, then shrugged. "I don't know, a little while."

Simon Firth considered, but just for a moment. He turned to Colin Mackenzie and said, "How much of our battle strategy do you have worked out?"

"Most of it is up here," Mackenzie said pointing to his head. "But Edna and I got some of it down. Well, the transportation, at least. I figure we can get everyone in one of our buses and that Land Rover Nurse Harriet drives."

The Wing Commander looked at Trevor Warwick. "What do you think?"

"You know what I think," Trevor said, in a low growl as he doubled up his fists.

Firth smiled and turned to Mackenzie. The Captain smiled back. "That's enough strategy for now," said the Wing Commander. He turned to the men in the room. "Listen up, men!" he shouted. "Get on your battle clothes! Get your weapons! And get out to the garage in back!" He looked at his watch. "You've got fifteen minutes!"

For a moment the room was absolutely silent. Then it exploded with loud voices and scuffling men, some limping or using canes, but moving.

56

General Baker-Smythe smiled to himself. Stealth, he thought–what a useful word. Major General Cabot had used it as camouflage for his unscrupulous greed. And now *he* was using it to put an end to the traitor Cabot had become.

He was certain that the Major General had no idea he'd lied about setting up a meeting with the Prime Minister; that he had a fiat from Saxon to do what he felt necessary regarding Cabot. The traitor wouldn't know he was on his way to take care of that problem; nearly there, in fact.

The General leaned up so Ethan Evans in the driver's seat of the rental car could hear him. "Corporal, tell me again what the woman in Slaughter Bridge told you."

"Her name is Katherine Ingall," said Evans. "She owns a property that backs up to the tourist section of Slaughter Bridge; the bridge itself and the fields where the Arthurian battles supposedly took place."

"And there is access by a private road?"

"Yes, sir. So visitors at the bridge wouldn't notice," the Corporal assured him.

Baker-Smythe chuckled softly. "Sort of like a back door entrance."

"Well, we're about to find out," said Evans. "The turn off is just ahead."

Moments later they turned off the B3314 onto a dirt road. A short way up the road, the General had Evans slow down, then come to a stop. He instructed him to get out, walk back to the highway, and flag the other cars so they wouldn't miss the turn. Once all six of the vehicles had turned in behind them, they proceeded up the road until they came to a small house and barn.

Corporal Evans said, "She told me to knock. She'd come out and show us the way."

Baker-Smythe nodded toward the house. "Well, do it!" he said, and Evans went up and knocked on the door.

Katherine Ingall was a big woman, tall and large boned, a blonde with bobbed hair, wearing jeans and a T-shirt that provided ample evidence she was female. She gave the impression that she was all business and proved it by coming right up to the car and opening the back door.

"This is Katherine Ingall, General," the Corporal called from behind her, his voice a half octave higher than normal.

Katherine Ingall reached one of her meaty hands into the car and said, "I just had to meet a hero like you. When they called me from Base Chivenor, they told me you were leading a mission to preserve our nation." She gave the General a broad smile and a vice-like grip on his hand when he offered it.

Then Katherine looked at the other cars parked behind the General's. She shook her head. "Whew!" she exclaimed. "I didn't know it was this many men. It's going to be a squeeze when you get up near the bridge."

"I'm sure we can handle it," said the General. "These are commandos."

Katherine grinned. "Like a war movie in my own back acres."

The Corporal could almost hear impatience rumbling from the look on the General's face. He took a chance and interrupted.

"Excuse me, Ms. Ingall, but we have a timeline. Could you show us where to go?"

Katherine Ingall looked as if she snapped to attention. "Oh, of course!" she said. "You get in the car and just follow me."

She started walking even before Evans was back in the driver's seat. The caravan of rental cars crawled along behind her past the barn and what looked like a vegetable garden until she reached a fence. She opened a gate in the fence and pointed toward a set of tracks in the grass, an overgrown continuation of the dirt road.

When Evans and the General pulled up next to her, Katherine Ingall said, "It ends in a stand of trees. From there you can look across what we call Arthur's Field all the way to the bridge." Then, with a slight wave, she stepped aside, and as each of the seven cars passed, she blew them a kiss.

57

Even though it was his idea, Tom Warwick was a bit nervous about stopping at Slaughter Bridge. The place could be packed with tourists, and that wouldn't be good with Harry aboard. On the other hand, the historian in Tom was intrigued to see this place. If he allowed his cynical side a vote, it could also be a test for the two who called themselves Merlyn and Arthur. He still didn't have them settled in his mind.

Then, when he turned into the parking area of the visitor's center, weighing the negative against the positive went out the window. There were only two other cars in the lot, an older, green Vauxhall SUV with London plates and a white two-door Ford Fiesta hatchback from Devon with a rental sticker on the rear window.

Tom parked, and they clambered out of the Mini Cooper, groaning and stretching their arms and legs. "We're a bunch of–what is the fish?" Merlyn said.

"Sardines," said Vivian with a grin. "Poor Harry." She turned to him. "I hope I didn't flatten your lap for good."

Harry rubbed his thighs. "When we get back to London, I'm coming to your McDonald's. You owe me a Big Mac."

"A what?" Arthur asked with a quizzical frown.

"It's a kind of hamburger," said Tom.

Now Arthur turned his frown on Tom. "What's that?"

"Meat and bread," Merlyn offered. "I perceive some traveler's hunger here. Perhaps we should proceed to the visitor's center. There we may possibly find meat pies or some crisps."

"Excellent!" said Vivian. "You've been studying our time."

Merlyn smiled and started to walk toward the visitor's center. As the others followed, Arthur handed Harry's hat to him. "I believe the word is clandestine," he said.

Harry pulled the hat on with a grumpy look. "Or sneaky."

There was a family of four in the small visitor's center, the occupants of the SUV, Tom figured. The mother and father were in their forties. The boy was a pre-teen in jeans and a T-shirt with a soccer team logo. His sister was a seven or eight year-old with a blonde ponytail and big blue eyes.

It was the little girl who made everyone gulp. The minute she saw Harry, she pointed at him and said something to her mother. Her mother looked at Harry for a moment, then shook her head. She took her daughter by the hand and walked her over to the husband, who was chatting with a clerk at the front of the center. The man finished his conversation, thanked the clerk, and they all went outside.

As they left, Tom said, "I'm going to see if I can get a brochure," and walked toward the clerk.

The rest of the Mini crew wandered around looking at the displays, except for Arthur. He stood transfixed in front of a large poster on the wall near the entrance. It was a painting of a knight in armor with a bloody sword lifted high. The words ARTHUR'S LAST BATTLE ran along the bottom of the poster.

It wasn't long before Merlyn moved up behind Arthur. "Not a good likeness," he said.

Arthur glanced at him, then turned back to the poster. "I've got a bad feeling about this," he said.

"I think someone already used that line," said Merlyn. "In the future, actually."

Arthur rolled his eyes. "Wizards," he said, shaking his head. He moved off to see what else was there.

At the front of the visitor's center, Tom had picked up a brochure. "Not a very busy day," he said to the clerk, a balding man in his fifties with a stomach somewhat larger than the unbuttoned yellow employee vest he was wearing. The smile he revealed at Tom's comment was oversized, too.

"Just that family and you folks," he said.

Tom returned the smile. "Who was in the white car?" he asked.

"What white car?" said the clerk.

"It's a rental, parked out in front," Tom said.

The clerk shrugged. "No one has been in here. Must have taken a walk on the trail. Down to the bridge or up to Worthyvale Manor. You don't want to miss the Manor. That's where Arthur's Stone is, where the Battle of Camlann took place."

Tom hesitated a moment, then nodded. "Thanks," he said. "That's where we're headed." He turned and started for the door. "Okay, everyone. We've got directions," he called to the others, waving his brochure. "Let's go see some history."

Arthur got a few laughs when he added a somewhat surly, "Again."

Outside, while Tom was looking at the directions, deciding which trail they wanted, Arthur walked over to the Mini and tried to open the door. It was locked. Merlyn saw Arthur fooling with the door handle. From several feet away, he raised an index finger. There was a small click and, on his next try, the door opened for Arthur.

Vivian gave Merlyn a squinty look. "I saw that," she said.

Merlyn flexed his finger and smiled slightly. "An early remote control."

When Tom noticed what he was doing, Arthur had already slipped on the scabbard and was taking Excalibur out of the car "Whoa! Wait a minute," Tom said. "You can't walk around wearing that."

"Why not?" asked Harry. He pointed at the visitor's center. "I saw a whole pile of plastic swords in there. I bet kids all over this place play with them." He grinned and swished an imaginary sword back and forth.

Tom shook his head angrily. "That's no toy. It's got to go back in the car." No one moved. After a moment, Tom insisted, "Now!"

Another moment passed, then Merlyn stepped in. "I don't think I'd try to take it away from him."

Arthur slowly moved his hand to the hilt of Excalibur and smiled.

Tom stared intensely at the King for a few seconds. Then the tension dissolved. "Right," he said. "Come on, everyone. Worthyvale Manor is this way."

Tom started walking, and the others followed him, except for Merlyn. He turned back to the visitor's center. "Sorry," he said. Then he shrugged with an embarrassed smirk. "Nature calls. I'll catch up with you."

"Just take this trail straight ahead," Tom called over his shoulder. "Don't be too long. You don't want to miss the battle."

"If only I could," Merlyn whispered to himself. Then he pointed a finger at the Mini Cooper and turned off Tom's mobile phone.

58

The sails had been let down and the ketch was just drifting. In the cabin, Josie and Henri had been sitting at the table talking for nearly thirty minutes. After a while, Francine had stopped blubbering, dried her eyes with a dishtowel, and joined them. But King Charles and Camilla could only guess at the subject of the conversation.

Finally, Charles interrupted. With an embarrassed smile, he said, "We don't understand French. What are you talking about?"

Francine looked up. "Evasion!" she said with a child-like grin.

Josie smiled. "Franny is–" She tipped her head and closed her eyes as if she was listening for something, then heard it. "Dramatic? Yes, I think that is it. We were only discuss."

"Discussing what?" asked Camilla.

"What to do next." Josie said.

Charles and Camilla exchanged glances. The King said, "I trust we get a vote on that?"

Henri cleared his throat for attention. Then he held up a forefinger and thumb and slowly closed the gap between them until it was quite small. *"Petit choice,"* he said.

"He thinks his idea is best," said Josie.

Francine nodded vigorously. "Chausey!"

"I don't understand," Charles said. He turned and looked at Camilla. She shook her head.

Josie got up from the table, opened a drawer under the microwave, took out a map, and rolled it out on the table. She searched for a moment, then put her finger on a spot in the English Channel a hair's breath from the coast of Normandy.

Charles leaned over and squinted. "I don't see anything."

Now Henri smiled. "That is idea." He pursed his lips and blew out making a *poof* sound. "No one see!"

The King leaned over and looked closer. There was a tiny dot on the map where Josie had pointed. "Is that an island?" he said.

Henri puffed up slightly and said, *"Plus de trois cents."*

Camilla leaned in next to Charles. "I have to see this. I think he said more than three hundred."

Josie said something in French to Henri. He made a face as if he'd tasted a bad wine. Josie repeated whatever she had said, and they got into an exchange that finally ended with Henri nodding his sullen agreement.

Josie smiled at Charles and Camilla. "I will be his translator."

"Fine," said Camilla. "Did he say what I thought he said?"

"Yes. But he was, how you say, blowing up? The dot on the map is Chausey Islands. There are many, many islands there."

Charles was clearly skeptical. "Over three hundred?" he said.

Josie glanced at Henri and he nodded. "At low tide." She said, putting her hand on the table. Then she raised her hand slowly up until it was above her head. "But only fifty-two when tide is high."

Henri said something in French. Josie nodded and translated. "Only one island is inhabit; Grande Ile. It is small. Less than two kilometers long and one half kilometer wide."

"And people *live* there?" said Camilla.

"Many come!" Henri slipped in.

He and Josie engaged in another somewhat protracted conversation, then she explained. "In the summer, when the ferry from Normandy operates, visitors come and stay in the Hotel du Fort."

The King couldn't stifle a snort. "This place has a hotel?"

Henri opened his mouth, but Josie cut him off. "Yes," she said. "It is open all summer long and has eight rooms. People can also rent a gite, a small apartment, at the old farm."

"What about the rest of the year? Like right now?" Camilla asked.

"Closed. And also is the restaurant," said Josie.

"So, no visitors?" said Charles.

"No. Only people who live there," Josie answered.

"And that is how many?" Charles asked.

Josie spoke with Henri, and then turned back to the King. "Henri says about thirty."

With a wary frown, Charles said, "How does Henri know all this?"

Now both Henri and Josie grinned. "He was born and raised there. Five of the thirty people are his family. The rest are friends."

Except for the creaking of the ketch as it wallowed in the water, there was silence in the cabin. Then Charles grinned back at them and said, "Well, let's get those sails back up!"

59

"How did you like the Ford Fiesta?" said Merlyn.

Major General Jack Cabot whirled around with a startled look. He thought he was alone in the small stand of Sycamore trees near the river, hadn't heard anyone behind him. The old man was nearly close enough to reach out and touch him.

"Damn!" Cabot said. "Be careful who you sneak up–" He stopped short when he recognized him. It was the old man from the war memorial, from the inn last night. "You," he murmured. "What are you doing here?"

Merlyn ignored the question and raised an eyebrow. "Isn't that what you're doing? Sneaking up on people?"

The Major General didn't answer.

"They passed here, didn't they," said Merlyn. "You saw him; the one you're after; the Prince, and some others. Yet, you are still here?"

Cabot bore down on the Wizard with an icy stare. "I said what are you doing here?"

Merlyn smiled warmly. "Remembering," he said softly.

"*Remembering?*" said Cabot. "Do you *remember* I told you to stay away from me?"

The Wizard turned and gazed off into the field across the river in silence.

After a moment, Cabot said, "Remembering *what?*" He was in no mood for puzzles.

"King Arthur," said the Wizard. "And those he battled here at Camlann."

Cabot frowned. "Camlann is only a place of legend."

Merlyn smiled again and nodded. "I thought you might know of it. For you have reason."

"Most Britons know something of King Arthur," Cabot said.

"What do you know of Camlann?" asked Merlyn.

Cabot shook his head in frustration and sighed. "They say King Arthur's last battle was there. His illegitimate son, Mordred, had proclaimed himself king and stolen Arthur's wife while he was away fighting the Saxons. Arthur returned, they fought at Camlann, and the bastard son got what he deserved. Is that enough legend, old man? It has nothing to do with me."

"What he deserved?" said Merlyn.

Cabot stood there a moment scowling at the Wizard. Finally he said, "For trying to seize the throne, to claim power over the people."

"As others attempt to do now?"

"I told you to be careful, old man," said Cabot. He took a step toward Merlyn as he continued what clearly sounded like a threat. "You are close to the edge. Take care you don't slip and fall off."

"I must caution you also, Major General. For, you are not the only one using stealth. Another is using it against you even now."

That gave Cabot pause, at least for a moment. He stopped and looked around the surrounding woods. Then he shook his head and approached Merlyn. As he drew close, the Wizard seemed to relax.

Merlyn said, "I'm not concerned so long as you are here. After all, you hold the Victoria Cross, Britain's highest decoration for valor. For doing what is right. I believe you will do what is right now."

"Damn you, old man!" the Major General said. "You don't fool me. I know what you're getting at, but you are wrong! Your vision of right and wrong doesn't always apply. In times of great crisis, when leaders fail, it is sometimes necessary for someone to assume power, to make the difficult decisions."

"And, naturally, you would know when that time has come. It's in your heritage."

"What do you mean, my heritage?" demanded Cabot.

"Do you know so little of your family legacy?"

"I know that Cabot men have long dedicated their lives to the protection of the British Isles."

Merlyn nodded in agreement. "This is true," he said. Then he looked off toward the field again. A sudden breeze stirred the grass, rattling leaves on the few trees standing there. "But what of the other influence?" he asked. "The dark seed?"

Clearly aggravated, Cabot shook his head. He'd had enough. "I don't know what you're talking about," he exclaimed. "And I don't care!" he added as he turned and started to walk away through the Sycamores.

The Wizard waited for him to move four meters away, six meters. Then he said, "Do you know you are related to King Arthur–through his bastard son, Mordred?"

It stopped Cabot in mid-step. He whirled around and shouted, "That's a lie!" then caught his breath. He stood there a moment before he whispered, "Damn you to hell."

He was alone.

60

"What the bloody hell are you doing, Captain?" asked Wing Commander Firth.

He'd just stepped out the back door of the Camelford Veterans Home and found Colin Mackenzie leading what appeared to be an exercise class next to the bus in the parking lot. The Captain himself was on the concrete doing push ups. A few of the men were down there with him, struggling to lift their bodies with skin and bone arms. Most were watching, leaning on canes or umbrellas and cricket bats.

"Battle preparation!" Mackenzie said, puffing out air. He did one more push up, then got to his feet.

"What rubbish!" Firth said. "You're going to have our men exhausted before we even get there."

"Someone has to take command!" Mackenzie declared. "I've done a complete weapons check. Approved their uniforms. And I've tested our transportation. Both the bus and the Land Rover are full of petrol and both started on the first turnover."

"You *approved* their uniforms?" said Firth with a raised eyebrow.

Mackenzie tried to stifle a grin without much success. "Actually, I created them." He turned and looked at the group of men. They all had splotches of brown and green on their clothes. "At least the camouflage."

The Wing Commander sighed and slowly shook his head. "Colin, you've ruined a pair of pants and a shirt for every one of these men."

"They all agreed to it before I did anything."

"It's spray paint, isn't it," said Firth. It wasn't a question.

"I was all ready to go, walking around and around. I found a couple of cans in the maintenance shack," Mackenzie explained. "Don't worry, I checked it. It's fast drying."

The Wing Commander let a moment pass before he spoke. When he did, it was calmly and quietly. "Where are the rest of the men?"

The Captain glanced at the group standing by the bus. Only fourteen of the thirty-two men who had agreed to protect Prince Harry were there. "Twits!" he said, curling a lip. "We don't need those wankers! Should have used them for target practice."

"Colin, you're crashing around like a bull in—" Firth started.

Mackenzie butted in with, "Bugger you and your china shop! We *are* bulls, and we're going to see that traitor Cabot gets gored. And not just in the arse."

The Captain turned to the cluster of men huddled by the bus. "Isn't that right, Knights of Camelford?" he shouted. Five or six of them yelled back. As many more frowned and tilted their heads as if they couldn't hear him. One jabbed the air with a fist in a victory sign.

Simon Firth sighed again and changed the subject. "I asked Harriet Claiborne for permission to use her Land Rover. She said only if we let her drive, and I agreed. She's changing her clothes now. Let's get the men aboard the bus so we'll be ready when she comes out here."

Captain Mackenzie smiled. "An excellent decision, Simon–for once. Bringing Harriet along, I mean. This is going to be a blood red day. We may need a nurse."

The Wing Commander was a little worried about Mackenzie. The Scot was always loud and unruly, but this morning he thought the Captain seemed over the top. His normal ruddy complexion had gone pale. He was a little bug-eyed. And he was sweating through his shirt. As a concession and, hopefully to calm him down, Firth said, "Why don't you pick out two or three men to join you and ride with Harriet? She'll need your direction, possibly your protection."

Mackenzie reacted as if he'd been deeply insulted. "That's a job for a nancy like Kay," he declared. "I'll be driving the bus! Leading the attack!"

Clive Kay was in the group of men by the bus. He immediately started a quick stork walk toward Firth and Mackenzie shouting, "You take that back!"

The Wing Commander stepped forward to cut him off. "Stand down, Commander," Firth said. "I'm taking the assignment to ride with Nurse Harriet. I'd like you to take on another important task."

Kay had stopped. With a dour look, he said, "I will carry out my duty."

"Excellent," said Firth.

"What is it?" Kay asked.

"I want you to ride shotgun on the bus. You and Captain Mackenzie can work as a team. To make sure the men get through any enemy fire or other dangers on the way to Slaughter Bridge."

Both Kay and Mackenzie were caught speechless. Before either recovered, Harriet Claiborne came out the back door in jeans and a dark green hoodie carrying a medical bag.

The Wing Commander took advantage of the moment. "Listen up!" he yelled. "Sergeant Major Warwick, Major Guy Samson, and CPO Grimsley join me in the Land Rover. The rest of you, get on the bus. Next stop, victory!"

However, the next stop was far from what he or any of the men imagined. From the moment the bus pulled out of the parking area behind the Veterans Home, Captain Colin Mackenzie was louder and brasher than any of the men had ever seen him. He drove like he was a new member of the British Automobile Racing Club, roaring around turns, grinding through the gears and slamming his foot on the acceleration pedal in the straightaway. And all the while, he kept up a constant stream of orders. Sit down in back! Careful with your weapons! Stay alert! Be on the lookout for the enemy! Assemble in ranks outside the bus when we arrive! Don't engage the enemy until ordered!

It wasn't far to Slaughter Bridge, but the ride seemed as if it would never end. When it finally did, the men got their biggest shock.

Commander Clive Kay was in the front seat across from Mackenzie and the first to notice something was amiss. From the way he'd been driving, Kay thought the Captain would throw the lever to open the door and jump out of his seat. But nothing happened when the bus came to a stop. Mackenzie sat hunched over the steering wheel, gripping it tightly with both hands, staring straight ahead.

"Stay seated!" Kay called to the men. He leaned closer to Mackenzie. "We're here, Captain," he said. "You need to open the door."

Mackenzie didn't react.

Kay repeated, "You need to open the door."

After a moment, still hunched over, his hands still gripping the steering wheel, the Captain slowly turned his head to look at Commander Kay. There were tears in his eyes.

"I . . . can't," Mackenzie said.

"What do you mean? You can't move?" asked Kay.

He shook his head. "No, not that."

Kay waited.

Finally, Mackenzie said, "I can't go."

"Why?"

A tear slid slowly down the Captain's cheek. He tried to blink it away, but another followed. "We're just a bunch of old men," Mackenzie said. As he put his head down on the steering wheel, he whimpered, "I'm afraid. Oh, God, I'm afraid."

Commander Kay turned and looked at the faces of the men waiting to get off the bus, men willing to lay their lives down for something they believed in.

"It's all right," he said to the Captain. Then he reached over and shoved home the lever that opened the bus door. "Knights of Camelford, disembark!" he shouted.

61

The visitor's trail to Worthyvale Manor was lush with ferns, cherry laurel, and other flowering shrubs growing under a canopy of Oak, Silver Birch, and Sycamore trees. It gave Tom, who was leading the group from the map in his brochure, another chance to play history professor.

He started with a comment that drew groans from everyone. "We're walking through a verdant tunnel into the past."

Vivian chuckled and tried to save him with a touch of humor but without much success. "You mean this is a time tunnel and we're getting younger?"

Tom stopped and turned around. "No, really!" he said. He waved a hand around at the plants on either side of the trail. "These shrubs, flowers, and trees may be living pieces of history."

Harry joined in with a smile. "Funny, I don't remember that lesson at Eton. Was it in First Level Cornwall Flowers and Trees? Or in British Tunnels?"

Tom gave the Prince a piercing look, jerked around, and started down the trail again.

"Wait! I want to hear the rest," King Arthur called, surprising everyone, including Tom. "What history?" he asked.

Tom stopped again. "Well, I'm glad to hear we have at least one student of history."

Merlyn had just caught up with them, and this brought a smile to his face. "More than a student," he said. "Arthur Pendragon *is* history."

"All right, all right," said Vivian. "If we must have a lesson, let's get to it. Can you teach and walk at the same time?"

"Very funny," Tom said petulantly. He turned and started off again. After a few steps, he held up the brochure and waved it. "According to this, King Arthur's stone lies in the remains of an eighteenth century garden created by Charlotte Boscawen.

Vivian rolled her eyes, but let him go on with his *lesson*.

"She was Lady Falmouth, daughter of Hugh Boscawen, the first Viscount of Falmouth."

"You mean she actually planted some of these trees and flowers? That long ago?" asked Vivian.

"It's possible," Tom said, now smiling.

"Swell," said Harry. "What's King Arthur's stone?"

Tom nodded his approval. "That takes us further back in history." He glanced at a page in the brochure, then said, "It was first recorded by Cornish antiquary, Richard Carew in 1602."

"Cornish what?" Harry asked.

"Antiquary," said Merlyn. "One who deals in antiques or items from the past."

"Okay, so it's old. What is it?" said Harry.

"Your timing is excellent, Prince. We're about to see for ourselves," Tom said.

They had come to a fork in the trail and two signs with arrows, Worthyvale Manor and King Arthur's stone. Tom pointed to the latter, and they started down that path. It wasn't long before the land began to slope downhill, and soon they came to a stream. Under a small stand of Sycamores, at the dank edge of the water, lay a huge stone with an inscription carved into it. For a few minutes they were silent, simply looking at the stone in wonderment. It was more than 270 cm long with words from some lost language cut into its edge.

Finally, Arthur said, "What does the paper you hold say?"

Tom took a moment to read the brochure. "The inscription is Latin and Ogam, an ancient Celtic script. Because of its age and because some of it has been damaged, there have been many interpretations of its meaning throughout history. But everyone agrees that it's around fifteen hundred years old. According to legend, that's when–"

Arthur finished the sentence for Tom, "the battle of Camlann was fought."

"And that's the reason they call it King Arthur's stone?" asked Harry. "Fairly shaky, if you ask me."

Tom shook his head. "Actually, quite a few historians believe the inscription reads 'Here lies the son of Arthur, the Great' or something close to that."

Merlyn broke the silence that followed. "Arthur?" he said, with an eyebrow raised.

The King looked at him, and the Wizard nodded slightly.

"They are wrong," said Arthur.

"What?" blurted Tom. He knew he shouldn't. These were friends, but he felt challenged, and pushed back with an edge in his voice. "You simply walk up here, take your first look, and declare the experts wrong?"

"Tom Warwick!" Vivian scolded.

He glanced at her, but pushed on. "Do you even read Latin? Or Ogam?"

Arthur gazed into Tom's eyes for a moment, then shook his head. "I don't read at all."

With a smirk, Tom said, "I thought so."

"And this is not my first look at the stone," the King added. He pointed back the way they'd come. "It was up there on the top of this rise when I first saw it. It had the same markings then as now."

That silenced everyone for a moment. Finally, Tom managed, "When?"

"Before the Battle of Camlann," said Arthur.

"But who . . ." Harry asked.

Arthur glanced at Merlyn. Another nod. "The old ones," the King said. "Those who some called Druids."

The only sound was several intakes of breath. Then Tom said, "Crap! I had no right to attack you like that. I'm sorry."

"You should be!" said Vivian.

The King drew Excalibur out of the scabbard, just enough to expose the blade. "It could be dangerous," he said with a grin.

"I have to get used to it," said Tom. "With you around, the history professor becomes the student." Then suddenly, his eyes brightened. "Your Majesty, would you mind if I ask you a few questions?"

"You may call me Arthur."

Tom felt a mild blush crawl up his neck.

Before he could respond, Harry interjected, "You still have to address me as Prince."

"Careful, Harry," said Arthur. He pulled his sword out again to expose the blade, and they all laughed. Then he turned to Tom. "What do you want to know?"

Tom closed his eyes to think for a moment, then opened them. "Where exactly was the battle of Camlann?"

The King pointed across the stream. "In the fields beyond this water. It was a river then, much wider."

"I'm trying to picture it," Tom said. "Where were you, and where was Mordred with his men?"

"My knights and I were here, just across the water," said Arthur. Then he pointed at the far side of the fields. "Mordred and his army were hiding in the distant trees." After a few seconds, he added, "Just as those men are now."

"*What*?" Tom said. He looked where Arthur had pointed.

"Looks like a crowd of people to me," said Vivian.

Tom squinted. "Who are they? I can't tell."

Merlyn had reached into the pocket of his coat. He pulled out a tarnished nautical spyglass and handed it to Tom. "This may help," he said.

"Where in the world did you get this?" asked Tom.

"Pirates," Merlyn said.

Tom frowned and turned to Arthur.

The King shrugged. "Wizard."

Tom shook his head, and put the spyglass to his eye. It took him a couple of turns to focus. As he did, his smile evaporated. "I think they're military," he said.

62

From behind Tom, a quivering voice shouted, "You are wrong! We are not military."

Tom and everyone at the stream whirled around to find a bunch of red-faced, old men struggling down the slope toward them. All of them had green and brown spots on their clothes. Commander Clive Kay was in the lead, waving a Colt 45 around. Wing Commander Simon Firth was behind him carrying a parade sword. The rest of the codgers had cricket bats, canes, kitchen knives, and other dangerous arms such as umbrellas and frying pans.

When Kay made it down to the stream he stopped and stood there, bent over at the waist, holding his side, and tried to catch his breath. Simon Firth took advantage of the pause. "We are knights," he managed through his wheezing. "The Knights of Camelford."

From somewhere in the group still coming down the incline a female voice called, "And one nurse!"

It produced the first response from the group at the stream. King Arthur called back, "Harriet? Is that you?"

Between the gulps of air he was sucking in Commander Kay said, "Yes, Harriet is here. We all came."

Tom was frowning and obviously a bit angry. "Why in the world? We're not lost. We can take care of ourselves. I called and told Edna to let you know we were stopping here."

Simon Firth was recovering more quickly than Kay. "That's the problem!" he exclaimed. "Major General Jock Cabot, the Commandant of the Royal Marines, was at the Veterans Home last night. And again this morning. He was using another name and dressed in civilian clothes. We believe he's undercover, looking for Prince Harry."

There was obviously more, but Firth finally had to stop and take a breath. Clive Kay finished it off for him. "And he could be here at Slaughter Bridge."

Suddenly, everyone was talking.

Arthur said, "Give me that!" and reached out to Tom for the spyglass.

As he gave it to him, Tom said, "Crap!" for the second time this morning. "I told you we'd be at Slaughter Bridge. Why did you let him come here?"

"Tom!" Vivian chided. "You don't *let* the Commandant of Marines do anything."

"I didn't know he was with the Marines," said a breathy Harriet Claiborne, who had just made it down to the water. "He said he wanted to go somewhere interesting."

"Great," said Prince Harry. "As second in line to the British throne, I've always wanted to be interesting." He looked around at the group of old men. "Well, at least my protectors are. They wear polka dot uniforms."

"This situation is a long way from humorous, Harry," Arthur said. The King was still looking through the spyglass. "I count more than twenty-five men in those trees. They are all in uniforms. And they all have weapons."

It was more than enough to turn Harry serious, even somewhat frightened. "Are they coming this way?" he said.

His question hung in a long moment of silence. Then Merlyn said, "Not yet."

Arthur lowered the spyglass and turned to the Wizard. "They will?" he asked, although he was sure of the answer.

Merlyn simply nodded.

Arthur moved to Commander Kay, grasped him by the arm, and walked with him over to Simon Firth.

"What?" said the Wing Commander.

"This is not your battle," said Arthur. "Take your people back up the hill, back to the Veterans Home where they will be safe."

At first, they didn't understand, then both Kay and Firth looked at Arthur Pendragon, High King of all Britain, as if he were crazy.

"You've given these old men life, a reason to wake up in the morning. Would you now kill us all before the battle?" said the Wing Commander.

Kay glanced to the knights spread along the stream. "And darken every memory?"

"What about Tom's father?" said Arthur. "Is he well enough?"

The Commander huffed. "It would hurt him more to be singled out for special privilege than being wounded. Trevor nearly knocked me silly. He'll be in the advance wave."

Arthur turned to Merlyn, and the Wizard pointed a long, crooked finger back at him.

The King nodded. Then he sighed and turned to his army of knights, assessing their strengths and weaknesses. Some were still out of breath from the walk here. The postures of many indicated back or knee problems. Nearly all were wearing glass on their eyes, a few with thick glass. Many were overweight. Those who weren't, appeared to be weak bags of bones.

On the positive side, few would be likely to injure themselves with their own weapons. Another plus was that they were all veterans, and at least some had probably seen battle. They would have an idea of what to expect. They would follow orders, if they could hear them. Perhaps most important was the fact that they were here at all, and what that said about their hearts.

Arthur shook his head. It was a sad lot. Still, the Knights of Camelford could do well for the plan he now had in mind.

"Arthur?" said Merlyn, interrupting the King's thoughts. "They are moving this way."

Arthur took a quick look through the spyglass, then said, "Here, Tom. You'll need this." He tossed the spyglass back to him. "Go with Merlyn. Take your wife and Prince Harry into those trees." The King pointed toward a stand of Sycamores farther downstream.

Tom wasn't happy about it. "What is this? You always make the Warwicks run from the battle?" he asked.

"For a different reason this time," said Arthur. He put his hand on Tom's shoulder. "Sir Thomas of Warwick, I charge you with the safety of the Royal Prince."

When Harry tried to protest, Arthur put his hand on the handle of Excalibur. "It has to be," he said softly. "For both of you." It was enough to elicit weak smiles from both men.

Then the King raised his voice so everyone could hear him. "Knights of Camelford, we need your help now!" He pointed to Commander Kay and Wing Commander Firth as he shouted, "Follow your leaders across the stream and set up a defensive position against the enemy who is advancing across the fields to kidnap or harm your Prince."

Arthur glanced at Merlyn and got one more nod, this time with a somber face. The Wizard pointed out Harriet Claiborne standing on the edge of the gathered knights. The King moved to her and she smiled, with the warm and radiant look he remembered from their first meeting.

"Am I still speaking your language?" said Arthur.

Her smile softened. "Yes, but I'm not going to understand what you're about to say."

"I want you to be safe."

"This is my life. They need me."

"Not only them," the King said. He took her face gently in his hands and kissed her forehead. Then he turned and moved off. As he disappeared into the trees lining the stream, he could hear the knights splashing into the water.

63

"What the bloody hell?"

"Sir?" Corporal Ethan Evans said to the General.

Baker-Smythe handed the binoculars he'd been using to the Corporal. "What the hell is that by the stream, Evans Corporal?" he demanded, reverting to the snide tag he'd pinned on Evans. "That doesn't look to me like we're sneaking up on anyone. Order the Alert Platoon to halt until we figure this out."

"Yes, sir!" said the Corporal.

He stopped the advance, passing the word to the men to rest. Then he spent some time focusing the binoculars, panning along the stream in the distance. Finally he said, "It looks like an old age pensioner's picnic to me."

When there was no response, he kept panning slowly and then suddenly stopped. "One of those old men has a gun, a revolver," he said.

"God damn, Cabot! Let me see!" the General said. He reached out for the binoculars.

The Corporal made the mistake of shaking his head slightly, and vastly compounded it by saying, "It's not the Major General."

Baker-Smythe blew up. In the midst of reaching for the gun at his waist, he caught himself and instead yelled, "Give me those bloody glasses! And shut your mouth!"

Evans was stunned by what had just happened. His hand was shaking as he passed the binoculars to the General.

Baker-Smythe yanked them away and put them up to his eyes. He worked the focus, then panned left and right. After a fruitless minute, he said, "Where?"

The Corporal hesitated only momentarily.

And the General blasted him again. "I said, where, God damn it?"

"Moving back and forth among the group of men on this side of the stream. Tall and skinny, walks like a stork."

Baker-Smythe spent another minute looking before he found Commander Clive Kay. He studied the scene for a minute more. Then, in a considerably calmed voice, he said, "I don't know who he is, but I know *what* he is."

"Sir?" said the Corporal.

The corners of the General's mouth turned up slightly. "A diversion," he said. "All of those men are. Something unexpected. A distraction to take our attention off our goal."

Corporal Evans frowned, but said nothing.

Baker-Smythe chuckled softly, deep down in his chest. "Positive proof that our target is here." He handed the binoculars back to the Corporal. "Well, Corporal, you and your men are going to give them a show, a lesson on what happens to those who fool with General Ian Baker-Smythe, with the government of Great Britain."

Evans just stood there, waiting.

The General pointed toward the stream. "Resume your advance, Corporal," he said. "Your mission is to kill or capture every one of those men."

Corporal Evans hesitated. He was desperately trying to think of a way to question Baker-Smythe's order, when the General drew his revolver and used it to motion the platoon as he shouted, "Forward!"

It was enough to snap the Corporal into action. He twitched as if he'd been shocked, then turned to the platoon and called, "Weapons ready! The enemy is at the stream. Kill or capture." He took a breath, stepped out in front of the platoon, and as he started walking called, "Advance at my pace. Fire only when ordered."

The General watched with satisfaction as the platoon moved away from him toward the stream, ever closer to the destiny he believed was his.

64

"I knew we shouldn't trust him! I knew it from the beginning!" exclaimed Clive Kay. He was kneeling next to Simon Firth in the middle of the knights who had splashed across the stream. They were all soaked and covered with runny splotches of paint that might have earned a smile from Captain Mackenzie. For now, it actually looked like camouflage.

Wing Commander Firth rolled his eyes at Kay's outburst. "Quiet Commander!" he said in a rasping whisper. "What the bloody hell are you talking about? We shouldn't trust who?"

Bringing it down only half a notch, the Commander grumbled, "That snake oil shyster, Arthur. Or whatever his true name is."

Kay felt something move behind him. When he turned, he decided he might have been more selective with his metaphor.

It was nurse Harriet, crouched close behind him. She leaned up to his ear and said, "Commander, I would be careful when you defame a person who has a sword that has a name."

Kay suddenly stood. "Don't threaten me! I'm not the coward here!"

Simon Firth grabbed the Commander's arm and pulled, trying to get him to kneel back down. "Clive, get down!" he demanded. "The marines are coming."

Kay jerked away and started moving among the knights. "Arthur, the snake! He's the one who tricked us into helping him. He's the one who upset Colin. He's the one who ran away, leaving us to fight his battle!"

As the Commander passed by Trevor Warwick, the Sergeant Major stuck out his foot and Kay crashed to the ground.

"Idiot!" the Sergeant Major yelled. "I don't give a whit if you make yourself a target, but I refuse to let you make arses out of us all!"

He jumped on Kay's gangly legs, holding them down.

As Kay thrashed around trying to get up, Warrant Officer Evan Gray joined Trevor. He took the top half, sitting on the Commander's chest. "I wish I could make this funny, but it isn't," he said.

Almost immediately Clive Kay gave up thrashing and lay still. "I can't breathe," he said, gasping. "Get off!"

"You'll stay down and be quiet?" asked Trevor.

Kay nodded.

Warrant Officer Gray snickered. "Commander Clive Kay, being quiet? Now, *that's* funny!"

"All right, Evan, you got your joke," Trevor said. "Now let him up." He held onto the Commander's legs while Evan Gray got off his chest. When Kay didn't try anything, Trevor released the legs and sat up.

The Commander lay there while he took a couple of deep breaths, then struggled up beside Trevor Warwick. They looked at each other from only inches away.

"You are a bastard, you know?" said Kay.

"I am a Warwick and a Knight of Camelford," Trevor answered.

Clive Kay stared at him a moment, then closed his eyes and shook his head in frustration. When he opened his eyes, they were brimmed with tears. "Why did he leave us?" he asked. "We don't know what to do."

Trevor looked off across the field where the marines were still moving toward them. "You know what your problem is, Clive?" he said. "Your problem isn't King Arthur. Or what he does or doesn't do. Your problem is the same as Colin's, the same one all of us have. You're old. And you're afraid."

Commander Kay blinked and a tear started slowly sliding down his cheek. Just before it reached his chin, someone broke the knights' pitiable attempt at silence and yelled, "Look!"

It was their leader, Wing Commander Simon Firth, who yelled. He was standing and pointing toward the approaching marines.

65

Corporal Evans saw him out of the corner of his eye, a solitary man approaching the platoon from the trees and underbrush on the east side of the field. The corporal raised his hand and stopped the platoon. He'd only met the man face to face once. However, even in civilian clothes, even at this distance, he knew who it was.

Looking over his shoulder at his men, the corporal called, "Platoon, halt! Hold your fire!"

Then he moved a few meters in front of the platoon and waited. It was two minutes that seemed like years. When the man finally drew close, Corporal Evans saluted.

Major General Jock Cabot smiled. "Corporal Evans, isn't it?"

"Yes, sir!" said the Corporal. He was still holding the salute.

"At ease, Corporal," Cabot said.

"Yes, sir." Evans dropped his salute and stood at ease, his hands clasped behind his back, feet slightly apart.

"I thought I ordered you to have your men stand down, Corporal."

"Yes sir, you did," said Evans.

"What are you doing here?"

Evans hesitated. He turned and glanced back at General Baker-Smythe. The General was still standing at the edge of the trees where the cars were parked.

"It was ordered by the General," he said. "He told me he was in command of the platoon. Our mission was to capture or kill an assassin involved in the attack on the Royal Family." He glanced back at the General again. "At first, that is."

Cabot's brow furled. "What do you mean, at first?"

"When we got here and the General saw all of those men at the stream, he changed the mission. He said they were a diversion set up by the target and ordered us to capture or kill all of them. He said we would teach them a lesson."

"You know who they are?" asked Cabot. He didn't wait for an answer. "They're men from the Camelford Veterans Home. Most of them in their seventies and eighties."

"We used binoculars from those trees," Evans said. He pointed to the clump of Sycamores where their cars were hidden. "I saw that they were old men. They were all dressed in a sorry excuse for camouflage. And they were carrying a weird collection of things that might be used as weapons; cricket bats, frying pans, canes. One of them even had a revolver. But no, I didn't know they were veterans."

"They're not a diversion, Corporal. They're here trying to protect someone from me."

"What?" queried Evans. He was stunned. "I don't understand, sir. Who would they need to protect from you?"

Cabot smiled sadly. "Someone who can prove there is no assassin. There never was. The Royal Family was kidnapped by a small contingent of Royal Marines. They are being held on the Isles of Sicily."

"But . . . why?" said the Corporal.

"It's complicated." The Major General gave a slight shake of his head and continued. "King Charles refused to give his assent to a new act of Parliament, The Emergency Powers Act. It had a lot of good about it, but it would likely turn the Prime Minister into a dictator. A group of men, including me, thought they could force Charles to give his assent."

He sighed and shook his head again. "It has taken me far too long to admit it, but I know it was wrong. And I'm going to try to make amends."

Corporal Evans was speechless.

The Major General pointed toward the stream. "Those brave men are trying to protect the one member of the Royals who escaped, the one who can put an end to this conspiracy–Prince Harry."

With this extra shock, Evans found his voice. "Holy Jesus!" he said. "Why? What kind of person would do this?"

Over Evans shoulder, Cabot had been watching General Baker-Smythe stomp toward them. He tipped his head in the General's direction. "Maybe you should ask him to explain."

Evens twisted around just as Baker-Smythe stopped a few meters away. The General's face was flushed; a bulging vein throbbed at his temple. He gulped a couple of breaths, then pointed at Cabot and shouted, "Restrain this traitor! Immediately!"

Corporal Evans was completely taken aback. "But General, this is Major General–" was all he got out before Baker-Smythe cut him off.

"What kind of lies has he been telling?" he demanded.

Evans looked at Jock Cabot and something happened. The Corporal's face took on a resolute firmness. He was calm. He knew what he would do, what was right. He turned to the General and said, "No, General. You're out of order."

Without hesitation, General Baker-Smythe drew the 9mm Browning at his hip and shot Cabot in the chest.

Corporal Evans made the mistake of bending down, trying to help Cabot and ended up in the grasp of Baker-Smythe. With an arm around his neck and the Browning pressed against his temple, the General yanked Evans to his feet.

"Careful, gentlemen!" Baker-Smythe warned the men in the platoon. "It's not worth dying to try to stop me."

Still holding Evans, he started to slowly move away, backing toward the trees where the cars were waiting. Then, from behind Baker-Smythe, a commanding voice said, "You're wrong, General. This is as far as you go."

In one sudden move, the General let go of Evans and spun around right into the thrust of Excalibur. As the blade penetrated his heart, the gun in his hand fired wildly, his eyes widened in surprise, then life slowly faded from them. His body slipped from the sword and crumpled to the ground.

66

When he heard the first gun shot, Merlyn took nurse Harriet and Prince Harry by the hand. "Come with me. We need you," he said. The Wizard led them out of the trees and started toward the platoon of marines out in the field.

Suddenly there was a strong wind blowing, then they were there, next to the marines.

Prince Harry whirled around, looking back at the trees by the stream, then at the marines. "What the . . .?"

With a guilty smile, Merlyn shrugged and said, "Sorry. We needed to get here quickly."

Corporal Evans was still in shock, but he'd pulled himself together enough to retain command of the platoon. He'd ordered the men to remain in place. Then he spent a moment looking at the General, more to make sure he was dead than any concern for him.

Arthur was standing near the body, wiping blood from Excalibur. The Corporal clearly intended to stay his distance. His voice had a slight tremble in it as he said, "Thank you. I'm sure you saved my life." Then he tilted his head and looked more closely at Arthur. "Who are you? Where did you come from?"

The King sheathed Excalibur. "You don't want to know," he said. Then he flicked his hand toward Cabot. "You have your hands full with him."

Evans followed the flick and saw Jock Cabot still sprawled on the ground. He took Arthur's advice and hurried to the Major General. He was squatted, next to Cabot when Merlyn, Prince Harry and Harriet appeared.

Harriet pointed. "He's the man from this morning!"

"Cabot?" said Harry. "The one who's after me?"

The Corporal looked up. "You're wrong. I talked with him. He wasn't after anyone. He was trying to stop us from killing all of you. The General shot him."

Harriet shook her head in exasperation. "Is everyone just going to talk? This man needs help." She went to Cabot, shooed Corporal Evans away, and said, "Let me see him. I'm a nurse."

The Corporal said, Of course," He acted relieved, as if he didn't know what he was doing anyway. He stood and walked over to Harry and Merlyn.

Evans pointed toward Arthur who was still standing beyond the platoon close to the body of General Baker-Smythe. "The man with the sword saved my life," he said. "Maybe a good number of you people, too. He told me I didn't want to know who he is." With a nervous grin, he added, "And I'm not about to ask again."

The Wizard smiled. "Probably doesn't want to end up in court."

Harry rolled his eyes. "You know that is absolute rubbish!" he said to Merlyn. "I'm going to tell them who he is!"

Merlyn reached the flat of his hand out toward Harry's throat and whatever he was going to say didn't come out. "No, Prince," the Wizard said softly. "Tell them who *you* are."

Evans had heard enough for something to click. "Actually, you do look familiar," he said.

"He should," said Merlyn, putting his hand down.

Harry had a small coughing fit. He gave the Wizard an icy glare, but then shook his head and grinned. "Does Prince Harry ring a bell?" he asked the Corporal.

"Oh, my God," Evans murmured. He turned to his men. "Platoon, ten-hut!" he called and they snapped to. The Corporal took a breath to calm himself. Then he said, "This man is His Royal Highness, Prince Harry."

Despite being at attention, a round of exclamations, including a couple of Wah-Whos, popped out of the marines.

It stopped short when a high-pitched voice screamed, "Quiet!"

Everyone turned to Harriet who was sitting on the ground beside Jock Cabot. "What is it, Harriet?" said Merlyn.

"He's alive. I've got the bleeding stopped, but we need to get him to a hospital."

Corporal Evans was already on his mobile phone. "I'm requesting a helicopter. It should be here in less than twenty minutes."

Merlyn took the Corporal aside. "We would like the Prince to ride back to your base in the helicopter. There are still those who would try to stop him from telling the truth about the Royals."

"Certainly. The Major General told me about the kidnapping. We'll provide protection," said Evans. "So the Prince can tell all of England."

The Wizard then motioned to Harry and they moved a short distance away from the platoon. Merlyn filled Harry in on the agreement to have him go in the helicopter. Then he told him something else, and got a nod and a large smile.

67

Wing Commander Simon Firth wasn't sure what was happening out in the field. There had been two gunshots and the military men had stopped advancing. With his eyesight, the spyglass hadn't been much help. But he thought he could make out a man with Merlyn's stature and flowing white hair.

"What is he doing out there?" he asked.

"Who are you talking about?" said Commander Kay.

"It looks like Merlyn."

"Let me see," Kay said, reaching for the glass.

Firth gave him the spyglass with a cynical, "To prove what? Two blind men are better than one?"

Before Kay could come up with a comeback, they both flinched at a sudden thumping sound. A helicopter had appeared from nowhere and was descending for a landing near the group of military men.

All of the knights by the stream were on their feet, some moving toward the middle of the field. Shouting and waving, Firth and Kay were able to stop them and ordered everyone back to their positions.

Firth put Sergeant Major Trevor Warwick in command, then he and Kay set off across the field toward the helicopter. They hadn't gone far when a voice called from behind.

It was Tom Warwick. His wife, Vivian, was with him. "Wait for us!" he yelled. "We're all alone. Merlyn took Harriet and the Prince out there."

Clive Kay gave a derisive shake of his head. "It's a wizard's office party."

"Don't be rude," said Firth. "You could end up a frog."

"Better than that coward who calls himself Arthur. I still can't believe he ran off and left us to handle this."

The conversation ended there, drowned out by the deafening sound of the rotors as the helicopter touched down. While the blades were still rotating, the side doors slid open and two men jumped out. Crouching down, they ran toward the platoon.

Corporal Evans pointed to where Jock Cabot lay with Harriet holding a handful of bloodied gauze on his wound. She yelled something to the medics when they got there, then moved out of their way. The two men quickly got Cabot onto a collapsible stretcher one of them had and carried him to the helicopter.

As the medics finished loading Cabot into the copter, Corporal Evans and Prince Harry approached. The Corporal said something and pointed at Harry, and there was an obvious stiffening of posture, an immediate nodding. The two men smiled broadly and helped Harry on board.

A few seconds later the rotor blades began to wind back up. The grass in the field flattened. Hats blew off. Eardrums rattled. And then they were gone.

With the immediate crisis over, the attention turned to the General and what the platoon should do now. Corporal Evans started with an assurance that no one was in danger. His Alert Platoon was going back to Base Chivenor in Devon, and they would transport the General's body and report what happened here.

He smiled and said, "Prince Harry will be valuable in that task. Certainly as regards the Royal kidnapping and Major General Cabot."

Clive Kay huffed his way into the conversation as he did so often. When he had everyone's attention, he used his snide voice and said,

"Wing Commander Firth and I have both been completely left out of this operation. So, we have a question."

"Manners, Clive. Manners," warned Firth.

The Corporal smiled and nodded. "Of course," he said. "Go ahead."

"What the bloody hell *did* happen here?" Kay demanded.

Before anyone could say anything, Tom Warwick leaned out from behind the tall, gaunt figure of Kay. He gave Evans a wan smile and a little wave. "Hi! We are . . . friends," he said. "That's what we'd like to know, too. I think history may have been made here."

Vivian Warwick silently mouthed the word *history*. Then she closed her eyes and kneaded her temple.

Harriet sighed. "Excuse me," she said. "Before you get started, I have a quick question. Where is Arthur?" She looked around.

"Is that him over there with the white haired man?" Evans said, pointing toward Merlyn.

Commander Kay squinted that direction, then sputtered, "Oh, now the coward shows his face!"

Corporal Evans reacted immediately. "Coward? You'll be sorry if he hears that accusation. That man saved my life! And probably all of yours! He killed the man who shot Major General Cabot, the man who ordered us to capture or kill all of you."

Harriet Claiborne couldn't resist a small smile. "I think you may have earned yourself another enema, Commander," she said. Then she turned and walked off toward Merlyn and Arthur with her medical bag.

As she approached them a slight frown creased her forehead. Something was wrong, she thought. Arthur was sitting on the rotted stump of a tree cut long ago. Merlyn was standing over him, gesturing. It looked as though he was angry with Arthur, lecturing him. Before she got close enough to hear, Arthur pointed in her direction. Merlyn glanced her way and stopped his lecture. He turned toward her.

"Hello, my dear," Merlyn said with his usual smile.

Harriet nodded, but her eyes were on Arthur. His shirt was covered in blood. With some effort she forced a smile. "Are all Kings this messy? You shouldn't have wiped your sword on your shirt, Your Majesty."

Arthur looked down at his shirt, then back at her. He shook his head. "I cleaned Excalibur in the grass."

"That's what we were discussing," said the Wizard. He held up Baker-Smythe's 9mm Browning. "It's Arthur's blood."

"Oh God, no!" whispered Harriet.

68

Arthur reached a hand out toward Harriet and grimaced in pain. He bent over; his weight shifted, and he began sliding off the tree stump. Merlyn grabbed him and managed to sit him down on the ground leaning up against the stump.

"Help!" Harriet cried, waving to the others down in the field near the platoon. "We need help!"

"No!" Arthur yelled, shocking both Harriet and the Wizard.

Merlyn leaned down close to the King. "There is little time, My Liege," he said.

Arthur stared hard at him. "You will *do* your King's bidding!" he insisted.

They were both sounding so final, as if it were over. "I don't understand," Harriet said. "I can help stop the bleeding. We can get another helicopter."

The Wizard shook his head with a sad smile. "I have stopped the bleeding, but only on the outside. Something more must be done. However, I agree with the King regarding a flight to a hospital. It raises complications that don't need to be faced. Simply imagine the first questions asked. This is *who*? He was born *when*?" He shook his head again. "No, the purpose of our return has been achieved. It is time for us to leave."

As Merlyn talked, tears had welled up in Harriet's eyes. "What is Arthur ordering you to do?" she asked. Tears began to slide down her face.

The Wizard pointed toward the field. "Your cry for help has taken us halfway there."

Harriet turned to see several people rushing to their aid.

"The King must speak with one of his knights, must secure a pledge from him," said Merlyn.

Arthur started to say something, but was stopped by a wet, hacking cough. When he finally got it under control, he ran his fingers across his mouth and looked at them. They were bloody. He coughed once more to clear his throat, spat the result on the ground, then pointed at those coming to their aid.

"Bedevere," he said.

Corporal Ethan Evans was leading the group of five hurrying toward them. It included Tom and Vivian Warwick, Commander Clive Kay and Wing Commander Simon Firth. All were shocked when they saw King Arthur. Jaws dropped, eyes widened.

"What can we do to help?" Evans managed to get out between gasps for air.

"Thank you, Corporal, for offering to help," Merlyn said. "But you have your hands full with your platoon." He glanced at the General. "And the dead man. Our friends here will be help enough."

"Do I need to request another helicopter?"

The look on Harriet's face made the Wizard hesitate a moment, then he shook his head. "Thank you again, but we can handle transportation."

The closer to a potential argument by anyone came from Arthur. "I will be all right," he said with a bright smile that faded into another grimace as soon as Evans nodded and turned to go.

When the Corporal was barely out of earshot, Clive Kay piped up. "What the bloody hell is going on here?" he demanded. "This is King Arthur! A legendary hero! It looks like he's bleeding to death, and you're dancing around claiming everything is sunshine and flowers!"

Tom Warwick couldn't resist. "I thought *coward* was your description of Arthur."

Paying no attention to either of them, Arthur started pulling at Excalibur, trying to draw it out of its scabbard.

"No, your majesty," said Merlyn.

The King glanced at the Wizard, then turned to Clive Kay. "Help me, Kay," he said.

The Commander was momentarily flabbergasted, then he virtually beamed as he stepped over to Arthur and, together, they pulled the huge sword out. As it cleared the top of the scabbard, Arthur let go, leaving Kay holding Excalibur. Surprised by Arthur's release and the weight of the sword, the Commander nearly dropped it. When he recovered and had Excalibur balanced on its point in the earth, he gave an embarrassed chuckle and said, "What do I do with it?"

With another grimace, the King pointed at Wing Commander Simon Firth. "Bedevere," he said.

"What?" Kay and Firth asked in unison.

Merlyn leaned in to Arthur and whispered something. Arthur nodded and the Wizard turned to the group standing there. "Perhaps I should explain. It's quicker and easier on His Majesty." Then he beckoned to Simon Firth and the Wing Commander came forward.

"This is about my great grandmother, isn't it?" Firth said.

The Wizard nodded with a slight smile. "And one who came long before her. I believe you know the legend. Sir Bedevere was the only knight to survive the Battle of Camlann. Mortally wounded, King Arthur made him swear to return Excalibur to the Lady of the Lake."

"In Dozmary Pool?" Firth said.

Merlyn simply nodded. "Would you please help the King take the scabbard off, and put it on yourself?" he said.

When that was done the Wizard turned to Kay. "Commander, you will please help place Excalibur in the scabbard."

With some grunting and a curse or two, they managed to get the sword in place. Firth stood as straight as he could with the weight of Excalibur across his chest and saluted. "As you require, Your Majesty," he said. Then, he turned and started walking toward the stream and the bus and cars beyond it.

Harriet stopped him, calling, "Wait!" She walked to where he stood and took the keys to her Land Rover out of her pocket. "You'll need these," she said and slipped them into his pocket. "I'll ride back in the bus."

Simon Firth whispered something to her, then turned and continued toward the stream. Harriet returned to the group standing near Arthur.

As if they had been standing in line at a soccer game entrance, Merlyn now beckoned Tom Warwick to come over to Arthur. "The King also wants to speak to you," he said.

Tom moved closer to Arthur.

Pushing with his hands on the earth, the King sat up straighter. He smiled vaguely at Tom. "I ordered an ancestor of yours to run from battle. To save himself, to stay alive and spread my idea."

"Not might is right, might *for* right," said Tom.

Arthur tried to hide his pain as he chuckled. "The modern, short version." Curling a finger, he motioned for Tom to come even closer. "That Tom Warwick was a young lad, a page of mine. You are a grown man, schooled in history. I have a larger chore for you."

Tom glanced around to see who was listening, but there was only Vivian, and she wasn't close. "I will do whatever I can," he said.

"Tell the world what has happened here. And why," said the King. Then he nodded to Merlyn.

The Wizard stepped in and touched Tom on the shoulder. "I'm sorry, but we must hurry, and Arthur has one more to see."

As Tom moved back by his wife, Merlyn turned to Harriet.

"Me?" she said in a tiny voice.

Merlyn nodded. The ancient features of his face softened. "Most certainly, you," he said.

The Wizard stepped out of the way, making room for Harriet. She moved close to the King, kneeled on the ground in front of him and took one of his hands. She was still crying.

For a long moment, Arthur was silent, staring into her eyes. He took his hand away from hers and wiped tears off her cheek. "I'm so sorry," he said softly. "We would have been wonderful together." He opened his arms, beckoning her into his embrace. "I haven't felt like this for more than a thousand years."

Harriet smiled through her tears. She didn't even glance at his bloody shirt as she accepted his invitation. They held each other close with their eyes shut, dreaming of what might have been, but only for a minute or two.

Then Merlyn said, "It is time, My Liege."

Harriet took the King's face in her hands and kissed him lightly on the lips. Then she got up and looked around as if she was lost.

Vivian Warwick said, "Over here, Harriet." She motioned for Harriet to join her. When she did, Vivian handed her a few strips of gauze and started wiping the blood from the nurse's blouse with one. "I got them from your medical bag," she said.

Now Merlyn moved close to the King's right side and grasped under his arm near the shoulder. "You can do it," he said and lifted, trying to help Arthur to his feet. They made it halfway, but Arthur wasn't strong enough. His legs gave out. He moaned and sat back down hard.

The Wizard waited a moment for him to recover. Then he tried once more, this time with a shout. "Again!"

And the King rose smoothly to his feet, it seemed with little effort. Once balanced, he looked to his left and saw the reason why. Commander Clive Kay had helped from that side and was still helping him stand. Arthur smiled as much as he could. "Thank you, Kay," he said.

"My pleasure, Your Majesty," said Kay. "Where do we go from here?"

"Very good," Merlyn said in approval. He pointed to the nearest stand of trees and bushes. "We will walk him over there."

Harriet, Vivian, and Tom stood transfix and watched. "Then what?" Tom whispered.

Vivian sighed, then she smiled. "I think this is where I came in," she whispered back.

It was only a few minutes with Merlyn and Commander Kay helping Arthur. When they got to the edge of the trees, the Wizard stopped. "This is far enough," he said.

"Kay, my friend," said the King. "You have been a true knight."

The Commander stepped back from them. Slowly, a grin spread across his face; a rarely seen phenomenon during his entire life. "This is far enough?" he said. "I've *been* a true knight?"

He turned and looked across the field at Harriet, at the dead General, the platoon of marines, the Camelford Knights. "I don't have any plans. I don't have anywhere to go."

Taking Arthur's arm again, he said, "Except with you, Your Majesty."

The Wizard nodded and smiled knowingly at Kay. "I just wanted to make sure," he said.

Merlyn took the King's other arm. As Tom and Vivian and Harriet watched, all three men moved into the trees. After a few steps they faded, then they were gone.

69

Henri came hurrying across the garden area surrounding the Hotel du Fort carrying a boom box radio.

King Charles saw him first. "Here comes our entertainment for the day," he said to Camilla with a grin.

"I wonder if he ran all the way from his aunt's house?" Camilla asked, and they both chuckled. The entire island was only half a kilometer wide, and his Aunt Isabelle's cottage was *way over* on the other side.

In the short time they had known him, on the ketch and now here on Grand Ile in the Chausey Islands, the King and Queen Consort had grown quite fond of Henri. Despite their stormy introduction, they had learned that he was a truly warm human being and concerned for their safety and happiness. It was Henri who convinced the couple that oper- ated the hotel to let them stay in one of the rooms. Normally, during the off-season, all eight rooms would be closed. He also arranged for the restaurant to be open for them. Of course, that was easier since the manager and cook was his Cousin Marcel. Now it looked as through he had found them a radio.

Charles waved and called, "*Monsieur*!"

Henri was headed for the hotel lobby, but detoured when he saw them having coffee at one of the outside tables of the restaurant. He was all smiles as he came up the three steps from the garden. "*Tres bon!*" he said, nodding vigorously. "You learn much French."

"About enough to get arrested," said Camilla.

Suddenly Henri's eyes lit up. "Yes! Arrested!" He lifted up the radio and pointed at it. "You must hear."

Frowning, Charles said, "Hear what?"

Henri pulled out one of the empty chairs at the table and sat down. He lifted the boom box onto the table and started fumbling with the dials. When nothing happened, he slapped his forehead. "*Merde!* Is no *batterie*." He pulled an electrical cord out of the back pocket of his pants and held it up. "We go inside."

Charles and Camilla looked at each other and shrugged. "Inside it is," she said. The Queen Consort picked up the bamboo cane Henri had found for her, and all three got up and went into the lobby with the boom box in tow.

Henri found an outlet behind one of the chairs arranged around a glass-topped table and plugged in the radio. The cord was just long enough to set the radio on the table. Then, once again, he fumbled with the dials.

"Is London station," he said. He fiddled around a moment with the frequency knob and found it.

The voice was a woman's, but she had that reporter's brusqueness. "To repeat, once again, in a totally unprecedented move, British Prime Minister Alistair Saxon has been taken into custody as a result of the investigation into the purported assassination attempt on King Charles.

"We have more on this astounding story from David Elliot, live in the Isles of Scilly. David?"

"Thank you, Melody. As you said, the story is astounding, and not all of the threads have been sown into this dark blanket of deceit and crime. We do know this much for certain; there was no assassination attempt. However, a crime was perpetrated against the Royal Family. In fact, the entire family was kidnapped and secreted here on Tresco in the Isles of Scilly. They've been released and are now on their way to . . . well, for security reasons, I can't say where, but they are safe now."

Charles glanced and Camilla. "No mention of Harry," he whispered. "Or us," she said.

While they were whispering, David Elliot had thrown it back to Melody. She picked it up with sobering news. "One thing we should make clear, David. We're not sure this is over. The persons involved are desperate enough that they are turning on each other. With drastic results in the case of two of them. General Ian Baker Smythe, Supreme Commander of the British Armed Forces, has been killed in Cornwall and Royal Marine Commandant, Major General Jock Cabot, is in critical condition at a military hospital in Devon.

"Our Maurice Dobbs is at that hospital with a report," was the last thing they heard from Melody.

All three sitting at the glass topped table suddenly looked toward the lobby doors where an all too familiar noise was developing, the thumping of helicopter rotor blades.

Charles cursed under his breath and immediately got up and headed outside. Camilla and Henri looked at each other. As she was getting up, the Queen Consort shook her head. "This isn't for you, Henri," she said. Then, using her cane, she followed Charles. Henri was right behind her.

King Charles was standing just outside with his back to the lobby doors. When Camilla and Henri came through the doors, he held out his arms to block them from going any farther. Looking up, he said, "They're landing the bloody thing right in front of the hotel."

"Who comes?" Henri asked from behind both the King and the Queen Consort. His voice had gone shaky and up a half octave.

"We can't be sure," Camilla said.

Charles glared over his shoulder at his wife. The noise level was rapidly increasing, and he had to shout, "Bastards who don't know the game is over yet! And I'm not going to put up with it anymore!"

As the helicopter touched down, Charles lifted his shirt and drew the 9mm Browning from his belt. He crouched down and started running toward the helicopter.

"Charles! No!" Camilla screamed.

The King was still ten meters away when the side door on the copter slid open and a man in a flight suit and helmet jumped to the ground. Charles stopped and raised his gun. The man took off his helmet and put it under one arm.

"Haven't you two been on holiday long enough?" yelled Prince Harry.

Charles nearly keeled over, and did go down on one knee. He threw the gun away. With head bowed, staring at the ground, his entire body began to shake. Harry came to his father and knelt down beside him. Putting an arm around the King's shoulders, he said, "It's over."

After a moment, Charles turned his head enough to look at Harry. "My God, I nearly shot you," he said.

"But you didn't," said Harry.

Another moment passed, then the King said, "How did you know where we were?"

Prince Harry gazed off into the distance and smiled warmly. "A Wizard told me."

Epilogue

Prime Minister Alistair Saxon was tried in the Supreme Court of the United Kingdom and found guilty of treason, kidnapping, and conspiracy to commit murder. He was sentenced to life in prison with no chance of parole. For his protection, he is serving his sentence in solitary confinement at an unnamed prison somewhere in England.

Richard Thorne, aide to Prime Minister Alistair Saxon, was offered a deal by the prosecution for his testimony in the Alistair Saxon trial and those against General Ian Baker-Smythe and Home Secretary Michael Lyme. The agreement required Thorne to admit to failing to report anti-government activities to the authorities, which calls for six months in jail. He was released for time already served.

General Ian Baker-Smythe was tried in abstention in Military Court and found guilty of treason, kidnapping, and attempted second-degree murder. He was officially stripped of all military rank, dishonorably discharged from the British Army. He was buried in an unmarked grave in an unnamed military cemetery.

Home Secretary Michael Lyme was tried in the Supreme Court of the United Kingdom and found guilty of conspiracy to commit kidnapping and conspiracy to commit treason. He was sentenced to twenty years in prison and began serving that sentence in Belmarsh prison in the London Borough of Greenwich. Six months later, Lyme was murdered in the prison library with a fork. Authorities were unable to identify the perpetrator.

MI-5 Director Nigel Gibbon learned that Operation Thunderbolt was a failure before the others involved. He immediately had the Prime Minister, Richard Thorne, and the Home Secretary, Michael Lyme, taken into custody. He privately made propositions to each of them. He would keep the death penalty off the table for Alistair Saxon, see that Michael Lyme received the lesser charge of conspiracy, and Richard Thorne would serve no jail time. All they had to do was forget that he was involved in any way with Thunderbolt. His scheme worked perfectly until Jock Cabot woke up.

Major General Jock Cabot was airlifted to Bideford Hospital where he was in a coma for two months. Not expected to live, Cabot surprised doctors by regaining consciousness. He surprised them again by requesting a voice recorder and asking that military personnel witness him using the recorder. Then, with great difficulty, he told what he knew of Operation Thunderbolt from its beginning to the end. Finally, he named the men responsible for it: himself, Alistair Saxon, Ian Baker-Smythe, Michael Lyme, Geoffrey Kitterage, and Nigel Gibbon. Later that afternoon, Major General Jock Cabot slipped back into a coma. He passed away the following morning.

Royal Marines Major Rhys Mallory was tried in Military Court and found guilty of treason and murder. Both of these charges are reason for execution. However, the Court determined that there were mitigating circumstances in that Major Mallory was following orders. As a result, he was dishonorably discharged from the Royal Marines and sentenced to life in prison with no chance of parole. Mallory is serving that sentence at Belmarsh Prison in Greenwich.

Prince Harry's friend, Michael Christian did regain consciousness and, in time, recovered to carry on a normal life. Prince Harry and Michael remain friends to this day.

Jodrell Bank Observatory Deputy Director Margaret Kinsey was officially reprimanded with a note in her personnel file for not following Jodrell Bank established procedure by contacting the Cracking Haven Police before altering the Home Office. She also was given a forty-pound increase in her weekly salary.

Jodrell Bank Observatory Astronomer Dr. Hiram Feinberg was offered an appointment as Director at another British Observatory, but turned it down again. He was quoted as saying he would rather work with stars than people.

Constable Nyles Langston, Crackington Haven Police Station, the so-called hero of the Pencannow Point Incident, relished the spotlight, giving interviews to journalists and appearing on television news programs. However, as time passed, he kept asking himself the same question: who tied the tourniquet? Eventually, he came to an answer and joined the Pencannow UFO Group.

Marjorie Langston, wife of Constable Nyles Langston, stood by her husband through his hospitalization and rehab, and the media circus that descended on them. When Nyles began spending more and more time with the Pencannow UFO Group, she went with him and, in an effort to stay close, started reading science fiction. She never again asked her husband about his trip to London, or why the King needed him.

Commander Clive Kay was never heard from again. A few weeks after his *disappearance* at Slaughter Bridge, a memorial was held for him at the Camelford Veterans Home organized by Trevor Warwick and Simon Firth. It was attended by nearly all the staff and patients.

Sergeant Major Trevor Warwick continued to live at the Camelford Veterans Home and playfully *seduce* the young nurses working there. His favorite target was Nurse Harriet Claiborne and they developed a symbiotic relationship, for he was also always ready to tell a story about the Camelford Knights to newcomers and the slowly declining population of old friends.

Wing Commander Simon Firth walked all the way back to the visitor's center with Excalibur. When he got there, Captain Colin Mackenzie was still sitting in the driver's seat of the bus. Firth called to him for help. When Mackenzie saw the enormous sword, he couldn't resist. As they struggled to load Excalibur and the scabbard into the Land Rover, Firth told Mackenzie what had happened and what King Arthur had tasked him to do. Then he asked the Captain to join him in carrying out the task, and the old light, the one that had always shone there, returned to Colin Mackenzie's eyes. The two of them drove to Dozmary pool and, that night, returned Excalibur to the Lady of the Lake. In the process, they formed an unshakable friendship.

Nurse Harriet Claiborne, returned to her nursing duties at the Camelford Veterans Home. However, after a time, the memories and dreams of what might have been overwhelmed her. She knew better, but she began to use drugs that were available to her to blur the pain. Then one night she awoke to find Merlyn sitting on the edge of her bed. He told her Arthur had a request: help those who need you most. The Wizard smiled, then was gone. Harriet is now working for Doctors Without Borders and extremely happy.

Tom Warwick finished his schooling, receiving a PhD in History from King's College in London. Upon graduation, he accepted a position as Associate Professor at Cambridge University. During the summer prior to beginning at Cambridge, he wrote the novel, *Future King*.

Vivian Warwick informed the management of McDonald's that she was resigning her position as manager of the Soho restaurant and moving to Cambridge where her husband had been hired as Associate Professor at the University. McDonald's management refused to accept her resignation and appointed her District Manager for the Cambridge Region's fourteen restaurants. Her salary was nearly doubled.

Josie, Francine, and Henri sailed the ketch back to Martinique, feeling good about what they had done, but expecting to be fired from their jobs. When they arrived, they discovered that some anonymous person had purchased them their own ketch. It was free and clear.

The Knights of Camelford who pledged to protect Prince Harry and risked everything were invited to a ceremony at Buckingham Palace. King Charles gave them special Medals of Honor and a private tour of the Palace.

King Charles and Queen Consort Camilla returned to London and, as soon as it could be arranged, held an unprecedented television news conference, which included both of them plus Prince William and Prince Harry. They personally explained to the British people what had happened to them and committed themselves to working with the people's new elected leaders to solve England's problems.

The strong positive stance by the Royals caused a breeze of confidence to ripple through Great Britain and, within a few weeks, the Troubles began to turn around.

King Arthur and Emrys Myrddin. Legend has it that Arthur Pendragon and Merlyn are waiting in Avalon, and when England needs them, they will come back. But that is only legend.

END

Made in the USA
Lexington, KY
02 June 2013